The
Blue Boa

Also by Jenny Nimmo

Children of the Red King
Midnight for Charlie Bone
The Time Twister
The Castle of Mirrors

Milo's Wolves
Griffin's Castle
The Rinaldi Ring

The Snow Spider Trilogy
The Snow Spider
Emlyn's Moon
The Chestnut Soldier

For younger readers
Ill Will, Well Nell
Hot Dog, Cool Cat
Tatty Apple

Delilah and the Dogspell
Delilah and the Dishwasher Dogs
Delilah Alone

The
Blue Boa

Jenny Nimmo

EGMONT

For Gwenhwyfar, who found the boa,
with love.

First published in Great Britain in 2004
This paperback edition published 2005
by Egmont Books Ltd
239 Kensington High Street, London W8 6SA
Text copyright © 2004 Jenny Nimmo
Illustrations copyright © 2004 David Wyatt

The moral rights of the author and illustrator
have been asserted

ISBN 1 4052 1830 4

3 5 7 9 10 8 6 4 2

A CIP catalogue record for this title is available from the
British Library

Typeset by Dorchester Typesetting Group Ltd
Printed and bound in the UK by the CPI Group

Contents

The endowed children   viii

Prologue   xi

1. Someone dangerous   1

2. The invisible boy   23

3. Runner Bean is rumbled   45

4. Sparkling stones   63

5. The shape-shifter   85

6. The starling   109

7. Uncle Paton's return   125

8. A visit to Skarpo   135

9. A very old mouse   153

10. The wand   173

11. Bull, bells and golden bats   195

12. A sorcerer on the loose   213

13. The flames and a journey   235

14. The garden in Darkly Wynd   259

15. Lysander's plan   287

16. The night of wind and spirits   305

17. Ollie and the boa   327

18. A belt of black jewels   349

Beatrice Bloor
b.1835
Witch.

Bertram
Babington Bloor
b.1840
Having read Mary
Shelley's Frankenstein,
Bertram, a scientist-
magician, tried to make
a human being. He was
not successful.

m.

Donatella da
Vinci
b.1845
Daughter of an Italian
magician. She assisted
Bertram but was
electrocuted during one
of his experiments.

Gideon
b.1875
Mathematician. Knighted
for tutoring a royal prince.
Sir Gideon was not endowed
or interested in magic.

m.

Gudrun Solensson
b.1876
Amateur singer.

Ezekiel
b.1902
Spoiled, cunning, flawed
magician. Continued his
grandfather's experiments.

m.

Hilda Hansoff
b.1902
Botanist. Fatally
poisoned by a
rare plant.

Bartholomew
b.1930
Unendowed.
Mountaineer. Lost
in the Himalayas.

m.

Mary Chance
b.1930
Dancer. Danced herself
to death when Bart
disappeared.

Masie Jo
b.1935
Widow

Note:

Charlie Bone can hear
the voices of people in
photographs and
paintings. In certain
circumstances he can
meet them.

Harold
b.1955
Unendowed, but
interested in his
grandfather's
experiments.

m.

Dorothy de Vere
b.1957
Violinist.

Manfred
b.1985
Hypnotist.

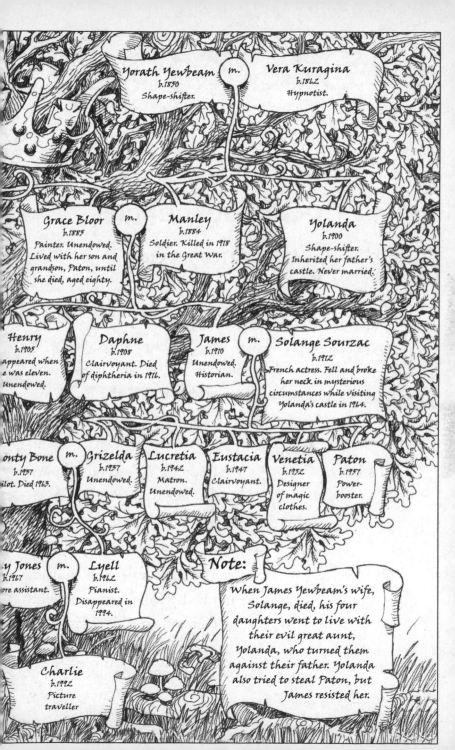

Yorath Yewbeam m. **Vera Kuragina**
b.1850
Shape-shifter.
b.1862
Hypnotist.

Grace Bloor m. **Manley**
b.1885
Painter. Unendowed.
Lived with her son and
grandson, Paton, until
she died, aged eighty.
b.1884
Soldier. Killed in 1918
in the Great War.

Yolanda
b.1900
Shape-shifter.
Inherited her father's
castle. Never married.

Henry
b.1905
...appeared when
...e was eleven.
Unendowed.

Daphne
b.1908
Clairvoyant. Died
of diphtheria in 1916.

James m. **Solange Sourzac**
b.1910
Unendowed.
Historian.
b.1912
French actress. Fell and broke
her neck in mysterious
circumstances while visiting
Yolanda's castle in 1964.

...onty Bone m. **Grizelda**
b.1937
...ilot. Died 1963.
b.1937
Unendowed.

Lucretia
b.1942
Matron.
Unendowed.

Eustacia
b.1947
Clairvoyant.

Venetia
b.1952
Designer
of magic
clothes.

Paton
b.1957
Power-
booster.

...y Jones m. **Lyell**
b.1967
...ore assistant.
b.1962
Pianist.
Disappeared in
1994.

Note:

When James Yewbeam's wife,
Solange, died, his four
daughters went to live with
their evil great aunt,
Yolanda, who turned them
against their father. Yolanda
also tried to steal Paton, but
James resisted her.

Charlie
b.1992
Picture
traveller

The children of the Red King, called the endowed

Manfred Bloor

Head boy of Bloor's Academy. A hypnotiser. He is descended from Borlath, eldest son of the Red King. Borlath was a brutal and sadistic tyrant.

Asa Pike

A were-beast. He is descended from a tribe who lived in the Northern forests and kept strange beasts. Asa can change shape at dusk.

Billy Raven

Billy can communicate with animals. One of his ancestors conversed with ravens that sat on a gibbet where dead men hung. For this talent he was banished from his village.

Zelda Dobinski   Descended from a long line of Polish magicians. Zelda is telekenetic. She can move objects with her mind.

Lysander Sage   Descended from an African wise man. He can call up his spirit ancestors.

Tancred Torsson   A storm-bringer. His Scandinavian ancestor was named after the thunder god, Thor. Tancred can bring rain, wind, thunder and lightning.

Gabriel Silk   Gabriel can feel scenes and emotions through the clothes of others. He comes from a line of psychics.

Emma Tolly   Emma can fly. Her surname derives from the Spanish swordsman from Toledo, whose daughter married the Red King. He is therefore an ancestor to all the endowed children.

Charlie Bone   Charlie can travel into photographs
                and paintings. He is descended from
                the Yewbeams, a family with many
                magical endowments.

Dorcas Loom   An endowed girl whose gift is, as yet,
                undiscovered.

The endowed are all descended from the ten children of
the Red King; a magician-king who left Africa in the
twelfth century, accompanied by three leopards.

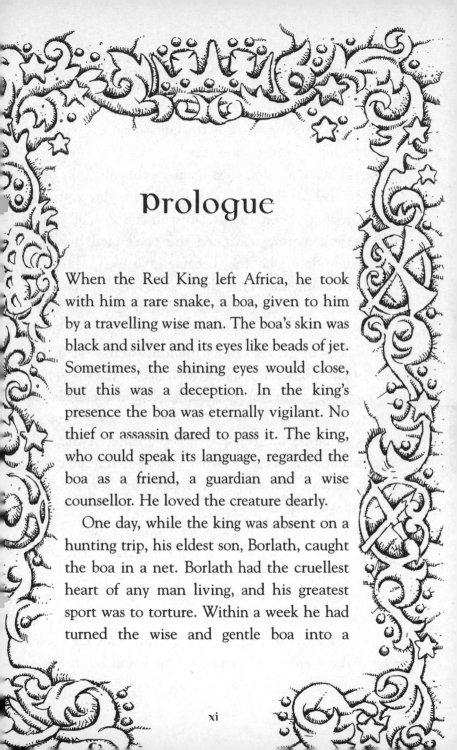

prologue

When the Red King left Africa, he took with him a rare snake, a boa, given to him by a travelling wise man. The boa's skin was black and silver and its eyes like beads of jet. Sometimes, the shining eyes would close, but this was a deception. In the king's presence the boa was eternally vigilant. No thief or assassin dared to pass it. The king, who could speak its language, regarded the boa as a friend, a guardian and a wise counsellor. He loved the creature dearly.

One day, while the king was absent on a hunting trip, his eldest son, Borlath, caught the boa in a net. Borlath had the cruellest heart of any man living, and his greatest sport was to torture. Within a week he had turned the wise and gentle boa into a

creature that lived only to kill. It would squeeze its victims into oblivion within minutes.

The king's daughter, Guanhamara, horrified by the boa's new and deadly nature, rescued the creature and cast a spell, hoping to cure it. Alas, Guanhamara's spell came too late and merely weakened the boa's fatal hug. Its victims did not die, but they became invisible.

When Guanhamara died, the boa fell into a deep sleep. It shrivelled into a thing that was neither alive nor dead. Hoping one day to reawaken the creature, Guanhamara's seven daughters (every one of them a witch) sealed the boa in a jar of liquid made blue with herbs. They also put in a bird with delicate, shiny wings. But the embalmed creatures were stolen by Borlath and passed down through his descendants, until Ezekiel Bloor, using a method recommended by his grandfather, managed to revive the boa whose skin had become a silvery blue. He was less successful with the bird.

Ezekiel was now a hundred years old. He had always longed to become invisible but, as far as he knew, the boa's hug was permanent, and he didn't dare to let the creature hug him. The old man still searched for a way to reverse invisibility, while the boa lived in the shadowy attics of Bloor's Academy, keeping its secret, until someone could bring it the comfort of understanding – and listen to its story.

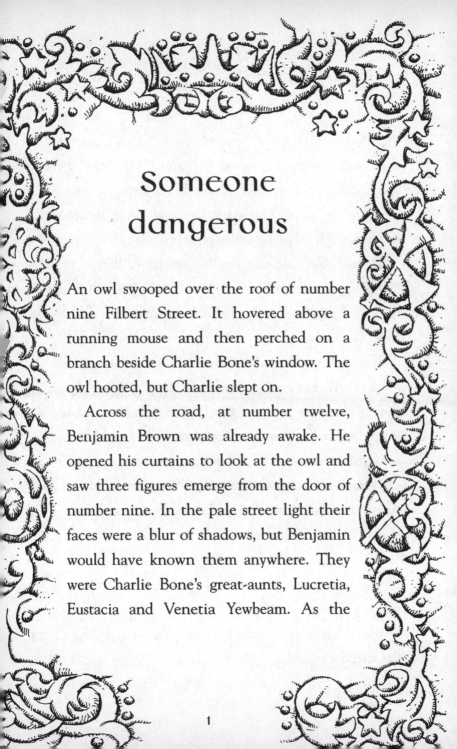

Someone dangerous

An owl swooped over the roof of number nine Filbert Street. It hovered above a running mouse and then perched on a branch beside Charlie Bone's window. The owl hooted, but Charlie slept on.

Across the road, at number twelve, Benjamin Brown was already awake. He opened his curtains to look at the owl and saw three figures emerge from the door of number nine. In the pale street light their faces were a blur of shadows, but Benjamin would have known them anywhere. They were Charlie Bone's great-aunts, Lucretia, Eustacia and Venetia Yewbeam. As the

1

three women tiptoed furtively down the steps, one of them suddenly looked up at Benjamin. He shrank behind the curtain and watched them hurry away up the road. They wore black hooded coats and their heads tilted towards each other like conspirators.

It was half past four in the morning. Why were the Yewbeam sisters out so early? Had they been in Charlie's house all night? They've been hatching some nasty plot, thought Benjamin.

If only Charlie hadn't inherited such a strange talent. And if only his great-aunts hadn't got to know about it, perhaps he'd have been safe. But when your ancestor is a magician *and* a king, your relations are bound to expect something of you. 'Poor Charlie,' Benjamin murmured.

Benjamin's big yellow dog, Runner Bean, whined sympathetically from the bed. Benjamin wondered if he'd guessed what was going to happen to him. Probably. Mr and Mrs Brown had spent the last two days cleaning the house and packing. Dogs always know something is up when people start packing.

'Breakfast, Benjamin!' Mrs Brown called from the kitchen.

Mr Brown could be heard singing in the shower.

Benjamin and Runner Bean went downstairs. Three bowls of porridge sat on the kitchen table. Benjamin tucked in. His mother was frying sausages and tomatoes and he was glad to see that she hadn't forgotten his dog. Runner Bean's bowl was already full of chopped sausage.

Mr Brown arrived still singing and still in his dressing-gown. Mrs Brown was already dressed. She wore a neat grey suit and her straight straw-coloured hair was cut very short. She wore no jewellery.

Benjamin's parents were private detectives and they tried to look as inconspicuous as possible. Sometimes, they wore a false moustache or a wig to disguise themselves. It was usually only Mr Brown who wore the false moustaches, but on one occasion (an occasion Benjamin would like to forget), Mrs Brown had also found it necessary to wear one.

Benjamin's mother swapped his now empty bowl for a full plate and said, 'You'd better take Runner across to Charlie as soon as you've cleaned your teeth. We'll be off in half an hour.'

'Yes, Mum.' Benjamin scoffed down the rest of his

breakfast and ran back upstairs. He didn't tell his mother that Charlie hadn't actually agreed to look after Runner Bean.

The Browns' bathroom overlooked Filbert Street and while Benjamin was brushing his teeth, he saw a tall man in a long black coat walk down the steps of number nine. Benjamin stopped brushing and stared. What on earth was going on in Charlie's house?

The tall man was Paton Yewbeam, Charlie's great-uncle. He was wearing dark glasses and carried a white stick. Benjamin assumed the dark glasses had something to do with Paton's unfortunate talent for exploding lights. Paton never appeared in daylight, if he could help it, but this was an extraordinary time to be going out, even for him. He walked up to a midnight blue car, opened the boot and carefully placed the wand (for that's what it was) right at the back.

Before Benjamin had even rinsed his toothbrush, Charlie's uncle had driven off. He went in the opposite direction to his sisters, Benjamin noted. This wasn't surprising as Paton and his sisters were sworn enemies.

'You'd better go over to Charlie's,' Mrs Brown called

from the kitchen. Benjamin packed his pyjamas and toothbrush and went downstairs.

Runner Bean's tail hung dejectedly. His ears were down and his eyes rolled piteously. Benjamin felt guilty. 'Come on, Runner.' He spoke with an exaggerated cheerfulness that didn't fool his dog for one minute.

The boy and the dog left the house together. They were best friends and Runner Bean wouldn't have dreamt of disobeying Benjamin, but today he dragged his paws very reluctantly up the steps of number nine.

Benjamin rang the bell and Runner Bean howled. It was the howl that woke Charlie. Everyone else in the house woke briefly, thought they'd had a nightmare and went back to sleep.

Charlie, recognising the howl, staggered downstairs to open the door. 'What's happened?' he asked, blinking at the street lights. 'It's still night, isn't it?'

'Sort of,' said Benjamin. 'I've got some amazing news. I'm going to Hong Kong.'

Charlie rubbed his eyes. 'What, now?'

'Yes.'

Charlie stared at his friend in bewilderment and then

invited him in for a piece of toast. While the toast was browning, Charlie asked Benjamin if Runner Bean would be travelling to Hong Kong with him.

'Er – no,' said Benjamin. 'He'd have to be quarantined and he'd hate that.'

'So where's he going?' Charlie glanced at Runner Bean and the big dog gave him a forlorn sort of smile.

'That's just it,' Benjamin said, with a slight cough. 'There's no one else but you, Charlie.'

'Me? I can't keep a dog here,' said Charlie. 'Grandma Bone would kill it.'

'Don't say that.' Benjamin looked anxiously at Runner Bean, who was crawling under the table. 'Now look what you've done. He was upset already.'

As Charlie began to splutter his protests, Benjamin quickly explained that the Hong Kong visit had been a complete surprise. A Chinese billionaire had asked his parents to trace a priceless necklace that had been stolen from his Hong Kong apartment. The Browns couldn't resist such a well-paid and challenging case but as it might take several months, they did not want to leave Benjamin behind. Unfortunately this didn't apply to Runner Bean.

Charlie slumped at the kitchen table and scratched his head. His bushy hair was even more tangled than usual. 'Oh,' was all he could say.

'Thanks, Charlie.' Benjamin shoved a large piece of toast into his mouth. 'I'll let myself out.' At the kitchen door he looked back guiltily. 'I'm sorry. I hope you'll be all right, Charlie.' And then he was gone.

Benjamin was so excited he had forgotten to tell Charlie about his uncle and the wand, or the visit of his three aunts.

From the kitchen window Charlie watched his friend dash across the street and jump into the Browns' large green car. Charlie lifted his hand to wave, but the car drove off before Benjamin had seen him.

'Now what?' mumbled Charlie.

As if in answer, Runner Bean growled from beneath the table. Benjamin hadn't thought to leave any dog food for him, and Mr and Mrs Brown were obviously far too busy to think of such mundane items.

'Detectives!' he muttered.

For five minutes Charlie struggled to think how he was going to keep Runner Bean a secret from Grandma Bone.

But thinking was exhausting so early in the day. Charlie laid his head on the table and fell asleep.

As luck would have it, Grandma Bone was the first person downstairs that morning. 'What's this?' Her shrill voice woke Charlie with a start. 'Sleeping in the kitchen? You're lucky it's Saturday. You'd have missed the school bus.'

'Um.' Charlie blinked up at the tall, stringy woman in her grey dressing-gown. A snowy pigtail hung down her back and it swung from side to side as she began to march about the kitchen, banging on the kettle, slamming the fridge door and plonking hard butter on the counter. Suddenly she swivelled round and stared at Charlie. 'I smell dog,' she said accusingly.

Charlie remembered Runner Bean. 'D-dog?' he stammered. Luckily, the heavy tablecloth hung almost to the ground and his grandmother couldn't see Runner Bean.

'Has that friend of yours been here? He always smells of dog.'

'Benjamin? Er – yes,' said Charlie. 'He came to say goodbye. He's going to Hong Kong.'

'Good riddance,' she grunted.

When Grandma Bone went into the larder, Charlie grabbed Runner Bean's collar and dragged him upstairs.

'I don't know what I'm going to do with you,' sighed Charlie. 'I've got to go to school on Monday, and I won't be back till Friday. I have to sleep there, you know.'

Runner Bean jumped on to Charlie's bed wagging his tail. He'd spent many happy hours in Charlie's bedroom.

Charlie decided to ask his Uncle Paton for help. Slipping out of his room he crept along the landing until he came to his uncle's door. A DO NOT DISTURB sign hung just above Charlie's eye level. He knocked.

There was no reply.

Charlie cautiously opened the door and looked in. Paton wasn't there. It was unlike him to leave the house in the morning. Charlie went over to a big desk covered with books and scraps of paper. On the tallest pile of books there was an envelope with Charlie's name on it.

Charlie withdrew a sheet of paper from the envelope and read his uncle's large scrawly handwriting.

Charlie, dear boy,
    My sisters are up to no good. Heard them plotting in

the small hours. Have decided to go and put a stop to
things. If I don't, someone very dangerous will arrive.
No time to explain. Will be back in a few days – I hope!
　　Yours affectionately,
　　Uncle P.
　　P.S. Have taken wand.

'Oh no,' Charlie groaned. 'When are things going to stop
going wrong today?'

Unfortunately they had only just begun.

With a long sigh, Charlie left his uncle's room, and
walked straight into a pile of towels.

His other grandmother, Maisie Jones, who was carrying
the towels, staggered backwards and then sat down with a
bang.

'Watch out, Charlie!' she shouted.

Charlie pulled his rather overweight grandmother to
her feet and, while he helped to gather up the towels, he
told Maisie about Paton's note and the problem of Runner
Bean.

'Don't worry, Charlie,' said Maisie. Her voice sank to a
whisper as Grandma Bone came up the stairs. 'I'll look

after the poor pooch. As for Uncle P – I'm sure it'll all turn out for the best.'

Charlie went back to his room, dressed quickly and told Runner Bean that food would be coming, if not directly, then as soon as Grandma Bone went out. This could be any time of day, or not at all, but Runner Bean wasn't bothered. He curled up on the bed and closed his eyes. Charlie went downstairs.

Maisie was filling the washing machine and Amy Bone, Charlie's mother, was gulping down her second coffee. She told Charlie to have a good day, pecked him on the cheek and rushed off to the greengrocer's where she worked. Charlie thought she looked rather too chic for a day weighing vegetables. Her golden brown hair was tied back with a velvet ribbon, and she was wearing a brand new corn-coloured coat. Charlie wondered if she'd got a boyfriend. He hoped not, for his vanished father's sake.

Five minutes after his mother had left, Grandma Bone came downstairs in a black coat, her white hair now bundled up under a black hat. She told Charlie to brush his hair and then walked out with an odd smile on her pinched face.

As soon as she'd gone, Charlie ran to the fridge and pulled out a bowl of leftovers: last night's lamb stew. Maisie grinned and shook her head, but she let Charlie take some of it to Runner Bean in a saucer. 'That dog should be exercised before Grandma Bone comes back,' she called.

Charlie took her advice. When Runner Bean had wolfed down the stew, Charlie took him out into the back garden, where they had a great game of hunt the slipper: a slipper that Charlie despised because it had his name embroidered in blue across the front.

Runner Bean was just chewing up the last bit of slipper, when Maisie flung open an upstairs window and called, 'Look out, Charlie. The Yewbeams are coming!'

'Stay here, Runner,' Charlie commanded. 'And be quiet, if you can.'

He leapt up the steps to the back door and ran to the kitchen, where he sat at the table and picked up a magazine. The aunts' voices could be heard as they climbed the front steps. A key turned in the lock and then they were in the hall: Grandma Bone and her three sisters, all talking at once.

The great-aunts marched into the kitchen in new spring outfits. Lucretia and Eustacia had exchanged their usual black suits for charcoal grey but in Aunt Venetia's case, it was purple. She also wore high-heeled purple shoes with golden tassels dangling from the laces. All three sisters had sinister smiles, and a threatening look in their dark eyes.

Aunt Lucretia said, 'So here you are, Charlie!' She was the eldest apart from Grandma Bone, and a matron at Charlie's school.

'Yes, here I am,' said Charlie nervously.

'Same hair, I see,' said Aunt Eustacia, sitting opposite Charlie.

'Yes, same hair,' said Charlie. 'Same hair for you too, I see.'

'Don't be cheeky.' Eustacia patted her abundant grey hair. 'Why haven't you brushed it today?'

'Haven't had time,' said Charlie.

He became aware that Grandma Bone was still talking to someone in the hall.

Aunt Venetia suddenly said, 'Tah dah!' and opened the kitchen door very wide, as if she were expecting the

Queen or a famous film star to walk in. But it was Grandma Bone who appeared, followed by the prettiest girl Charlie had ever seen. She had golden curls, bright blue eyes and lips like a cherub.

'Hello, Charlie!' The girl held out her hand in the manner of someone expecting a kiss on the fingers, preferably from a boy on bended knees. 'I'm Belle.'

Charlie was too flustered to do anything.

The girl smiled and sat beside him. 'Oh my,' she said. 'A ladies' magazine.'

Charlie realised, to his horror, that he was holding his mother's magazine. On the cover a woman in pink underwear held a kitten. Charlie felt very hot. He knew his face must be bright red.

'Make us some coffee, Charlie,' Aunt Lucretia said sharply. 'And then we'll be off.'

Charlie flung down the magazine and ran to the coffee maker while Grandma Bone and the aunts sat babbling at him. Belle would be going to Charlie's school, Bloor's Academy, and Charlie must tell her all about it.

Charlie sighed. He wanted to visit his friend, Fidelio. Why did the aunts always have to spoil everything? For

half an hour he listened to the chattering and giggling over the coffee and buns. Belle didn't behave like a child, thought Charlie. She looked about twelve, but she seemed very comfortable with the aunts.

When the last drop had been squeezed out of the coffee pot, the three Yewbeam sisters left the house, blowing kisses to Belle.

'Take care of her, Charlie,' Aunt Venetia called.

Charlie wondered how he was supposed to do that.

'Can I wash my hands, Grizel – er – Mrs Bone?' Belle held up her sticky fingers.

'There's the sink,' Charlie nodded to the kitchen sink.

'Upstairs, dear,' said Grandma Bone, with a scowl in Charlie's direction. 'Bathroom's first left. There's some nice lavender soap and a clean towel.'

'Thank you!' Belle skipped out.

Charlie gaped. 'What's wrong with the kitchen?' he asked his grandmother.

'Belle has tender skin,' said Grandma Bone. 'She can't use kitchen soap. I want you to lay the dining room table – for five. I presume Maisie will be joining us.'

'The *dining room*?' said Charlie in disbelief. 'We only eat

there on special occasions.'

'It's for Belle,' snapped Grandma Bone.

'A *child?*' Charlie was amazed.

'Belle is not just any child.'

So it seems, thought Charlie. He went to lay the dining room table while Grandma Bone shouted instructions up to Maisie. 'We'd like a nice light soup today, Maisie. And then some cold ham and salad. Followed by your lovely Bakewell tart.'

'Would we indeed, your highness?' Maisie shouted from somewhere upstairs. 'Well, we'll have to wait, I'm afraid. Oops! Who on earth are you?'

She had obviously bumped into Belle.

Charlie closed the dining room door and went to the window. There was no sign of Runner Bean in the garden. Charlie had visions of a dog's lifeless body lying in a gutter. He ran to the back door, but just as he was about to open it, a sing-song voice called, 'Charleee!'

Belle was standing in the hall, staring at him. Charlie could have sworn that her eyes had been blue. Now they were green.

'Where are you going, Charlie?' she asked.

'Oh, I was just going into the garden for a . . . a . . .'

'Can I come with you?'

'No. That is, I've changed my mind.'

'Good. Come and talk to me.'

Was it possible? Belle's eyes were now a greyish brown. Charlie followed her into the sitting room where she sat on the sofa, patting a cushion beside her. Charlie perched at the other end.

'Now, tell me all about Bloor's.' Belle smiled invitingly.

Charlie cleared his throat. Where should he begin? 'Well, there are three sort of departments, Music, Art and Drama. I'm in Music so I have to wear a blue cape.'

'I shall be in Art.'

'Then you'll wear green.' Charlie glanced at the girl. 'Haven't my aunts told you all this? I mean, are you staying with them, or what?'

'I want to hear it from you,' said Belle, ignoring Charlie's question.

Charlie continued. 'Bloor's is a big grey building on the other side of the city. It's very, very old. There are three cloakrooms, three assembly halls and three canteens. You go up some steps between two towers, cross a courtyard, up

more steps and into the main hall. You have to be silent in the hall or you'll get detention. The Music students go through a door under crossed trumpets, your door is under the sign of a pencil and paintbrush.'

'What's the sign for the Drama students?'

'Two masks. One sad and one happy.' Why did Charlie get the impression that Belle knew all this? Her eyes were blue again. It was unnerving.

'There's another thing,' he said. 'Are you – er – like me; one of the children of the Red King? I mean, was he your ancestor too?'

Belle turned her bright blue gaze on him. 'Oh, *yes*. And I'm endowed. But I prefer not to say how. I'm told that *you* can hear voices from photographs, and even paintings.'

'Yes.' Charlie could do more than *hear* voices, but he wasn't going to give anything away to this strange girl. 'Endowed children have to do their homework in the King's room,' he said. 'There are twelve of us. Someone from Art will show you where it is: Emma Tolly. She's a friend of mine, and she's endowed too.'

'Emma? Ah, I've heard all about her.' Belle inched her way up the sofa towards Charlie. 'Now, tell me about you,

Charlie. I believe that your father's dead.'

'He's *not!*' said Charlie fiercely. 'His car went into a quarry, but they never found his body. He's just – lost.'

'Really? How did you find that out?'

Without thinking, Charlie said, 'My friend Gabriel's got an amazing gift. He can feel the truth in old clothes. I gave him my father's tie and Gabriel said that he wasn't dead.'

'Well, well.' The girl gave Charlie a sweet, under-standing smile, but the effect was spoiled by the cold look in her eyes – now a dark grey. And, was it a trick of the light, or did he glimpse a set of wrinkles just above her curved pink lips?

Charlie slipped off the sofa. 'I'd better help my other gran with lunch,' he said.

He found Maisie in the kitchen, throwing herbs into a saucepan. 'All this fuss for a child,' she muttered. 'I've never heard of such a thing.'

'Nor me,' said Charlie. 'She's a bit strange, isn't she?'

'She's downright peculiar. Belle indeed!'

'Belle means beautiful,' said Charlie, remembering his French. 'And she is very pretty.'

'Huh!' said Maisie.

When the soup was ready Charlie helped Maisie to carry it into the chilly dining room. Grandma Bone was already sitting at the head of the table, with Belle on her right.

'Where's Paton?' asked Grandma Bone.

'He won't be coming,' said Charlie.

'And why not?'

'He doesn't eat with us, does he?' Charlie reminded her.

'Today, I want him here,' said Grandma Bone.

'Well, you won't get him,' said Maisie. 'He's gone away.'

'Oh?' Grandma Bone stiffened. 'And how d'you know that?' She glared, first at Maisie and then Charlie.

Maisie looked at Charlie.

Charlie said, 'He left a note.'

'And what did it say?' demanded Grandma Bone.

'I can't remember all of it,' Charlie mumbled.

'Let me see it!' She held out a bony hand.

'I tore it up,' said Charlie.

Grandma Bone's eyebrows plummeted in a dark scowl. 'You shouldn't have done that. I want to know what's going on. I must know what my brother said.'

'He said he'd gone to see my great-grandpa, your father, although *you* never go to see him.'

His grandmother's tiny black eyes almost disappeared into their wrinkled sockets. 'That's none of your business. Paton visited our father last week. He only goes once a month.'

Charlie only just stopped himself from mentioning his own visit to his great-grandfather. Because of the family feud it had to remain a secret. But Uncle Paton had never told him what caused the feud or why he mustn't talk about it. He'd have to tell another lie. 'It was an emergency.'

This seemed to satisfy Grandma Bone, but Belle continued to stare at Charlie. Her eyes were now dark green and a chilling thought occurred to him. Uncle Paton had gone to stop someone dangerous from arriving. But perhaps that person was already here?

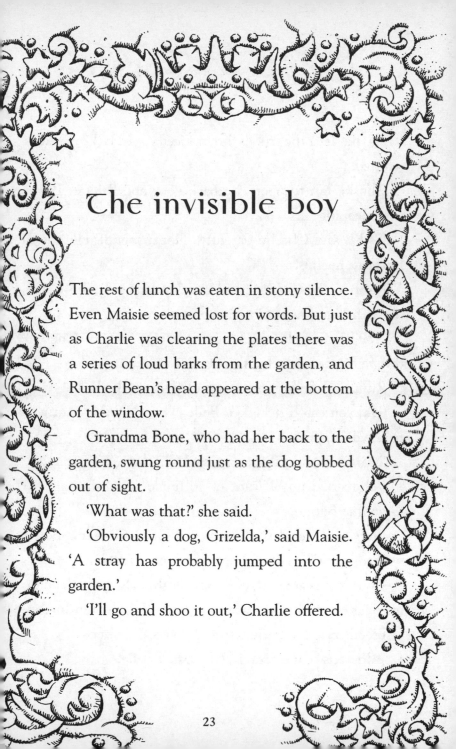

The invisible boy

The rest of lunch was eaten in stony silence. Even Maisie seemed lost for words. But just as Charlie was clearing the plates there was a series of loud barks from the garden, and Runner Bean's head appeared at the bottom of the window.

Grandma Bone, who had her back to the garden, swung round just as the dog bobbed out of sight.

'What was that?' she said.

'Obviously a dog, Grizelda,' said Maisie. 'A stray has probably jumped into the garden.'

'I'll go and shoo it out,' Charlie offered.

As he left the room he noticed that Belle looked worried.

Charlie ran to open the back door and Runner Bean came leaping in.

'Sssh!' said Charlie urgently. 'Not a sound!' He put a finger to his lips.

Runner Bean appeared to understand this and obediently followed Charlie up to his room.

'You've got to be quiet, or it's curtains for you.' Charlie drew a finger across his throat.

Runner Bean grunted and curled up on the bed.

'Did you catch it?' asked Belle, when Charlie returned to the dining room.

'No, I just shooed it away,' said Charlie.

Belle stood up. 'I want to go home now,' she said to Grandma Bone.

'Very well, dear.' With surprising speed, Grandma Bone walked into the hall and put on her coat and hat.

Charlie was amazed. His grandmother always had a nap after lunch, even if it was just a snack. The golden-haired girl seemed to have some sort of power over her.

'Where is home, exactly?' he asked Belle.

'Don't you know where your great-aunts live?' she said.

Charlie had to confess that he didn't. He'd never been invited to their home, and never been told where it was.

'I expect you'll find out soon enough,' said Belle mysteriously.

'There's no need for him to know,' said Grandma Bone, helping her into a smart green jacket.

'Bye-bye, then, Charlie!' said Belle. 'I'll see you at Bloor's on Monday. I'm going to be on the green bus. Watch out for me.'

'I'll be on the blue bus. But I expect I'll see you some time.'

The strange girl smiled and tossed her golden curls. Her eyes were blue again.

When Belle and Grandma Bone had gone, Charlie went to help Maisie with the washing-up.

'Where *do* the aunts live?' he asked Maisie.

'Some big house at the end of one of those creepy alleys,' said Maisie. 'Darkly Wynd, I think the road's called. Funny name – perhaps it's winding and twisty.'

'I've never been there.'

'Nor me,' said Maisie. 'And I jolly well wouldn't want

to.' She handed him a bowl of leftovers. 'Here, take this to Runner. I don't know how long we're going to be able to keep this up. Grandma Bone's bound to smell a rat, you know.'

'As long as it's not a dog,' said Charlie, trying to make light of the problem.

Maisie just shook her head.

On Sunday, Charlie managed to sneak Runner Bean in and out of the house before Grandma Bone woke up. They had a good race round the park and then Charlie fried bacon and eggs for their breakfast. Apart from a brief run in the garden after dark, Runner Bean spent the rest of the day on Charlie's bed.

On Monday morning Charlie's mother promised to take the dog for a walk when she got back from work, and Maisie agreed to keep him fed. But as Charlie got ready for school he began to worry.

'You must keep quiet,' he told Runner Bean. 'No barking, understand? I'll see you on Friday.'

With mournful eyes the big dog watched Charlie close the door between them.

*   *   *

As Charlie and his friend, Fidelio, walked up the steps to Bloor's Academy, Fidelio said, 'There's a very pretty girl trying to get your attention.'

'Oh.' Charlie turned to see Belle looking up at him from the bottom of the steps.

'Hullo, Belle. This is Fidelio,' he said.

Belle gave Fidelio a dazzling smile. 'I see you're in Music. Violin?' She nodded at the case Fidelio was carrying.

'Yes,' murmured Fidelio. He seemed rather lost for words, which was unusual for him.

'See you later.' Belle skipped into the hall. 'I remember,' she whispered, 'no talking.' And off she waltzed, towards the pencil and paintbrush sign. Her green cape floated round her in a particularly stylish way as she bobbed into the green cloakroom.

'Wow!' said Fidelio, as soon as they had passed under the two trumpets. 'Who is she, Charlie?'

'I'm not sure,' Charlie muttered. 'She's staying with my great-aunts. What colour would you say her eyes were?'

'Blue,' said Fidelio. 'Bright blue.'

'Well, the next time you see her, they'll probably be

green or brown,' said Charlie.

'Really?' Fidelio looked interested. 'I can't wait to see that.'

They went into assembly where Fidelio joined the school orchestra and Charlie took his place beside Billy Raven, the youngest child at Bloors. He was an albino, with snow white hair and spectacles that made his round red eyes look permanently surprised.

After assembly Charlie had a trumpet lesson with old Mr Paltry. He hadn't practised over the holiday and found himself out of breath and out of tune. Mr Paltry rapped his knuckles, shouting, 'No, no, no! A *flat*, not sharp!' His squeaky voice almost deafened Charlie, and when the bell went he was so eager to escape he almost fell over Olivia Vertigo as he raced for the garden door.

Today her hair was striped black and gold, her face was covered in white powder and her eyes were ringed with black. She looked more like an exotic racoon than anything else, though Charlie refrained from saying so.

Unfortunately, Fidelio didn't. 'Hi, Olivia! Are you playing a racoon this term?' he asked as he strolled up.

'Who knows,' said Olivia. 'Manfred's writing the end-

of-term play – with Zelda's help, of course.' She nodded at a group of sixth formers on the other side of the playing field. Manfred, the head boy, was talking earnestly to Zelda Dobinski, a tall, skinny girl with a large nose.

Charlie noticed that Manfred's sidekick, Asa Pike, was staring at Belle walking arm in arm with Dorcas Loom. Asa broke away from the group of sixth formers and walked across to the two girls. He had a crooked smile on his pale, weaselly face and, as he approached the girls, he ran his fingers through his red hair, almost as if he were trying to tidy himself up.

Charlie grabbed Fidelio's arm. 'Look!' he said. 'Asa's speaking to a junior. I bet that's never happened before.'

'Except when he's been telling them off,' said Fidelio.

'That girl with Dorcas is really pretty,' muttered Olivia.

'Her name's Belle,' Charlie told her. 'She's living with my great-aunts.'

Olivia whistled. 'I can't imagine any child living with them. By the way, have you seen Emma?'

The boys shook their heads and Olivia sauntered off to look for her friend. She eventually found Emma sitting on a log by the old castle walls. She was holding what

appeared to be a small, neatly-written letter.

'What's up, Em?' said Olivia, perching beside her.

'I found this by Mr Boldova's desk.' Emma held up the letter. 'It must have fallen out of his pocket. I didn't mean to read it. I meant to give it back, but then I saw something and . . . well, look.'

Olivia took the letter and read,

> My dear Samuel,
>
> We have it on good authority that the shifter is heading your way. What form it will take God only knows. But it will recognise you, so get out of that place, Samuel, as soon as you can. I have resigned myself to losing Ollie, although your mother still grieves. She can't stop herself from buying the jam he so loved. We have a room full of the stuff now, and it breaks my heart to see it. I know you feel your brother's loss as deeply as we do, but you must give up the search. We could not bear to lose you, too. Come home soon.
>
> Dad

'What d'you think?' said Emma.

'Interesting,' said Olivia. 'But I think you should put the letter back on Mr B's desk. It's none of our business who he is, or what he's up to.'

'But it *is*.' Emma pushed her long blonde hair out of her face. She was very agitated. Olivia knew her friend liked Mr Boldova. He was young for a teacher, but he was good at art, and he seemed to be on the children's side whenever there was trouble.

'You remember when Manfred locked me in the attic, well someone let me out, and whoever it was had a passion for jam. I heard Manfred teasing him about it. I know this sounds peculiar but he, or she, seemed to be invisible. And then there was this boy, Ollie Sparks, who was lost in the attics ages ago. He got out eventually and everyone thought he'd gone home, but maybe he didn't. Maybe he was punished. Maybe he's still up there.' She glanced up at the tiled roof of the academy.

'Hmm. So what d'you want to do about it?' asked Olivia.

Emma shook her head. 'I don't know.'

A hunting horn sounded across the garden and the two friends agreed to talk again in the afternoon break.

Emma's next lesson was French, but first she ran to the

art room. It was empty and she was just sneaking the letter on to Mr Boldova's desk, when he walked in.

'Emma?' He looked surprised. 'Shouldn't you be in another lesson?'

'French, sir. But, it's just that I . . . well, I'm really sorry, but I read your letter and . . .' Suddenly Emma found herself telling Mr Boldova about the invisible presence in the attic, the person who liked jam.

Mr Boldova listened intently and then he sat at his desk and said, 'Thank you, Emma. Thank you very much. Will you promise not to tell anyone else about this?'

'But I've already told Olivia Vertigo, and she might tell some of our friends.'

'Can you trust them, Emma?'

'With my life,' said Emma.

Mr Boldova smiled. He looked a rather outdoor sort of person for an artist. His face was tanned and his dark brown hair was drawn back in a ponytail, somewhat like Manfred Bloor's, only Manfred's hair was black and stringy.

Emma said, 'What happened to Ollie, sir? We thought he'd gone home after he escaped from the attics.'

'I'm afraid not,' sighed the teacher. 'Our parents live a long way from here. Dr Bloor agreed to put Ollie on a train in the company of the matron's sister, a Miss Yewbeam. She told us that Ollie went to get an orange juice from the station cafeteria, and never came back.'

'I bet he never even got as far as the train,' said Emma hotly. 'Those Yewbeams are evil. They're Charlie Bone's great-aunts, you know, and they make his life a misery.'

'Ah, Charlie Bone,' Mr Boldova said thoughtfully.

'I'd like to help Ollie,' Emma went on. 'He helped me, you see, and I could probably find the place where he's kept.'

'Better leave it to me, Emma. It could be dangerous.'

'Sounds like it could be dangerous for you too, sir.'

'I can take care of myself,' Mr Boldova said cheerfully. 'Now run along to your French lesson.'

Emma went, but she didn't hurry. She had too much on her mind. She was ten minutes late for her French lesson, and Madame Tessier was furious. She was an excitable woman and always hated the first day of term. She missed the sunny French city where she had been born, and complained constantly about the gloomy, grey academy,

with its creaking floorboards, erratic heating and poor lighting. She was only there because Dr Bloor offered her a salary she couldn't resist.

'Go! Go!' she shrieked at Emma. 'You don't want my lesson, you don't come in. It eez too late. So *allez – allez!*' She waved her long fingers at Emma. 'Get out!'

Emma got out – quickly.

'You too,' came a husky whisper.

Emma looked down the corridor and saw Charlie Bone standing outside the history room. He had just said that Napoleon was the Emperor of Russia. Mr Pope, the history teacher, had screamed at Charlie, telling him he was an ignoramus, and he didn't want to see him in his class a minute longer.

'I didn't really hear the question.' Charlie's loud whisper echoed across to Emma. 'I was thinking about a dog.'

Emma glanced up and down the corridor. There was no one about. 'What dog?' she whispered.

In as quiet a voice as he could manage, Charlie told Emma about Benjamin and Runner Bean. 'Why were *you* sent out?' he asked.

'I was just late,' said Emma. She recounted her conversation with Mr Boldova.

Charlie's eyes gleamed with interest. Yet another mention of someone dangerous on the move. Was it possible that they were one and the same?

'So you reckon Ollie Sparks is in the attics?' He paused and looked thoughtfully at the ceiling. 'Let's go and look, shall we?'

Emma was horrified. 'What, *now?*'

'I can't think of a better time,' said Charlie. 'We've got half an hour before the end of the lesson. Everyone else is in class, so who's going to see us? I'm bored stiff hanging around out here.'

Before Emma could think of an excuse, Charlie had sprinted off towards a staircase at the end of the corridor. Emma wished she hadn't told Charlie about the attics. He was inclined to rush into things without thinking them through. But she felt she had no choice but to follow.

They crept up one staircase after another. Once they bumped into Dr Saltweather, who interrupted his humming to ask where they were going. 'We've been sent to get books from the library,' said Charlie. And Dr

Saltweather waved them on, although they were nowhere near the library. But Dr Saltweather was oblivious to everything but his precious music.

They ran along dark passages and through empty, creaking rooms and, as they drew near to the west wing of the building, Emma became increasingly nervous. She still had nightmares about the time when her only escape was to become a bird and fly.

Memory, or instinct, led her to the cell-like room where Manfred Bloor had once imprisoned her. Light from a tiny window showed dark walls patched with green slime, a narrow bed covered in filthy blankets and black, broken floorboards.

'What an awful place,' Charlie murmured.

'Manfred locked me in,' said Emma. 'But then someone turned the key on the other side, and the door opened. I rushed to see who it was but there was no one there. Manfred caught me and brought me back, but – and this is the strange part – he said to someone, "Any more trouble and you won't get jam for a week." That's why I thought it might be Mr Boldova's brother, Ollie. Because he liked jam.'

'Perhaps he's been locked in some other gruesome room like this one.' As Charlie turned to the door it suddenly slammed shut. Charlie lifted the latch and pulled. Nothing happened. The door appeared to have jammed. 'Must have been a draught,' muttered Charlie.

'There isn't any draught,' said Emma.

'But what else could it have been? No one came in. We'd have seen them.'

'Maybe they were invisible.'

'Hey!' called Charlie. 'Is anyone there?'

No reply.

'What on earth are we going to do?' cried Emma. She looked at her watch. 'We've only got twenty minutes.'

'This is stupid.' Charlie rattled the door while Emma pulled the latch.

'It must be Ollie,' said Emma. 'Ollie! Ollie Sparks, are you there?'

Silence.

'Ollie, we've come to help,' Charlie explained. 'If you're there open this door, *please!*'

Emma and Charlie waited. There was a soft creak. A key turned in the lock. Charlie pulled the door and it

swung inwards. There was no one in the passage outside.

The two children stepped out. They squinted down the shadowy passage, searching for a door, a recess, any place where someone could be hiding. Emma's foot touched an empty jar and it rolled away, filling the passage with a loud rumble. When the jar finally came to rest, faint footfalls could be heard receding into the distance.

'He's running away,' Emma whispered.

They chased the footfalls down the passage, up a rickety set of steps and into a long room with a narrow skylight. The floor was littered with empty jam jars and comic books. At the far end of the room there was a bed with a clean-looking pillow and a patchwork cover. An oil lamp sat on a small bedside table and a huge cupboard stood just inside the door. There was nothing else in the room except a spindly chair and a battered desk that had been placed beneath the skylight.

'Ollie,' Emma said softly. 'Ollie Sparks, are you here?'

'What if I am?' said a rather mournful voice.

'Why can't we see you?' asked Charlie.

There was a pause before the voice replied, 'Cos I'm invisible, aren't I?'

'What happened to you?' asked Emma.

'The blue boa got me.'

'Boa?' said Charlie and Emma.

'Snake,' went on the mournful voice. 'Awful thing. I saw it, see. No one's meant to see it. It's a secret. A secret weapon.' There was a croaky laugh. 'Once I'd seen it, they weren't going to let me tell about it, so they brought me back here, and it – well, I was like a guinea pig – they let the boa squeeze me, only I didn't die, I just got invisible.'

'Hell!' gasped Charlie.

'It didn't get all of me.' A breathless sort of giggle shivered on the air. 'It missed my big toe.'

In horrified fascination Charlie's eyes were drawn towards the floor. Emma couldn't help screaming. She had already seen it: a small pink blob, lying just a few steps away from them.

'Sorry,' said the voice. 'It used to have a bit of sock and shoe on it, but the shoe got too small, and the sock wore out. A toe's a bit disgusting on its own, isn't it?'

'Not at all,' said Charlie cheerfully.

'They tried to get all of me back,' said the voice. 'They made me drink revolting potions, and threw smelly liquid

over me, and once they covered my bed in spiderwebs while I was asleep.'

'That is so gruesome,' said Emma.

Charlie said, 'Ollie, why don't you escape? The door's not locked. You could easily run away. No one would see you.'

'You try it.' The voice sounded very aggrieved. 'I came out once. People walked into me, knocked me down – some of them screamed. I couldn't get out of the main doors, no one can. I didn't feel safe, so I came back here.'

'It must be so horrible, all alone,' said Emma. 'What do you eat?' She was actually wondering *how* Ollie ate, but was too polite to ask.

'The food's mostly disgusting, but Manfred gives me nice jam. I suppose he does it to keep me quiet. And, in case you're wondering, I eat just like anyone else. Only you can't see the food once it's inside me.'

Emma hoped Ollie couldn't see her blush.

Charlie had an idea. 'If you come down to the dining hall at suppertime, we'd all be sitting still. No one would bump into you, and I could make room for you between me and my friend, Fidelio. The food's not so bad on the

first day of term.'

Silence. Perhaps Ollie was thinking.

Emma remembered the most important thing of all. 'Ollie, your brother's here,' she said. 'He's come to look for you.'

'What? Samuel? I can't believe it. Wow!' Suddenly the pink toe jumped into the air and there was a small thud as two feet landed back on the floor.

'So, if you come down to supper, you can see him,' said Charlie.

'Yes. Oh, yes . . .' A pause. 'But I won't know the time. I haven't got a watch.'

Charlie took off his watch and held it out. 'You can borrow this.'

It was disturbing to see a watch gradually disappear into thin air.

'Don't worry, it'll come back when I take it off. Everything I wear becomes invisible,' Ollie explained. 'Everything I eat or hold or put on.'

Emma glanced at her own watch and cried, 'We've only got five minutes. We'll never make it.'

She dashed out of the room and down the steps while

Charlie followed, calling, 'Sorry, Ollie. Got to get back to class. Hope to see – er – hear you later!'

Emma and Charlie tore down the empty passages, often taking the wrong turn, or the wrong staircase, but ending up, at last, on the landing above the entrance hall. Their relief was short-lived. Approaching them from the other side of the landing was Dr Bloor.

The big man strode towards the children. 'Why aren't you two in class?' he boomed.

Emma and Charlie froze. They couldn't think of an explanation.

Dr Bloor stared down at them with cold, pale eyes. Suspicion was written all over his big face with its dull grey skin and thick, bluish lips. 'Well, I'm waiting.'

'We – er . . .' Charlie floundered.

'Ah, there you are,' said a voice, and Mr Boldova appeared behind the headmaster. 'I've been looking for these two,' said the art teacher. 'Did you find it?'

Charlie swallowed, 'Um . . .'

'That rat's such a rascal.' Mr Boldova turned to the headmaster. 'I brought it along for the children to draw, but it keeps escaping. When I saw these two idling away I

asked them to look for it. Any luck, Charlie?'

'No, sir.'

'And now we're late for our next lesson,' said Emma meaningfully.

'Dear, oh dear,' said Mr Boldova. 'I'd better explain to your teachers. All my fault. Come along, kids. Sorry about this, Dr Bloor.'

Mr Boldova propelled the two children past Dr Bloor towards the corridor that led to the classrooms.

Dr Bloor swivelled round to watch them go. 'That rat must be found,' he shouted. 'See to it, Mr Boldova.'

'Of course, Headmaster.'

As soon as they were out of earshot, Charlie whispered, 'Thanks, sir. I think we were heading for detention.'

'Keep walking,' the art teacher said quietly.

But Emma couldn't remain silent any longer. 'We found Ollie,' she said softly.

Mr Boldova almost tripped. He gripped the children's shoulders and said, 'What? Tell me how – where?'

As they hurried on to their classrooms, Charlie and Emma took turns to tell the teacher about poor Ollie and his invisibility.

'Ollie's going to try and get down to supper tonight, sir,' said Charlie. 'So you might . . . well, he might be able to talk to you.'

'I can hardly believe it,' murmured Mr Boldova. 'Invisible or not, Ollie's here, and he's alive. I thought they'd taken him to one of those awful castles of theirs. I've spent almost a year trying to find out which one.'

'Do they have many, sir?' asked Charlie.

'At least five,' said Mr Boldova. 'This is so incredible. I shall take Ollie home at the first opportunity. We'll find a way to cure him when we get home.'

They had reached Madame Tessier and Mr Pope, who stood fuming outside their classrooms. Mr Boldova quickly explained that he had borrowed Emma and Charlie to search for his rat, Rembrandt, who had escaped from his cage. The two teachers grudgingly accepted his apologies and told the children to hurry along to lunch.

'I'll see you two at suppertime,' said Mr Boldova, giving the children a big smile. And he walked away, whistling merrily.

Would Charlie's plan for Ollie work? He was sure it wouldn't be as easy as Mr Boldova seemed to think.

Runner Bean is rumbled

On his way to the dining hall Charlie had to pass the portraits. They hung on either side of the long, softly lit passage: haughty-looking women in lace and silk, men in dark robes or wearing velvet coats and white breeches. You might think that Charlie would be curious to know what they had to say but, to tell the truth, he was beginning to find their bad-tempered whispering, rude demands and boring jokes rather tiring. He was also afraid that one of them might come leaping out at him. So he usually tried to avoid looking at them.

Except for today. Something had jogged

his memory.

'Ah, there it is.' He stopped before a portrait of a bold-looking woman in red velvet. She had dark ringlets, and a necklace of rose-coloured jewels sparkled at her throat. SELENA SPARKS said a small bronze plaque at the bottom of the frame.

'Selena Sparks,' Charlie murmured.

'What about her?' Fidelio said over Charlie's shoulder.

'Ssh!' hissed Charlie. He waited for a voice, but Selena had nothing to say to him. Perhaps she was shy. 'I knew I'd seen that name,' Charlie muttered. 'All these people are descended from the Red King. So maybe Ollie is too.'

'Ollie who?' asked Fidelio. 'I wish you'd talk sense, Charlie.'

'Emma and me . . .' Charlie began.

He was interrupted by a shout from Manfred, the head boy. 'Move on, you two, you're cluttering up the passage.'

The boys hurried on, but Charlie, glancing back, saw Manfred stop and stare at Selena Sparks. Charlie hoped Manfred wouldn't guess why he was so interested in the portrait.

As they took their places in the long underground

dining hall, Charlie whispered, 'Can you leave a gap, Fido? Someone might want to sit between us. Someone invisible who's hungrier than we are.'

'Really?' Fidelio raised his eyebrows. 'It didn't take you long to get tangled up in something, did it?' He moved closer to his neighbour, leaving a small space between Charlie and himself.

It happened to be one of the best meals Charlie had eaten at Bloor's; morsels of chicken and bacon floated in a creamy sauce, and he was tempted to eat every scrap, but he pushed a few pieces to the side of his plate, in case Ollie turned up.

'He can have all of mine,' said Fidelio, who was a vegetarian.

'I'll have it,' said his neighbour, a large boy called Morris who played the bassoon.

'No, you won't,' said Fidelio. 'It's for Cook's dog. He hasn't been well.'

Morris gave him a funny look, then ran his thumb round his own almost-empty plate and licked it. This was against the rules.

Charlie wondered if Ollie had got lost. He scanned the

three long tables, looking for signs of a disturbance. He couldn't see Emma, who sat somewhere on the Art table. The Drama table was in the middle, and it was by far the noisiest, even though Manfred sat at the head. Apart from Asa and Zelda, who sat on either side of Manfred, everyone in Drama faced away from the head of the table. They perched rather crookedly on the benches, with the shoulder nearest to Manfred slightly raised. No one wanted to be caught by the head boy's hypnotising stare when they were halfway through a meal.

Aside from these strange postures, Charlie couldn't detect anything out of the ordinary amongst the purple capes, so he turned his attention to the far end of the room, where the teachers sat at a table on a raised platform. From here they could keep an eye on the children below them.

'Who are you looking for?' Billy Raven goggled at Charlie through a fringe of thin white hair. He was sitting on the other side of the table, a few places away from Charlie. His spectacles made his red eyes look far too large for his head.

'I'm not looking for anyone,' said Charlie. 'I thought I

saw a bat.'

This wasn't so unlikely. Hundreds of bats lived in the old building.

As Billy looked away, Charlie felt something push against his side. Fidelio gave him a surprised look, and then a piece of chicken disappeared from the side of his plate.

'Thanks,' came a disembodied whisper. 'Delicious.'

Several more pieces disappeared, and no one seemed to notice, until Gwyneth Howells, sitting opposite Charlie, gulped, 'Uh! Your meat just . . .' and the fork that was halfway to her mouth dropped to the floor, laden with peas.

Gwyneth bobbed under the table to retrieve her fork and let out an ear-splitting scream. She came up for air, her round, brown eyes starting out of her head. 'I saw . . . I saw . . .' she cried. 'There's a . . . there's a . . . under the table, there's a . . .'

'There's a what?' said her neighbour, Rosie Stubbs.

'There's a TOE!' cried Gwyneth, and she fainted backwards over the bench, landing in an untidy heap on the floor.

Several girls, and even boys, screamed and a husky voice gasped 'Yikes!' in Charlie's ear. His plate went flying and his tumbler rolled to the floor, water spilling all over the table.

'I'd better get out of here,' whispered the voice, while Rosie Stubbs shouted, 'Gwyneth's fainted.'

Dr Bloor stared out from his seat at the head of the high table. Matron Yewbeam and Miss Chrystal came down the steps into the main hall and ran up to Gwyneth. The matron shook Gwyneth's shoulder, but as the poor girl was obviously unconscious, she lifted her up and, helped by Miss Chrystal, carried her out of the dining hall.

Mr Boldova had come to the edge of the platform and Charlie caught his eye. The art teacher gave a slight shrug and Charlie shook his head.

Ollie had fled and Charlie knew it would be hard to coax him back again. In fact this time he might even be locked in. From the end of the Drama table, Manfred was watching Charlie suspiciously. He had seen him looking at Selena Sparks, and he knew Ollie's toe was still visible. Perhaps he had put two and two together.

After supper Charlie gave Fidelio a better explanation

about what had happened to Ollie Sparks. He spoke in an undertone as they hurried up the long passage leading from the dining hall. This time he didn't even glance at Selena, in case Manfred was watching.

'Here we go again,' said Fidelio. 'Another problem for you, Charlie.' They had reached the blue cloakroom, and here the two friends parted; Fidelio taking books and pens to his classroom, while Charlie had to carry his homework upstairs to the King's Room.

How did he manage always to be late, even when he thought he'd been hurrying? All the other endowed children had got to the room before him. As Charlie bounded through the tall black doors, Manfred was making an announcement.

'Two of the endowed have left the school.' Manfred glared at Charlie as he dropped his books on to the round table. 'Quiet, Bone!'

'As I was saying, Beth and Bindi have left us, but we have a new member.'

It had been such an extraordinary day, Charlie had almost forgotten Belle. But here she was, sitting between Asa and Dorcas. Asa's weaselly features were screwed into

an odd smirk and his scraggy red hair stuck out in oily spikes. If it hadn't been for his yellow eyes, you would have found it hard to believe he could turn into a beast.

'Her name's Belle,' Manfred continued.

'Belle what?' said Tancred, his pale hair bristling with electricity.

'It's not important,' Manfred waved his hand.

'It is to me,' Tancred persisted. 'I like to know a person's whole name.'

Charlie wished Tancred would look away before Manfred did something nasty. The head boy had an angry, hypnotising stare coming on.

Tancred's friend, Lysander, gave him a warning nudge. 'Leave it, Tanc.'

But Tancred was like a dog with a bone. 'My name's Torsson,' he said, looking at Belle, 'and what . . .?'

'Donner,' Belle said suddenly.

'Belledonner? That's deadly nightshade,' said Gabriel. 'It can kill you.'

'Actually, that's *belladonna*,' said Belle. 'In small quantities it dilates the pupils. Eyes become shinier, more lustrous and beautiful.' All at once, her own round blue

52

eyes flashed with purple lights.

The effect was so startling even Tancred was speechless. All round the table, books were opened and pens clutched. Homework began in silence.

Above the door the Red King stared out from his portrait. The cracked and ancient painting always raised Charlie's spirits. But he'd never managed to hear the King's voice. Sometimes he caught a low muttering, sometimes a creak and the swish of a cloak, but then a shadow would fall behind the king, like a dark stain on the canvas; a hooded figure that chilled the blood just to look at it. And Charlie knew that the sinister shadow was blocking his contact with the king.

Eleven of us now, thought Charlie. Last term there had been twelve endowed children. What would happen if there were ten, like the original ten children of the Red King? Would the pattern be repeated, five on one side, five on the other? And this time, who would win?

'Get on with your homework, Bone!' Manfred's voice made Charlie jump.

'Yes, Manfred.' Charlie looked down at his open book.

After homework, Emma caught up with Charlie as he

made his way to the dormitories. 'It was Ollie, wasn't it?' she said breathlessly. 'The toe under the table?'

Charlie nodded. 'I don't think we'll be able to get him back again,' he whispered. 'He was terrified. And I've got a nasty feeling Manfred knows.'

'I'll tell Mr Boldova,' said Emma.

As they approached Emma's dormitory, they saw two girls standing outside the door. Their heads were close together and their furtive giggling seemed to imply that they were sharing an unpleasant secret.

'Belle and Dorcas,' Emma observed. 'It's as if Belle has put Dorcas under a spell. They go everywhere together.'

'Good luck, Em,' Charlie muttered as Emma slipped into the dormitory.

'Trying to ignore me, Charlie Bone?' said Belle as Charlie walked past.

'Not at all,' Charlie called without looking back. 'I can see that you're busy.'

'You ignore me at your peril, Charlie!'

Was it Belle who had spoken? Charlie couldn't be sure. The voice belonged to someone much older. Someone whom it would be foolish to disobey.

Charlie hurried on.

Belle and Dorcas were seldom seen apart after that day. Charlie became convinced that Belle wasn't what she pretended to be. And then there was Ollie Sparks. The summer term was proving to be more than a little interesting.

'You'd better watch it, Charlie,' said Fidelio one day. 'If you go up in the attics again, you're bound to get detention.'

'Or worse,' muttered Olivia.

'Hypnotised for life,' said Emma. 'Like Manfred tried to do to me.'

They were sitting on a log pile in blazing sunshine. It promised to be a brilliant summer, which was just as well because the school play would be performed in the open air.

'What's Belle like as an artist?' Charlie asked Emma. 'I mean, can she draw?'

Emma shrugged. 'Who knows? She makes things. We've been asked to design clothes for the play, and the set.'

The hunting horn sounded and the four children slid off the logs and headed towards the academy.

'I wish we could do something about Ollie,' said Emma as they reached the garden door. 'Maybe if we got detention and stayed in school till Saturday . . . What about you, Charlie?'

Charlie was tempted but he had other responsibilities. 'Runner Bean,' he said. 'I've got to get home to look after him.'

It had just been decided that they would all meet on Sunday to discuss Ollie's problem, when Fidelio suddenly announced, 'I can't. I've got to play in a concert.'

Charlie was sorry to hear this. Fidelio was such a good person to have around in a crisis. He had excellent ideas, and he never gave up. But Fidelio was also a brilliant musician. Charlie was afraid he would be seeing less and less of his friend this term.

When Charlie got home on Friday evening, so many things went wrong he forgot all about Ollie. He had expected to see his great-uncle, but Paton hadn't returned and there was not even a word from him.

'I'm a bit concerned,' said Maisie. 'It's not like Paton. And I'm afraid it gets worse, Charlie. I've got to leave

here tomorrow.'

'What!' Charlie was really worried. His mother had to work on Saturday, and the thought of spending a day alone with Grandma Bone was unpleasant to say the least. 'Where are you going? Can't I come with you?'

'No chance, Charlie.'

Maisie's sister, Doris, had been taken ill. Maisie would have to go and look after her. There was no one else. But something would have to be done about Runner Bean. While Charlie was at school there'd be no one in the house to feed him and look after him.

'You'd better take him for a run now,' said Maisie. 'I haven't had time. You can't keep him hidden much longer, Charlie; a lively dog like that is bound to be rumbled.'

As Charlie ran up to his room he could hear him whining and scratching the door.

'Ssssh!' Charlie leapt into the room and slammed the door behind him.

Runner Bean put his paws on Charlie's shoulders and licked his face.

'Thanks, but yuk!' whispered Charlie.

There was a creak on the landing and a voice called, 'Is that you, Charlie, slamming doors?'

'It's me, Grandma,' Charlie shouted. 'I'm changing out of my school stuff.'

When Charlie put his head out of the door, Grandma Bone had gone back to her room.

'Come on, Runner,' Charlie said softly.

He ran downstairs with the dog bounding behind him. They left by the back door and slipped into the narrow street that led to the park. An hour later, Charlie and the dog arrived back at number nine, exhausted and hungry.

His mother was getting anxious and Charlie explained that he didn't know the time because he'd sort of lost his watch. Mrs Bone sighed, 'Honestly, Charlie. I suppose you'd better wear mine until you find yours.' She handed him her watch, which was fortunately not too feminine. 'I'm just going to help Maisie with her packing,' she said. 'Back in a tick.'

Charlie searched for the tins of dogfood Maisie had hidden. He'd just spotted a tin of Bonio in the larder, when there was a loud scream and then a growl.

Charlie looked round to see Grandma Bone rooted to

the spot, just inside the door. 'WHAT'S THAT DOING IN HERE?' she screeched, pointing at Runner Bean.

'It's Benjamin's dog,' Charlie said nervously. 'You know, Runner Bean.'

'Of course I know, but why isn't it in Hong Kong?'

Before Charlie had time to answer, Runner Bean, snarling horribly, rushed at Grandma Bone, who shrieked again.

'Get it out!' she shouted.

'Er . . .' Charlie played for time.

Runner Bean bared his teeth and snapped at the old lady's ankles.

'That's it!' yelled Grandma Bone. She backed out of the kitchen, shouting, 'I'm ringing pest control – the dogs' home – the police. They'll have to put that dog down. It's dangerous.'

'Grandma, you can't,' Charlie pleaded.

But Grandma Bone was already on the phone, giving her address, telling someone about the killer that needed exterminating. 'They'll be round at half past six, and I'm not coming downstairs until that wretched Bean has gone.'

Charlie was horrified. He didn't know what to do. Maisie and Mrs Bone came running down to see what all the fuss was about. But they didn't know what to do either. Maisie was so worried about her sister, she said she couldn't think straight.

'If only Uncle Paton was here,' Charlie wailed. 'He'd know what to do.'

Charlie felt like taking Runner Bean and rushing over to Fidelio's or Emma's, or even Olivia's place. But could they hide the big dog, or would they want to, with Runner Bean looking so wild? He hated being shouted at; his eyes were rolling and low rumbles kept coming from his throat.

'We'll explain to whoever comes, that he must on no account be put down,' said Mrs Bone. 'We'll tell them that he's never bitten anyone, ever.'

'Perhaps he'll go to a nice dogs' home where you can visit him,' Maisie said hopefully.

'He'd hate it,' cried Charlie. He took a large dish of goose liver pâté and ten slices of honey-roast ham out of the fridge, and poured them into the dog bowl that Maisie had hidden under the sink.

'Grandma Bone's specials,' said Maisie in hushed tones.

'I don't care,' said Charlie. He knelt beside Runner Bean and stroked the dog's wiry head.

It was very satisfying to see his grandmother's favourite food being wolfed down a shaggy throat.

The time was twenty-five minutes past six.

Charlie stood up. 'I've made a decision. I'm going to ask Fidelio to hide Runner until Benjamin comes back.'

'With all those noisy musicians?' said Maisie. 'He wouldn't last a minute.'

And then someone rang the doorbell.

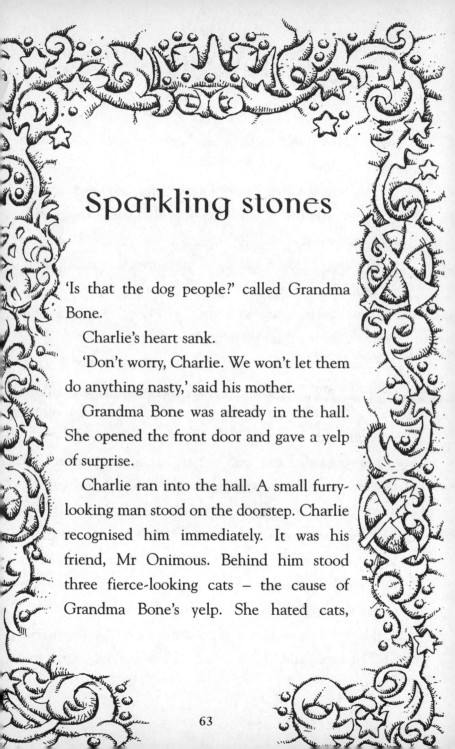

Sparkling stones

'Is that the dog people?' called Grandma Bone.

Charlie's heart sank.

'Don't worry, Charlie. We won't let them do anything nasty,' said his mother.

Grandma Bone was already in the hall. She opened the front door and gave a yelp of surprise.

Charlie ran into the hall. A small furry-looking man stood on the doorstep. Charlie recognised him immediately. It was his friend, Mr Onimous. Behind him stood three fierce-looking cats – the cause of Grandma Bone's yelp. She hated cats,

particularly orange cats. These were orange, yellow and copper-coloured.

'Are you the dog exterminator?' she said suspiciously. 'I've seen you before, and these peculiar cats.' She took a step backwards.

The man held up a card. 'Orvil Onimous, madam. Pest control.'

'You'd better come in and get the dog,' said Grandma Bone. 'Charlie, if it's got a lead, fetch it.'

Charlie leapt back into the kitchen, followed by Mr Onimous and the cats.

'It's OK,' Charlie whispered to Maisie and his mother. 'Mr Onimous has come.'

Maisie pulled the lead out of her apron pocket and handed it over. 'You be good to that dog,' she insisted.

Mr Onimous winked.

There was some good-natured growling and sniffing between cats and dog as Mr Onimous clipped the lead to Runner Bean's collar, but the big dog seemed very happy to see them all again.

'How did you know about Runner?' Charlie whispered.

'The cats,' said Mr Onimous. 'They wanted to pay you

a visit. I didn't know nothing till I got here. Come and see us at the café, Charlie.'

Grandma Bone called, 'Come on, come on! Get that dog out of here.'

Mr Onimous led the cheerful dog away, and Runner Bean looked back, just once, to give Charlie an encouraging bark.

'Cheerio, folks,' said Mr Onimous.

Grandma Bone slammed the door. Luckily it was Charlie who answered the bell when the real pest controller turned up. 'It's OK,' Charlie told the man, 'we found the dog a home.'

With one problem solved, Charlie had a good night's sleep. In fact he overslept. The next thing he knew, Maisie was shaking him awake.

'I'm off now, Charlie. The taxi's waiting. Your mum's already gone to work, and Grandma Bone's off somewhere.' She put a scrap of paper on Charlie's pillow. 'It's the Yewbeams' address. In case you need them. After all, they are your aunties. I hate leaving you on your own, love, but I've got no choice.'

'I'll be OK,' yawned Charlie. He couldn't imagine why he would need to call on the Yewbeams.

Maisie gave him a peck on the head, and then she was gone.

It seemed unnaturally quiet. Charlie couldn't remember ever being completely alone in the house before. Uncle Paton had always been there. Always. What *had* become of him?

After breakfast Charlie called in at the greengrocer's to see his mother. She was weighing apples for an impatient-looking man and there was a long queue behind him.

'I can't stop now, Charlie,' she muttered. 'See you at teatime. You'll be all right, won't you?'

'Sure. I'm going over to Emma's,' Charlie said cheerfully.

Emma lived with her aunt, Julia Ingledew, in a bookshop behind the cathedral, but as Charlie began to make his way up the steep road to Ingledew's, he found himself pulling Maisie's scrap of paper out of his pocket. His aunts had a very strange address: number thirteen, Darkly Wynd.

'Darkly Wynd,' murmured Charlie. Was that a road, an

alley, or another town entirely? Charlie went into a newsagent's. He bought a tube of peppermints and showed his scrap of paper to the woman behind the counter.

'Darkly Wynd? You're not going *there*, are you?'

'I thought I might,' said Charlie.

'Not a good idea. It's a nasty place. Not suitable for young lads like you.'

Charlie was intrigued. 'Why?'

'Very dark. No street lights.'

'But it's daytime,' Charlie pointed out.

'Things have happened in that place, love. Better not go.'

'I've got relations there,' said Charlie.

The woman leaned over the counter, staring at Charlie. 'What sort of relations?' she asked.

'Aunts. Great-aunts. I'm sure I'll be all right. Please tell me where it is.'

The woman sighed and said, 'All right, but don't say I didn't warn you. Turn right at the top of this road, then go on till you get to Greybank Crescent. It's off there somewhere.'

'Thanks.' Charlie left the shop before the woman could

utter any more gloomy warnings.

Greybank Crescent was what it sounded like: a crescent of tall, grey buildings facing a semicircle of dusty grass. A huge fir tree stood in the centre, lending an air of shadowy menace to the place.

Exactly halfway round the crescent there was a gap in the terraced houses and a faded sign nailed to a side wall said DARKLY WYND. Charlie turned into a narrow, murky alley. On either side grimy windowless walls towered up to the sky. A damp wind swirled into his face and it was hard to believe that only a moment ago, he'd been standing in sunlight.

The alley broadened into a courtyard surrounded by gaunt, ancient-looking houses. Like giant walls they seemed to lean inwards, blotting out the light. Above them hung the darkest cloud Charlie had ever seen.

He shivered and began to walk past the houses, counting the numbers on the doors. Nearly every house appeared to be deserted. Windows had been boarded up, peeling doors nailed shut. Someone or something had driven all the former residents away. At number five a group of youths burst out of the door, fighting and

screaming. Charlie hurried on. At number nine, a rough-looking man emerged from the basement. He bellowed at Charlie, who began to run. At number eleven a dustbin lid crashed to the pavement and a rat ran between Charlie's legs.

Darkly Wynd didn't lead anywhere. At the end of the courtyard a block of buildings, taller than the others, stood facing Charlie. They had strange turrets and iron-framed balconies, tall arched windows with pediments of gnomish faces and unlikely beasts. The first house was number thirteen.

Charlie mounted the stone steps. On the black door at the top a brass knocker, shaped like a hand, hung above the number thirteen. Charlie didn't knock. Of course he didn't. Instead he leaned over the railings and peered into a long window. The room beyond was filled with dark, looming furniture. He looked through the window on the other side of the porch and saw portraits of grim and serious people, hanging three deep on every wall. The house was silent. It appeared to be empty.

As Charlie retraced his steps he noticed that the next house was also numbered thirteen, and so was the next.

'Poor postman,' muttered Charlie. The second house was also silent and gloomy, but from the third came a whirring, ticking sound.

To get a better view, Charlie ran down the basement steps and climbed on to a narrow ledge beneath the long window. Standing on tiptoe he could just see into the room beyond.

What he saw there was more interesting than he could have hoped for. A long oval table almost filled the room. It was covered with scraps of cloth, sparkling sequins, feathers, buttons, tiny squares of mirror, velvet, leather and reels of cotton. A row of lights in bell-like brass shades hung over the table, illuminating three figures. Belle sat at a sewing machine, while Aunt Venetia and Dorcas stood side by side, watching her. Aunt Venetia was holding a long hatpin with a black beetle on the tip. Belle said something and Venetia stuck the hatpin into a piece of red velvet. The velvet immediately became a writhing mass of shiny black beetles.

Dorcas gasped – and so did Charlie.

Belle looked at the window and her violent blue stare sent Charlie toppling back on to a row of dustbins.

Looking down at him from the front door, was Asa Pike.

'Wh-what on earth are you doing here?' asked Charlie, picking himself up.

'I could ask you the same question.' Asa, who usually went about wearing a tatty disguise, looked extremely smart. He wore a leather jacket, white shirt, blue checked tie and stone-coloured trousers. As if this wasn't surprising enough, he was carrying a bunch of tulips.

'My aunts live here,' said Charlie.

'So why are you spying instead of going in?' asked Asa.

'Mind your own business.'

Asa shrugged and rang the doorbell, while Charlie leapt up the basement steps. When he reached the pavement, a sound from above made him glance up. A man looked out from a high barred window; he had dark hair and a solemn face. Charlie felt sure he knew him. He got the impression that the man was a prisoner.

Charlie ran on, down Darkly Wynd, trying to get the horrible picture of crawling beetles out of his mind.

'Have you been to a horror movie?' said Emma, as Charlie leapt into Ingledew's. 'You look awful.'

'I've been somewhere horrible all right,' said Charlie. He told Emma about the beetles and Darkly Wynd.

Emma's eyes widened and then she said, 'To tell the truth it doesn't surprise me. Your great-aunts are so gruesome. My auntie's making sandwiches. D'you want some?'

Charlie certainly did. Julia Ingledew made delicious sandwiches with very exotic fillings. Today was no exception. Unfortunately, Saturday was Ingledew's busiest day, so they all had to eat sitting behind the counter and Miss Ingledew kept jumping up to help the customers.

A man with an expensive taste in books, and suits by the look of it, had just left the shop with a rare book on fish. But Miss Ingledew didn't look as happy as she should have, considering the huge sum of money she'd been given. She nibbled a sandwich, cleared her throat and said, 'Charlie, what's happened to your uncle?'

'I don't know. He's gone off somewhere.'

Miss Ingledew looked anxious. 'It's just that he usually comes to the shop at least twice a week, and there's been no word.'

Charlie was pleased to see that she reddened slightly. It

meant that his uncle's crush on Miss Ingledew wasn't entirely hopeless.

'He left a note saying the aunts were plotting,' Charlie explained. 'And he had to stop someone dangerous from arriving.'

'Wow!' exclaimed Emma. 'I wonder if he succeeded.'

'Me too,' said Charlie.

'I do hope he's all right,' said Miss Ingledew anxiously. 'I don't know what I'd do without . . . I mean, he's so dependable, isn't he, Charlie?'

'Certainly is,' agreed Charlie.

Charlie got home in time for tea, but wished he hadn't. Grandma Bone decided to put in an appearance, which meant that he had to eat a disgusting vegetable pie, instead of his usual chips.

There had been no word from Uncle Paton, but Grandma Bone didn't seem worried any more. 'I'm sure he's having a lovely holiday,' she said.

This convinced Charlie that the opposite was true. He also had a sneaking suspicion that his grandmother now knew where Paton had gone. Her smug expression could

only mean one thing. His uncle was in danger.

After a painful half hour, Grandma Bone left Charlie and his mother to do the washing-up.

Charlie gave a sigh of relief. 'Mum, I'm worried about Uncle Paton. How can we find out where he's gone?'

'We can't, Charlie. Your uncle knows what he's doing.' She glanced at herself in the mirror and brushed her shoulders.

'You haven't got another boyfriend, have you?' Charlie asked.

His mother's answer wasn't very reassuring. 'What makes you think that?'

'Please don't forget Dad,' said Charlie.

She smiled pensively. 'Of course I won't, Charlie.'

On Sunday afternoon Charlie went to the Pets' Café as usual. It was a good place for friends to meet, as long as they didn't forget to bring a pet.

Today the bouncer, Norton Cross, let Charlie in without a pet. 'Mr Onimous told me all about Runner Bean,' said the big man. 'Your pet's waiting for you, Charlie.' He pointed to a table where Gabriel sat, feeding

biscuits to Runner Bean.

The yellow dog gave a happy bark when he saw Charlie and jumped up, almost knocking Charlie over. After making a big fuss of Runner, Charlie sat beside Gabriel, whose lap was covered in gerbils.

'I'm surprised Runner didn't eat those,' Charlie remarked.

'I don't think he eats things that move,' said Gabriel.

The Pets' Café door clanged open and three more customers came in: Olivia and a white rabbit, Emma carrying a strange-looking bird in a cage, and a surprising visitor, Mr Boldova. He held up his black rat, Rembrandt, and Norton Cross waved him on into the café.

While the girls came over to Charlie's table, Mr Boldova went to the counter.

'Mr B came into the bookshop yesterday,' Emma explained. 'He wants to talk about Ollie and the boa thing, Charlie. So I brought him here.'

Mr Boldova arrived at the table with a tray of cakes and orange juice. 'My treat,' he said. 'Pass them round.'

The art teacher took a seat between the girls while the cakes were divided as fairly as possible.

'Emma says you want to talk to me, sir,' said Charlie, biting into a giant flapjack.

Mr Boldova lost his cheerful expression. 'Yes, Charlie. I'll come straight to the point. There's a new girl in Art. Belle Donner. Apparently she's staying with your aunts. Does that mean she's related to you, Charlie?'

Charlie choked on a crumb. 'I hope not,' he croaked.

'Hey, what's going on?' asked Olivia. 'Is there something we ought to know?'

'Yes, what *do* you know about Belle?' said Mr Boldova.

'Nothing,' said Charlie, 'Except her eyes keep changing colour and . . . and . . . I saw . . .'

'What?' said Olivia impatiently.

Charlie told them about Darkly Wynd and the beetles. 'It was one of my aunts who did the beetle thing, but I'm sure Belle had something to do with it. She's got some sort of power over them.'

'It must be her.'

'Her who?' said Olivia.

Mr Boldova gave a grim smile. 'Emma has probably told you by now that my younger brother, Ollie, was a pupil at Bloor's. Just over a year ago he disappeared. When I came

to Bloor's to try and discover what had happened to him, I had to take on a new identity. There are people in Bloor's who would certainly want to get rid of me if they knew who I was.'

'Get rid of!' said Emma.

'I'm afraid so.' Mr Boldova took a thoughtful bite of his fruit cake. 'One way or another.'

'About Belle . . .' Charlie prompted.

'Ah, Belle.' Mr Boldova wiped his mouth on a brown Pets' Café napkin and said, 'Beyond the mountains in the north-east, there's a castle. It was built in the twelfth century and once it had another name. Now it's known as Yewbeam Castle.' He looked at Charlie.

Charlie muttered, 'Yewbeam,' but he didn't interrupt.

Mr Boldova continued. 'For centuries the descendants of the Red King have lived in Yewbeam Castle. Most of the owners have been endowed. In the year 1900, a baby was born in the castle. She was named Yolanda. Her father was a shape-shifter, her mother a hypnotist. On her twenty-first birthday, Yolanda inherited the castle, although . . .' Mr Boldova glanced at the children's expectant faces, '. . . although it cannot be said that her

father was thoroughly dead.'

'*Thoroughly* dead?' squeaked Olivia. 'What does that mean?'

'It means that one can never be sure when a shape-shifter has ceased to exist. Yolanda is now over a hundred, and she can still take the shape of a twelve-year-old girl.'

'You mean,' breathed Charlie, 'that Yolanda is – Belle?'

'I'm fairly certain,' said Mr Boldova. 'And I'm afraid that she's recognised me. My home isn't far from hers, and she has always resented the people in Sparkling Castle. There used to be so much fun, so much sparkle, but since Ollie went, we don't enjoy making things glitter any more, my father and I. Yes, we both have the talent. Sadly, Ollie doesn't. His gift is musical; he was also blessed with boundless curiosity, and I was always afraid this would lead him into trouble.'

'There's a portrait of Selena Sparks, sir. Was she a sparkler?' Charlie asked.

'Selena – ah, yes, a wonderful lady by all accounts. We're descended from her brother, who didn't have the gift. Selena never married. Having too much fun, no doubt.'

Charlie longed to ask how the sparkling happened, but he thought that the time wasn't quite right. Olivia had no such qualms.

'What d'you do, sir?' she asked. 'How d'you make things sparkle?'

'Never mind about that,' said the teacher. And then, seeing the disappointed faces, he said, 'Oh, well,' and reached into his pocket. He brought out a fistful of small stones and, holding them over the table, he let the stones roll gently in his open palm. Four heads bent closer, and suddenly the stones began to sparkle. The children could feel the heat from the dazzling radiance the stones threw out, and Runner Bean, the rabbit, the parrot and the gerbils all began squeaking and barking in unison.

The rat, Rembrandt, being used to such spectacles, watched in silence.

Mr Boldova closed his fist and the sparkle died. Emma's bird immediately cried, 'I'll be darned!'

'They can be dangerous,' said Mr Boldova, slipping the stones into his pocket.

'How can you hold them, sir, when they're so hot?' asked Gabriel.

'To tell the truth, I've no idea,' said the teacher.

Mr Onimous appeared beside the table, wanting to know what had been going on. 'Who's been upsetting my customers?' he said, meaning the animals.

Mr Boldova was about to confess when Mr Onimous suddenly put a finger to his lips. 'No. Don't tell me, you're one of them, aren't you, sir?' He winked at Charlie and went on, 'What d'you think of old Runner Bean? Looks happy enough, doesn't he?'

'He looks great, Mr Onimous. How's he getting on with the cats?'

'No problems, Charlie. They're pals. Speaking of the flames, they've been showing a lot of interest in that school of yours just lately. Is everything OK there?'

For a moment, Charlie hesitated, then looking at Mr Boldova, he said softly, 'No, it isn't.' He lowered his voice and told Mr Onimous about Belle and invisible Ollie.

'Strike me!' murmured Mr Onimous. 'No wonder the cats are curious.'

At that moment a group of very noisy customers arrived: four black dogs with square muzzles and dangerous eyes. The two youths who accompanied them looked mild

enough, but Charlie sensed something awkward about them. They were both overweight, with sandy hair and pink, freckled faces. You could tell that they hadn't spent much time training their dogs.

'Rottweilers,' muttered Gabriel. 'You'd better watch Runner. They're nasty fighters.'

Mr Onimous hopped away to attend to the barking that had broken out, while Runner Bean began one of his low grumbles. He would have liked to get closer to the Rottweiler gang, but didn't dare chance it.

The children finished their tea and, after several hugs, Charlie led Runner Bean to safety behind the counter. 'See you next week,' he said to the yellow dog.

As he walked towards the door the Rottweilers moved into his path. Their growls had a menacing edge and for a moment Charlie didn't dare to pass them.

'Sorry, mate.' One of the youths gave a reluctant grin and pulled the Rottweilers out of the way.

Gabriel already had the door open and Charlie sprinted through it, almost knocking over the girl standing outside: Dorcas Loom.

'Hi!' said Charlie. 'What're you doing here?'

'I'm waiting for my brothers,' said Dorcas.

'Haven't you got an animal?' asked Gabriel.

'Don't like them,' said Dorcas.

At that moment Mr Boldova came through the door, followed by Emma and Olivia.

'Oh!' Dorcas's eyes grew very round. 'Fancy seeing *you* here, sir.'

The art teacher gave a slight smile. 'Hullo, Dorcas.'

And then Dorcas caught sight of Emma's bird. 'How cute,' she said. 'What is it?'

'A mynah. I wouldn't . . .' She was too late to stop Dorcas poking her finger into the cage.

'Coochy! Coochy!' said Dorcas.

The mynah pecked her finger and Dorcas gave an ear-splitting shriek.

One of the Rottweiler youths stuck his head out of the door, and said, 'What's the matter, Dorcy? What happened?'

'Beastly, rotten, vile, smelly bird bit me!' cried Dorcas.

'You shouldn't keep vicious pets,' said the youth, glaring at Emma.

Mr Boldova said, 'Don't be stupid. I'd say four

Rottweilers posed more of a threat than a mere mynah.'

The youth raised his fist, thought better of it, and withdrew behind the door, saying, 'We'll be out in a sec, Dorc.'

Dorcas had by now calmed down a little but when Emma apologised for her mynah's behaviour, Dorcas wouldn't even look at her.

'Bye, Dorcas,' the others called as they walked away.

Dorcas turned her back and sucked her finger.

When they reached the high street, Mr Boldova said, 'Now, look. I don't want any of you to try and rescue Ollie again.'

'But . . .' Charlie began.

'No. It's too dangerous,' Mr Boldova said forcefully. 'Believe me. I'm grateful for your help, Charlie and Emma, but it's up to me now. OK?'

The children grudgingly agreed and the art teacher walked off in the direction of Bloor's Academy. Emma and Olivia took a street that led to Ingledew's bookshop, and Gabriel and Charlie headed up to the crossroads.

Before they parted, Charlie said, 'D'you think Dorcas was spying on us? She's changed a lot lately. Ever since I

saw her in the house in Darkly Wynd, I've had this feeling that she's not what we all thought she was.'

'She's certainly lost weight,' said Gabriel.

'It's not just that,' Charlie said with a grin.

'Well, she's endowed. But we don't know how – yet. As for spying, I thought Billy Raven was the spy. We all know he's in league with Manfred and that horrible old Mr Ezekiel.'

'There's always room for another spy,' said Charlie thoughtfully. 'And Billy might not be any use to them, now that we all know. Besides, I feel kind of sorry for Billy, being an orphan and having to live in that dark old building all the time. Never going home, ever. Imagine!'

'Can't,' Gabriel admitted with a shiver. 'See you tomorrow, Charlie!'

Gabriel loped away with a gerbil clinging to a clump of his floppy hair. It looked so funny Charlie couldn't help smiling, but then his thoughts turned to Belle and his smile faded.

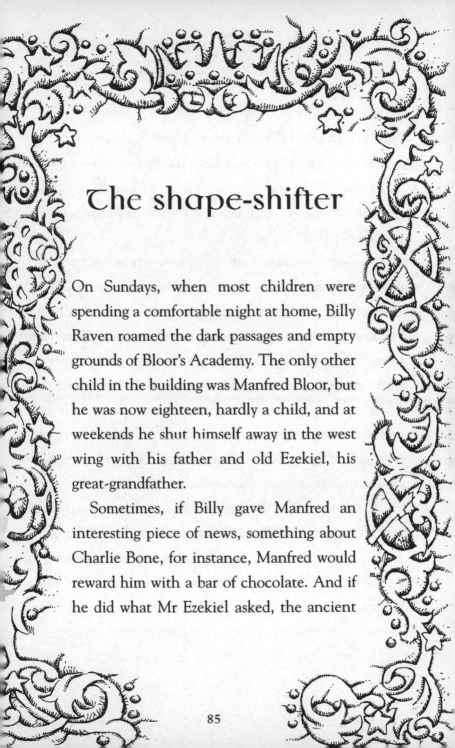

The shape-shifter

On Sundays, when most children were
spending a comfortable night at home, Billy
Raven roamed the dark passages and empty
grounds of Bloor's Academy. The only other
child in the building was Manfred Bloor, but
he was now eighteen, hardly a child, and at
weekends he shut himself away in the west
wing with his father and old Ezekiel, his
great-grandfather.

Sometimes, if Billy gave Manfred an
interesting piece of news, something about
Charlie Bone, for instance, Manfred would
reward him with a bar of chocolate. And if
he did what Mr Ezekiel asked, the ancient

man would give Billy a late-night mug of cocoa.

Today it was Billy's eighth birthday, but so far no one had remembered. Last year Cook had made him a cake, but the Bloors had let the day pass without so much as a 'Happy birthday, Billy!'

You might wonder how Billy knew it was his birthday; after all, no one had spoken of it since he was a year old. Billy knew because the date was fixed firmly in his head. He knew because the animals knew, and they had told him.

Billy was a baby when his parents died. He was brought up by an aunt who was kind but strict. When Billy was two, a beautiful cake had arrived in the post. The aunt's dog ate it, candles and all. For this the dog was beaten, and so was the cat, for good measure.

On 4 May, when Billy was three, the dog and the cat said, 'Cake day, Billy!' But no cake arrived. The same thing happened when Billy was four and five. By this time, out of the aunt's hearing, Billy and the animals had been having long conversations. When Billy turned six, he said to the aunt, 'Am I going to get a cake today?'

The aunt said, 'Who told you that it was your birthday?'

'The dog and the cat,' said Billy.

The aunt gaped at him. At last she said, 'You can talk to animals, then?'

'Oh yes,' said Billy, thinking that this was something everyone could do. 'I talk to them a lot.'

The aunt said no more, but the very next week, Billy was sent to Bloor's Academy.

He felt lonely in the dark, massive building. He kept getting lost, and he began to think that people were trying to keep things from him. They didn't want him to know who he really was. Cook was kind, though, and he often talked to the dog, Blessed, an old fat creature with a hairless tail. He might have been ugly, but Billy loved him all the same. The old dog always had time to listen to him.

Last term Billy had kicked Blessed. He didn't mean to. It had just happened and Billy regretted it bitterly. Blessed wouldn't tell him something he badly wanted to know, and he'd lost his temper. Now Blessed wouldn't speak to him, and there were only the mice and an occasional rat to talk to. Mice were boring; they were only interested in food and babies. Rats were better. Mr Boldova had a rat that told jokes. Its name was Rembrandt.

Today Mr Boldova had taken Rembrandt for a walk. Billy wondered where they had gone. Hoping for a treat of some kind he began to make his way to the top of the west wing, where Mr Ezekiel lived. The old man had a huge, musty room crammed with ancient stuff; urns and pots, bones and swords and jars full of dead things. Mr Ezekiel was a magician, but not a very good one.

Billy had just reached the top of a rickety staircase when he heard a scream. He peered down the long gas-lit passage that led to Mr Ezekiel's room. Something was coming towards him; a short fat dog howling its head off.

'Blessed!' Billy grunted in the dog's language. 'What's the matter?'

'Tail! Tail!' cried Blessed. 'Tail hurt!'

The old dog rushed up to Billy. 'Can you see?' he begged.

Blessed used to have an ugly bald tail. What he had today was even worse. A tiny pink stub stuck out from his bottom.

'Not much tail left, I'm afraid,' said Billy. 'What happened?'

'Snake,' said Blessed. 'Blue snake. Blessed bit snake. Mr

Zeke said no. Snake squeezed tail. Blessed ran.'

'Looks like he bit it off,' Billy observed.

'No, no, no! Tail still there,' whined Blessed. 'Squashed. Squeezed. Hurt.'

'Honestly, it's not there,' said Billy.

'Liar!' cried Blessed. 'Tell Cook.'

Billy didn't like the sound of this blue snake. He decided to give Mr Ezekiel a miss. He would go and look for Cook instead.

Billy would never forget his eighth birthday. He didn't get a card, or a present. He didn't even reach Cook in her kitchen. Something happened on his way there. He was walking across the landing above the entrance hall, when the new girl, Belle, appeared. She came from the small door that led to the music tower. Almost at the same time, Mr Boldova walked out of the green cloakroom at the other end of the hall.

The girl and the art teacher stared at each other for some time. All at once, Belle said, 'Good evening, Samuel Sparks.'

The art teacher said, 'And you are . . .?'

'No prizes for guessing who I am,' cackled Belle. Her

voice was old and deep.

'Yolanda,' the teacher whispered as if he was afraid of the name.

'Yesssss!' The girl flung out her arms, and as she did this, a veil of grey, like thin smoke, began to swirl around her body. 'Now you see me, now you don't,' she sniggered.

'I *can* see you, unfortunately,' muttered the art teacher.

'Sad Samuel! You've come to find your little brother, haven't you? Well, you never will.' Belle was changing shape. White hairs drizzled into the blonde curls, her pretty features stretched and sagged, and she was growing taller and taller. Now she was an ancient woman, with yellow skin that hung in folds beneath her chin, and a huge crag of a nose.

Billy didn't want to go on watching, but he couldn't help himself. He sank to his knees and peered between the oak railings.

Mr Boldova approached the hag. He pulled something out of his pocket and opened his fist. A cluster of small stones lay in his palm; gradually they began to glow, and then fierce red sparks flew out of the teacher's hand.

Billy gasped, his spectacles slid off his nose, and he only

just managed to catch them. The people below were too intent on each other to notice him.

'Those won't help you, Mr Sparks,' sneered Yolanda. 'Ollie was a wicked boy, he had to be punished. And now I've got to punish you.'

'We'll see about that!' Mr Boldova raised his fist and flung the burning stones at the old woman. She screamed as her hair and bits of grey clothing began to smoulder, and then, in a deep, chilling voice, she said, 'You've done it now!'

She stared at the teacher. Stared and stared. He took a step towards her and faltered. He took another and stopped. His face was white and his eyes looked frightened and faraway. Desperately, he felt in his pocket, searching for more sparkling stones, but he couldn't withdraw his hand. He couldn't move. He seemed almost to have stopped breathing.

'That'll teach you,' said Yolanda. She patted her hair and the scorch marks on her dress, and then she turned on her heel and disappeared through the door to the music tower, leaving Mr Boldova as still and silent as a statue.

Suddenly, with a loud squeak, a black rat jumped out of

Mr Boldova's pocket and ran across the hall. He began to leap up the stairs, and when he got to the top he came racing up to Billy.

'Help!' squeaked the rat. 'Help! Help!' He gazed up at Billy imploringly. 'Help Rembrandt,' he wailed. 'Help master.'

'I'll try,' said Billy. He picked up the rat and walked slowly along the landing. The art master hadn't moved. Billy descended the wide staircase. The burning stones lay scattered across the hall and Billy had to step between them. The stones were losing their colour now; some were already ash-grey, like dead coals.

Mr Boldova didn't appear to see Billy. The white-haired boy moved closer and said, 'Sir, your rat.' He held Rembrandt out to him.

'What!' Mr Boldova stared at Rembrandt. 'What's that?'

'Your rat, sir,' said Billy.

'I haven't got a rat.'

Rembrandt gave a squeak of distress.

'Honestly, it is yours, sir. It's called Rembrandt.'

Mr Boldova began to move, but he clearly wasn't

himself. He turned and walked in the opposite direction. 'Take it away!' he shouted. 'Bin it!'

If rats could pass out, Rembrandt would have done just that. As it was, he went quite limp. Billy tucked him under his sweater and ran up to his dormitory.

'Gone,' muttered the rat as Billy sank on to his bed.

'What's gone?' said Billy. 'D'you mean Mr B?'

'Dead,' said Rembrandt. 'Light gone out.'

Billy realised what the rat meant. 'You mean his real self, don't you? His soul?'

Rembrandt sighed.

Billy was so shaken by what he had seen, he couldn't stop shivering. Belle wasn't a girl at all, but an old, old woman. She had changed her shape, but she had also done something terrible to Mr Boldova. Belle was a hypnotiser, like Manfred Bloor.

'Two endowments,' Billy murmured. He lay back on his bed and closed his eyes. He wished he could go home and talk to someone. But there was no home to go to. Mr Ezekiel had promised he would be adopted, but the kind parents he mentioned had never turned up.

'Tell Cook,' said a voice.

Billy opened his eyes. The rat was sitting on his chest, staring at him.

'Tell Cook,' the rat repeated. 'Cook knows many things.'

At the mention of Cook's name, Billy realised he was very hungry. He slipped off the bed and, tucking Rembrandt under his sweater, he left the dormitory and made his way downstairs.

When he reached the hall, he found that the lights had come on and the burning embers had been removed. It was hard to believe that, only an hour ago, a battle of shifting shapes and flying sparks had taken place. Billy hurried on towards the dining hall. But as he passed the prefects' room, Manfred Bloor emerged.

'Ah, there you are, Billy,' said the head boy. 'You look startled. Anything been happening?'

Billy hesitated. He felt that Belle's shape-shifting was something he shouldn't have seen. 'N-no, Manfred.'

'Nothing to tell me, then?'

Billy wanted to talk about Belle and Mr Boldova, but he'd have to mention the rat. And he desperately wanted to keep him. He shook his head. 'No.'

'Nothing? No titbits about Charlie Bone?' Manfred's coal black eyes glittered.

Billy couldn't be hypnotised. He had found this out soon after he had arrived at Bloor's. Manfred had tried to practice his horrible skills on him, but it had never worked. Perhaps it was because of his dark red eyes. 'Nothing to report,' he said.

Manfred looked disappointed. 'What's that under your sweater?'

'My gloves. I was feeling cold.'

'Aww!' said Manfred in a mocking voice.

'It's my birthday today,' said Billy.

'Too bad. I haven't got anything for you. Now, if you'd got some news for me, well, I might be able to find a bit of chocolate.'

Billy loved chocolate. And it *was* his birthday. All he had to do was to tell Manfred what he'd seen, and hand over the rat. But what would Manfred do to Rembrandt? Billy gave a small shudder and said, 'As a matter of fact I've had a very boring day.'

'You're a hopeless case. Did you know that, Billy?' said Manfred scornfully.

'Sorry, Manfred.' Billy scuttled away from the head boy.

'I'm afraid I can't come to your birthday party,' Manfred shouted after him.

'What birthday party?' Billy muttered as he sped past the portraits, past three canteens and down and down into the underground dining hall.

And there he found that someone *had* remembered his birthday. A large iced cake sat at the end of the Music table. It had Billy's name on it, surrounded by eight flaming candles.

Billy gasped and took a seat beside the cake. Rembrandt poked his head out of the top of Billy's sweater and said, 'Oh, my! Cake and candles.' And then Cook appeared, singing 'Happy Birthday' in a high, trembly voice.

'Thanks, Cook.' Billy blew out the candles, made a secret wish and cut himself a large slice of cake.

'You've brought a guest, I see.' Cook nodded at Rembrandt. 'Where did you find him?'

Billy looked at Cook's kind, rosy face and suddenly it all came pouring out: Blessed's tail, the flying sparks, shape-shifting Belle and the horrible battle he'd just witnessed.

Cook wiped her pink brow with the hem of her apron

and sat beside Billy. She looked worried but not surprised.

'So it's *her*,' she muttered. 'I knew there was something not right about that girl. But whatever possessed Samuel Sparks to come here?'

'He came to find his little brother,' Billy told Cook.

'Ollie Sparks? Is he still here, then?' Cook seemed very surprised.

'Yes. That's what the old woman said. And she said no one would ever find him.'

'Oh, my goodness. Where've they hidden the poor boy? I was always worried about him. What's he been eating? If only I'd known.'

'D'you think they're starving him?' said Billy.

'Oh, I hope not, Billy. Dear, oh dear. What's to be done?' Cook got up and straightened her apron. 'I advise you not to eat all of that cake, Billy. When you and the rat have had what you want, I'll come and put the rest away for next weekend.'

As Cook made her way towards the kitchen, Billy called out, 'I know people think I'm a spy, but I won't tell Manfred or Mr Ezekiel about what I saw. I promise.'

Cook turned and looked at Billy. 'I'm sure they know

already. As for you being a spy, I don't blame you, Billy. One day you'll get the parents you want; if the Bloors don't see to it, then I will. But right now I'd better go and find the poor dog that's lost its tail.'

As Cook hurried up the corridor of portraits, a cold draught rushed round her ankles. This meant that the main doors had been opened. She reached the hall in time to see a figure slip through the doors before Mr Weedon slammed them shut.

'Who was that?' asked Cook.

'What's it to you?' said Weedon sourly.

Cook drew back her shoulders and said, 'I asked a civil question. The least you could do is to give me a civil answer.'

'Ooo!' mocked Weedon. 'Hoity-toity!'

'Are you going to tell me?' asked Cook.

'No.' Weedon bolted the doors and walked off.

Cook, who was extremely intuitive, knew another victim had been led into a trap. And from what Billy had told her, she could guess who that victim was.

She was right.

Mr Boldova, carrying a suitcase, walked across the

courtyard and under the arch between the two towers of Bloor's Academy. He descended the steps into the cobbled square, and there his gaze was drawn to the fountain of stone swans in the centre. The cascade of water glowed gold in the last rays of the sun.

Mr Boldova frowned. Why was he here? Where was he going? Who was he?

A black car pulled up at the other end of the square. The driver, a grey-haired woman, beckoned to Mr Boldova. He walked over to her.

'Can I give you a lift?' asked the woman.

'Er . . .' Mr Boldova scratched his head. 'I don't know where I'm going.'

'I do,' said the woman. 'I'm clairvoyant. Jump in, Samuel.'

'I'm not sure . . .'

'Do hurry up. We haven't got all day, have we?' The woman's laughter was cold and shrill. 'My name's Eustacia, by the way.'

Mr Boldova passed a hand over his eyes. There didn't seem to be anywhere else to go. He walked round the car and got into the passenger seat. There was something he

ought to do next, but what?

'Forget the safety belt!' Eustacia gave another wild laugh, and the car roared off at an alarming speed.

At first break, on Monday morning, when Charlie and Fidelio were hanging their capes in the blue cloakroom, Billy Raven came in with a bulge under his sweater. The bulge moved and Charlie asked Billy what he was hiding.

'Nothing,' said Billy, turning pink.

'Come on, Billy. It can't be nothing,' said Fidelio. 'It squeaked.'

Billy was about to deny this when the head of a black rat appeared at the top of his sweater.

'That's Rembrandt,' said Charlie. 'What are *you* doing with him?'

Billy pouted, and then he mumbled, 'Mr Boldova gave him to me.'

'I bet he didn't,' said Charlie.

Billy rushed out and ran along to the garden door, with Charlie and Fidelio in pursuit.

'It's OK, Billy,' Charlie called out. 'We're not accusing you of anything. That rat's always escaping.'

Billy didn't stop. He kept on running until he was lost in a sea of bobbing figures. Out of that same sea, two girls came rushing towards the boys.

'Something awful's happened,' Emma panted.

'What?' said the boys together.

While Emma gulped for air, Olivia said, 'Mr Boldova's left the school.'

'He can't have,' said Charlie. 'He'd have told us.'

Emma got her breath back. 'Exactly. Something awful's happened to him. I just know it. And I've got a horrible feeling those two are responsible.' She looked over at Dorcas and Belle, who were sitting on the grass, whispering to each other.

Having missed the meeting in the Pets' Café, Fidelio hadn't a clue what they were talking about. So the four friends walked round the grounds while Charlie filled Fidelio in. They were soon joined by Gabriel, who announced that he'd just seen Billy Raven feeding bits of toast to a black rat. Could it be Rembrandt?

'It could,' said Charlie. 'In fact it is. And now they say Mr Boldova's left, but I think something terrible has happened to him.'

'Something to do with *her?*' said Gabriel, eyeing pretty, blonde Belle, who was now combing her curls.

Olivia suddenly stopped dead in her tracks. 'If that girl's a shape-shifter, it's going to be hard to know where she is. She could look like anyone.'

'Or any *thing,*' said Fidelio darkly.

This thought was so awful they all fell silent.

On his way to homework that evening, Charlie caught up with Billy Raven, his arms full of books.

'Have you got Rembrandt with you?' Charlie asked.

'No. I put him in the dormitory cupboard,' Billy said quietly.

'I think we'd better find a different place for him,' said Charlie. 'Matron'll hear him scratching, and who knows what she would do if she found a rat in the dorm.'

Billy shuddered. 'He's going to be such a good friend. Already he's told me a lot of things I didn't know.'

'Has he told you why Mr Boldova left?' asked Charlie.

Billy's ruby eyes gazed over the top of his spectacle frames. He shrugged.

It occurred to Charlie that Billy might have seen what happened to the art teacher. 'You know something, Billy,

don't you?' he said.

They had reached the tall black doors of the King's Room and, ignoring Charlie, Billy pushed at the doors and rushed in. His books spilled out of his arms and tumbled to the floor.

'Calm down, Billy Raven!' Manfred shouted. 'What's the hurry?'

From her seat between Asa and Dorcas, Belle smiled at the albino. 'Don't be mean, Manfred. He's only small,' she said.

Manfred gave her a surprised look.

As Charlie bent to help Billy retrieve his books, he noticed that the small boy's hands were trembling. He was very frightened.

Once, twelve endowed children had sat evenly spaced at the round table. But gradually their positions had changed. Now there were two distinct groups. Manfred, Asa, Zelda, Belle and Dorcas sat on one side of the circle, while Lysander, Tancred, Gabriel, Emma and Charlie sat on the other. Billy was the odd one out.

'Sit next to me, Billy,' Charlie said softly.

Billy gave him a grateful smile and piled his books next

to Charlie's.

After homework Charlie kept close to Billy as they made their way to the dormitory. Gabriel caught up with them and, always interested in animals, wanted to know what had become of Rembrandt. When he heard that the rat was shut in a cupboard, he suggested they take him to the art room, where Mr Boldova had kept him in a large, airy cage.

'But could I visit him?' Billy asked. 'I don't belong in Art.'

'Course you can,' Gabriel assured him. 'Emma's always in the art room. Just ask her.'

'OK.' Billy rushed off and by the time the others had reached the dormitory, he was waiting for them, with Rembrandt under his cape.

The art room was on the same floor as the boys' dormitories. It was a vast space with a high ceiling and long windows facing north towards the castle ruin. Easels stood in various positions all round the room, and canvases were stacked three or four deep against the walls. Rembrandt's cage was in a corner beside the paint cupboard.

There was no one in the art room except Emma. She was painting a large white bird flying through a forest. She left the picture to show the boys where Mr Boldova had kept Rembrandt's food, at the bottom of the paint cupboard.

When the black rat had been made comfortable with fresh water and plenty of grain, Emma secured the cage door.

'I can't stop thinking about Mr B,' she said. 'We all miss him in Art. He seemed to be, you know, always on our side.'

Without any warning, tears began to gush down Billy's cheeks. 'I know, I know,' he sobbed. 'I saw.'

'*What* did you see?' said Charlie.

Billy ran his sleeve across his face and, in a frightened, choking voice, recounted the terrible events of his eighth birthday: Blessed's tail, the ancient woman who'd emerged from Belle's body, the flying coals and the sudden and dreadful stillness that had fallen over the art teacher.

'He didn't want Rembrandt,' sobbed Billy. 'He seemed to have forgotten everything – even who he was.'

'Hypnotised,' Charlie murmured.

The others stared at him in horror, and Emma said, 'There isn't much that Belle can't do, is there? How are we going to help Ollie now?'

'Do you know where he is?' asked Billy.

Charlie couldn't decide whether to tell him. He was sorry for the small albino, but he had been Manfred's spy. It would be better not to give him too much information until they were quite sure he could be trusted. The others had obviously come to the same conclusion.

'No, we don't know where he is,' said Gabriel. 'I think we'd better get back to our dormitories now, or Matron will be on the warpath.'

Billy begged to be given a few more minutes with Rembrandt, and the other three left him crouching beside the cage, squeaking softly at the black rat.

Billy stayed talking to Rembrandt much longer than he had intended. When he finally slipped out of the art room, Matron had already called, 'Lights out!'

He tore along the passage, clamping his spectacles to his nose, and tripping over his own feet.

'Where've *you* been, Billy Raven?' Manfred stepped out of a doorway, blocking his path.

Billy was too scared to lie, but he decided to tell a half-truth. 'I've . . . I've been feeding Mr Boldova's rat,' he said. 'I found him in the passage.'

'I don't think that's true, Billy,' Manfred said coldly.

'It is, it is,' said Billy desperately.

'I think you saw something, Billy. I think you rescued that black rat when our dear departed art teacher had a little accident.'

'No, no!'

Manfred glowered down at Billy. 'What did you see?'

'I didn't see anything,' mumbled Billy, looking away from Manfred's dreadful black eyes.

'Liar. You saw what happened to Mr Boldova and you told Charlie Bone, didn't you?'

Billy had a nasty feeling that if he told the truth it would get Charlie into trouble. 'No,' he said defiantly. 'I didn't see anything, and I didn't tell Charlie anything.'

Manfred gave a sigh of irritation. 'You probably think I'm leaving Bloor's at the end of this term, don't you?'

Billy hadn't thought about it. He shook his head.

'All the sixth formers will be leaving. It's the summer term. We have exams to do. That's why I'm rather busy at

the moment. But *I* shan't be leaving. I'll be here, with time on my hands to keep an eye on you.'

'I see,' said Billy in a small voice.

'So, you'd better remember who you're working for, Billy. Or you'll never get the nice kind parents that you want.'

The starling

Billy sat on the end of his bed. Everyone else in the dormitory seemed to be asleep, but Billy had never felt more awake. Before his horrible encounter with Manfred, he'd had the most amazing conversation with Rembrandt.

The black rat had talked of a house full of sparkling light and laughter. A house of books and music and pictures, where once a family had been happy. There had been a boy called Oliver, a gifted flute player. He was expected to develop an even greater gift, like his father and his brother, who could turn stones into fire. But he was sent

away to school and never came home again.

Billy remembered Ollie Sparks. He was in Music and used to stay with a friend at weekends. Ollie had been a very nosy boy, and this used to annoy people. He got into trouble for going where he shouldn't.

Rembrandt had told Billy that Ollie was still in the academy. The rat had smelled him out and found him in one of the attics. But Ollie couldn't be seen, except for one toe. There was also a snake up in the old part of the building. A dreadful blue thing. It was so ancient Rembrandt's brain could hardly fathom it.

'Mind-boggling,' Billy murmured.

'Billy, are you all right?'

Billy almost fell off the bed. He hadn't heard Charlie Bone creep up on him.

'I was just thinking about Rembrandt,' Billy whispered. 'He told me so much. I can't work it all out.'

'D'you want to come and stay next weekend?' Charlie asked. 'You could bring the rat.'

'Could I?' said Billy. 'OK, thanks.'

Charlie tiptoed back to bed, while Billy crept under his covers and had the best night's sleep he'd had in ages.

Over the next few days, Charlie was made aware just how seriously the academy took its summer play. Every break Olivia could be seen walking round the field learning her lines. Sometimes, Emma walked beside her, holding a folder that contained the scenes Manfred had printed out.

Fidelio spent more and more time in the music room, practising the incidental music for the play, and Charlie found that his breaktime companions were usually Gabriel Silk and Billy Raven. It soon became clear that Billy had learned all there was to know about the invisible boy from Rembrandt. But it seemed that he hadn't passed on the information to Manfred. Did this mean he could now be trusted? One day he even suggested that he should go and look for Ollie.

'At night I'm allowed to visit Mr Ezekiel,' said Billy, 'so if I'm caught Matron won't be surprised.'

'I don't like the sound of it, Billy,' Charlie confessed. 'Matron's capable of giving you a very nasty punishment.'

'Besides, there's that boa thing lurking about,' said Gabriel. 'We don't want two invisible boys stuck in the attics.'

'The boa must have got Blessed's tail,' said Billy thought-fully. 'Rembrandt says it's so old he can't fathom it.'

'Rats can't understand time,' said Gabriel know-ledgeably.

Charlie muttered, 'I'm not sure I can.'

He was just going indoors at the end of break when Olivia clutched his sleeve. 'Wait a minute, Charlie,' she hissed. 'We've got something to tell you.'

Charlie hung back as Billy and Gabriel were swept away with a crowd of children surging into the hall.

'What is it? I'll be late for my trumpet lesson.'

'I'm going out tonight, to look for that room where we met Ollie,' Emma said softly. 'And I'll have to be alone.'

'You're going to *fly*?'

Emma nodded. 'I can look in from the outside. Maybe fly in if there's a window open. I don't think I can rescue him yet. I just want him to know that we're still trying.'

'It'll be dark,' said Charlie. 'How are you going to see?'

'It gets light ages before we're up,' Olivia whispered. 'I think it's a brilliant idea. But we've got to make sure there's an open window on our floor, so Emma can get back in. Can you do that, Charlie? Belle sleeps next to me.

She's bound to close the dormitory window if I open it. She watches me like a hawk.' Olivia glanced at Emma. 'Well, perhaps not a hawk, more of a viper – no offence to vipers.'

Charlie grinned. He lost his smile when Asa looked out at them and shouted, 'What are you three doing? You look a mess. You'll be late for your classes if you don't hurry up.'

The three friends leapt into the hall and separated, each rushing to a different cloakroom. Charlie managed to reach Mr Paltry's wind room just before the old man turned up, complaining about all the extra work he had to do for the school play.

'You don't need to worry, Charlie Bone,' said Mr Paltry. 'It'll take years for you to reach the standard required for the school band.' And he added in an undertone, 'Probably never will.'

Charlie just grinned. Trumpet playing wasn't one of his priorities.

Before supper that night he met Gabriel and Fidelio coming out of the music room. When he told them of Emma's intended mission, they were eager to help. Fidelio suggested they leave as many windows open as possible,

but Charlie was worried this would be too obvious. Matron Yewbeam and her assistants were bound to go round the building checking all the windows.

'I just want you to cover for me when I leave the dormitory,' he told them. 'Say I'm in the toilet or something.'

'Matron never believes a word I say,' Gabriel muttered, 'but we'll do our best.'

Charlie waited until he heard the cathedral clock strike midnight. The sound of those twelve chimes never failed to send a shiver down his spine. It was on the stroke of twelve, eight years ago, that his father, Lyell, had been put into a trance from which he couldn't wake. Manfred Bloor was responsible. Even as a small boy he had tremendous power. Lyell's car had been found at the bottom of a deep quarry and everyone believed that he was dead, but Charlie knew that this wasn't true. Grandma Bone had destroyed every photo of his father and Charlie couldn't even remember what he looked like, but he was determined that one day he would use his endowment to find Lyell and wake him. In the meantime he would do everything he could to stop the Bloors getting their own

way and ruining people's lives.

Charlie got out of bed and crept to the door. It was pitch dark in the passage and he kept close to the wall until he found the staircase leading to the girls' dormitories.

The old treads creaked under his feet even though he climbed on tiptoe. When he reached the top, Charlie gave a sigh of relief and moved quickly to the faint patch of light coming from a small window. He opened it, just wide enough to admit a small bird, and was about to dash back to the stairs, when a shadowy figure caught his eye. It came gliding out of the darkness on the other side of the window, and Charlie was too shocked to move.

'What are you doing?'

The voice belonged to one of the last people Charlie would have wanted to meet.

'Belle!' he said. 'I couldn't sleep. Thought I'd take a walk.'

'On the girls' floor?' She moved closer and Charlie could see the glimmer of her horrible changing eyes.

'Wasn't thinking,' Charlie murmured.

'Tch! Tch! The window's open. No wonder it's so cold.'

Belle slammed the window shut and latched it. 'Better run back to bed before Matron finds you.'

'Er, yes.' Charlie walked back to the staircase. When he looked over his shoulder, Belle was still standing there. He would have to find a less conspicuous window.

The art room, thought Charlie. If it was hard to find his way upstairs, it was even worse getting back again. Charlie wished he had the torch Cook had given him last term. Matron Lucretia Yewbeam had confiscated it. She was probably keeping it in Darkly Wynd, Charlie thought. No chance of getting it back from there.

He found the right door, at last, and crept into the art room. If it hadn't been for pale starlight filtering through the long windows, Charlie would have crashed straight into a group of easels. As it was, he just managed to step round them and up to the windows. Here he realised that only a small section, at the top of each window, could be opened. It was impossible for Charlie to reach that high.

In a far corner, a spiral staircase led down into the sculpture room. Hoping to find an easier window there, Charlie made his way between easels and paintboxes, and

was about to descend when he heard a grinding noise and then a squeak. He could just make out Rembrandt's dark form, standing up at the bars of his cage.

'It's OK, Rembrandt, it's only me.' Charlie wished he could speak the rat's language, like Billy. But Rembrandt seemed reassured by Charlie's voice and went back to some serious nibbling.

Charlie tiptoed down the cold spiral of iron steps. As he reached the bottom he heard tapping, and noticed a tiny light coming from a far corner. Someone else was in the sculpture room. Charlie froze. Mr Mason, the sculpture teacher, was a strange man. It wouldn't have surprised Charlie to find the teacher still working at midnight.

A voice said, 'Who's that?' and a beam of light swung in Charlie's direction. 'Charlie? What are you doing here?'

'Wh-who's that?' stuttered Charlie.

'It's me, Tancred. Lysander's here, too.'

'Phew!' Charlie walked across to the source of light. He found Lysander sitting beside a block of wood, while Tancred stood behind him with a torch. They were both wearing green capes over their pyjamas.

'What are you doing?' asked Charlie.

Lysander explained that he was experimenting. 'Gabriel passed on the word about Ollie Sparks,' he said. 'Thought if I could, kind of, carve a likeness of Ollie, I might get the ancestors to give the invisible boy a bit of body – you know?'

Charlie didn't know. He couldn't understand what the African was talking about. 'D'you know what Ollie looked like?'

'Course I do,' said Lysander. 'I remember him well. Nice kid, but nosy. Too nosy. I can see him like it was yesterday.'

'Sander can do that,' said Tancred admiringly. 'He can remember details perfectly. He'll carve that piece of wood until it's so real you can see it breathing.'

'Really?' The block of wood was already taking on the shape of a boy and yet Charlie didn't see how it could help Ollie. Lysander's endowment was truly remarkable if he could turn a block of wood into a living, breathing person. But the real Ollie was trapped in the attics. How could having another Ollie help him? 'We don't need two Ollies,' Charlie said.

Lysander explained that once his spirit ancestors had seen a perfect likeness of Ollie they could give the

invisible boy shape and substance; they could make him visible again.

'Ah!' said Charlie. 'That's amazing.'

'And now may we ask why you are here?' said Tancred.

'Emma's going out tonight,' Charlie told them. 'As a – you know – she's flying. She's going to look for Ollie's room, so he knows we're still trying to rescue him.'

'Better not tell him about Mr B just yet,' warned Tancred.

'No. Not yet,' Charlie agreed. 'Thing is, Emma won't be able to get back through all those old attics. She'd get lost in the dark. So I'm trying to leave a window open.' He told the others about Belle.

'Hmm.' Tancred looked at the windows. They were exactly the same as those in the art room. Only the small sections at the top could be opened, and at present these were securely fastened. 'Mr Mason sometimes opens them with a pole,' he said. 'But it's not here.'

The tall blond boy began to stride about the room, and Charlie could feel a breeze sweeping round his feet. Bits of wood and paper, fragments of clay and small chisels began to slither and shuffle across the floorboards.

'Watch it, Tanc!' said Lysander.

'OK. OK. I'm focused,' said Tancred. 'Here we go!'

Finding an empty space in the centre of the room, he spun round, his cape flying out like a green wheel. Charlie watched, mesmerised by the swirling starlit dust motes until, all at once, Tancred's spinning shape came to rest. He raised his arm, pointing to the top of the window, and a bolt of pure, icy wind left his fingers and soared upwards. There was a sharp crack, and a pane of glass fell out. It dropped neatly into Tancred's upheld cape.

'What about that?' he said proudly.

'Perfection,' said Lysander.

'Out of this world,' breathed Charlie.

Tancred hid the pane of glass among a stack of boards standing against the back wall. 'Mr Mason will never notice,' he said.

Charlie looked up at the empty window frame. 'I wish we could watch her,' he murmured. 'I've never seen Emma fly, or even become a bird.'

'Some things are better done in secret,' Lysander said mysteriously. 'I think we should pack up now and get back to bed, or we'll never wake up in the morning.'

Tancred led the way with his torch, up the iron spiral staircase and through the art room. Charlie's dormitory was only halfway down the passage but, with a whispered 'goodnight', the two older boys crept on to a dormitory at the far end.

At that moment Emma was opening a window in the corridor outside her dormitory. Before she flew she had moments of terrible anxiety. She was never sure if her arms would become wings, or if the wings would lift her off the ground. She had to close her eyes tight and think of a bird, and then believe in herself, and in the ancestor who had passed on this strange gift.

Tonight Emma had chosen the form of a starling. Hidden by a tall cupboard, she began to shrivel and dwindle, becoming smaller and smaller, while shiny dappled feathers covered her body. She put the note she held into her mouth and when the transformation was complete she lifted her wings. But as she flew out of the window, someone in a pale nightdress stepped towards her. Emma soared into the starlit sky and the window clanged shut behind her.

She tried not to think about how she would get back, but concentrated on finding the attic room where Ollie Sparks was imprisoned. Twice she flew round the huge, gaunt building, perching every now and then on a window ledge, a pediment or a gutter. But the black room behind the tiny attic windows gave nothing away. Not a light or a shadow, no rumpled beds, jam jars or pink toes could be seen.

So Emma flew down to the floor beneath the attics, and here she did see something: a candelit room where an old man, propped up by a mountain of cushions, sat in a four-poster bed. Emma had seen that dreadful, wizened face before, when she, too, had been imprisoned in the attics. Old Mr Ezekiel now wore a red nightcap and a black velvet bed jacket covered in beads of shiny jet. He laughed to himself as his bony finger travelled over the page of a huge black book, and Emma quickly flew on.

On the floor below she saw Lucretia Yewbeam, in a purple nightgown, brushing out the long strands of her grey-white hair. And further on, Emma found Manfred Bloor, in a black robe, his dark hair released from its ponytail and hanging in thin cords round his face. He had

his back to the window, but Emma could see his reflection in the long mirror he was gazing into. And then he saw her.

Manfred only saw a starling, sitting on the ledge outside his window. But he stared at the bird's reflection, and then swung round. Emma flew off, her heart beating wildly. She opened her beak and gave a shrill cry of alarm. And her note floated away on the wind.

He knew it was me, thought Emma. He saw the note. What will he do now?

Uncle Paton's return

Next morning, Charlie thought he was the last one down to breakfast, but just as he was hurrying past the portraits he heard someone shuffling behind him. He looked round to see Emma, pale-faced and sleepy-eyed. While Charlie waited for her to catch up, another figure appeared. It was Olivia. Who else would wear bright yellow shoes with black socks? It was amazing the weird clothes that Drama children managed to get away with.

Olivia was rolling along in a strange lopsided way. 'I've bust the heel,' she explained, holding up a foot in a yellow

shoe. 'They're Mum's. Hope she won't have a fit.'

Emma regarded the shoe and yawned.

'How did you get on last night?' Charlie asked her.

Emma frowned. 'Couldn't find Ollie's window. They all look the same. And I dropped the note.'

'What note?' said Olivia. 'You never said anything about a note.'

'I was carrying one. To leave for Ollie. But all the attic windows were shut.'

'Carrying in your . . .?' Charlie was about to say 'beak', but couldn't quite manage it.

'Mouth,' said Emma, giving him a funny look.

Charlie said quietly, 'Did you find the window in the sculpture room?'

Emma yawned again. 'Eventually. Thanks.'

'It was Tancred.'

They had reached the dining hall, and here they had to part, each going to their own table. Charlie noticed that Emma had to sit beside Belle. He was worried for his friend. Suppose someone had found the note she'd written. If the Bloors knew she was trying to rescue Ollie, there was no knowing what they might do. I'm glad she

126

can fly, he thought to himself.

Beside him, Fidelio polished off his last speck of porridge and said, 'I'm sure there are things going on that I ought to know about, Charlie. Music's taking over my life a bit, but I still want to know what's happening to you lot.'

'Come to the Pets' Café on Sunday,' said Charlie. 'We'll all be there. Maybe even Lysander and Tancred.' He noticed Billy, staring at him from the other side of the table. 'And Billy,' he added.

'Billy?' Fidelio lowered his voice. 'Is that wise?'

Charlie shrugged. 'I think he's changing his spots, if you know what I mean.'

'Hmm,' said Fidelio.

During the first break, while the others were rehearsing for the play, Charlie helped Emma search for the note she'd dropped. He was just peering into the shrubbery beside the garden door, when Belle and Dorcas walked up to him.

Belle said, 'I didn't know you were interested in horticulture, Charlie.'

'Haughty what?' said Charlie.

'Never mind. What are you looking for?'

'Nothing.' Charlie shoved his hands in his pockets and walked away from them. He looked for Tancred and Lysander, but they were nowhere to be seen. Perhaps Lysander was working on his carving. Billy was missing too, but he had a rat to feed and comfort.

A few minutes before the end of break, Charlie met Emma. She hadn't found the note either.

'I think it must have blown into the courtyard,' she said.

This was bad news. It was impossible for any of the children to go in there once the main doors were shut on Monday morning.

'What did the note say?' asked Charlie.

Emma bit her lip. *'Don't give up hope, Ollie. We haven't forgotten you. E.'*

'E? Just E?' said Charlie. 'That's not so bad.'

'E is for Emma,' Emma said gloomily. *'They'll* know.'

'We'll just have to hope that *they* don't find it,' said Charlie.

His next lesson was history and, as usual, he found it very hard to concentrate. Luckily, Mr Pope didn't ask him

any questions. He seemed to have given up on Charlie, which was just as well, as Charlie was wrestling with several other problems at once, and none of them had anything to do with Napoleon.

For one thing, who were *they*? The Bloors obviously, and Belle, of course. But Weedon, the gardener, was a nasty piece of work. And the matron, Charlie's Great-Aunt Lucretia, was definitely an enemy. What about the rest of the staff? It was very difficult to guess. If only he had Uncle Paton to talk to, but there was no word of him still.

Before Charlie knew it, the lesson was over and Mr Pope was shouting, 'Another lesson has passed you by, Charlie Bone. There'll be a test on Napoleon's campaigns first thing on Monday morning. If you don't get more than seventy per cent you'll have detention.'

Charlie's jaw dropped. This meant a whole weekend wasted on learning dates. He gathered up his books and marched grimly out of the history room.

Other children were faced with the same problem. News of tests abounded. The staff had apparently caught test fever. There were very few happy faces at supper that night.

'I don't think I'll be able to make it to the Pets' Café this Sunday,' said Gabriel, staring glumly into his soup.

'Nor me,' said Charlie.

Billy leaned across the table. 'I can still come home with you, can't I?' he begged.

Charlie didn't have the heart to say no. 'Course you can. You can test me on my dates.'

Billy beamed. 'You're on.'

On Friday, Charlie heard about Lysander's progress on the carving. He and Emma were caught up in the usual rush to the dormitories to collect their bags. In spite of the looming tests, a babble of excitement had broken out. No one could remain despondent when there were two days and three nights of freedom to look forward to. Steps were climbed two at a time, and dark passages rang with hurrying footsteps and happy laughter.

'I saw the carving last night,' Emma whispered to Charlie. 'It's fantastic, like a real boy. Lysander's just begun to paint it. A few more days and it'll be ready.'

'How's he kept it secret?' asked Charlie.

'He puts a sheet over it in the daytime. Mr Mason never pays any attention to it. He's too busy doing his

own sculpting.'

'Belle's in Art,' said Charlie anxiously.

'I don't need reminding. But, as far as I know, she hasn't seen the carving.'

They parted at the bottom of another staircase and Charlie went to find Billy.

It was true that Belle hadn't seen Lysander's carving, but she'd been aware of it. She had merely been biding her time. As soon as all the other children had climbed aboard the school buses, Belle went into the sculpture room. Mr Mason was tapping away at a chunk of stone by the window. He didn't even see Belle. She walked over to a white sheet that covered something almost exactly her size. Belle pulled off the sheet. A boy stood before her. Not exactly a boy, but something so very like a boy it was hard to believe he wasn't real.

The boy had brown hair and bright blue eyes. His mouth was quite small, and his nose was thin and pokey – an inquisitive nose. He was wearing a blue cape but, as far as Belle could see, the clothes under the cape were, as yet, unpainted. The shoes and trousers were the colour of light wood.

'So,' murmured Belle. 'That's their game.'

Charlie and Billy got off the blue bus at the top of Filbert Street. Rembrandt had fallen asleep under Billy's sweater but he was obviously having had dreams. He kept twitching and squeaking in his sleep. Billy reckoned that he'd been badly freaked by Mr Boldova's rejection.

'You'll have to make up for it, then,' said Charlie. 'You're his best friend now.'

Billy looked surprised and pleased. 'I suppose I am.'

'I'm afraid Mum doesn't know you're coming,' Charlie warned him. 'She's out all day on Saturday, and she doesn't get home till after four.'

'I don't mind,' said Billy happily.

'She'll leave us plenty of food.'

'Good. Can I give some to Rembrandt?'

'Course. Don't let my grandma see him. She can't abide animals. She'd probably kill him.'

'Oh,' said Billy, nervously.

About twenty paces from home, Charlie became aware of a car parked in the road outside number nine. Its colour might have been described as black. But then again, it wasn't quite black. It could have been midnight blue, but

it was so streaked with mud and ash and – was it rust? Or
had the vehicle been engulfed in flames? The bumper was
bent and the windscreen shattered.

'That looks like a car from hell,' said Billy.

'Or a car that's been *through* hell,' said Charlie. 'It
belongs to my Uncle Paton.'

The boys tore down Filbert Street. When they reached
number nine, Charlie bounded up the steps and let
himself in. Billy followed cautiously.

'There's no one here,' Charlie shouted from the
kitchen.

Billy watched Charlie cross the hall and begin to mount
the stairs.

'Shall I stay here?' he asked shyly.

'No. It's OK. Come on up.' Charlie didn't want to go
into his uncle's room alone. The DO NOT DISTURB sign lay
on the floor, and the hook on the door was bent almost
flat, as though someone had grasped it for support. The
signs were so ominous Charlie didn't know what to do.
Should he knock or walk in unannounced?

'I'd knock,' Billy advised.

Charlie knocked. Once. Twice. Three times.

No sound came from within the room.

Charlie held his breath, opened the door and walked in. Billy took just one step inside and then waited, his hand over the rat.

The first thing Charlie saw was the wand, lying on his uncle's desk. The once slim white cane was almost unrecognisable, but Charlie knew it from its size and the dented silver tip. The rest was a charred and blackened stick.

'What happened?' he murmured. Slowly he turned his gaze towards the bed, and there was his uncle, a figure all in black, lying stretched out on top of the covers, so tall that his feet in ash-covered shoes hung over the end.

Paton's face beneath streaks of soot was deathly white. But worst of all, to Charlie, was his uncle's hair. Once a luxurious black, it had turned ash grey.

'Is he dead?' Billy whispered.

'No,' said Charlie fiercely, but to tell the truth he wasn't sure. He touched his uncle's shoulder. There was no response. 'Uncle Paton,' he said softly, and then more urgently, 'Please, Uncle Paton, wake up. If you can.'

A visit to Skarpo

Paton's eyes remained closed. His face looked like carved ice. Not a muscle twitched. Charlie put his ear to his uncle's chest and caught the faint sound of a heartbeat.

'He's alive. But in a very deep sleep,' said Charlie. 'We'll just have to wait until he wakes up.'

It was no ordinary sleep, and yet it didn't seem like hypnotism. Paton must have been to Yewbeam Castle. But what terrible thing had happened to him there? Uncle Paton was the only person in the house who could stand up to Grandma Bone, and Charlie

shuddered to think what life would be like if his uncle never woke up.

'Let's get out of here,' he said.

Billy was standing very still beside the door and Charlie noticed that Rembrandt's head was poking out of the bottom of Billy's sweater. The rat's nose was twitching violently. Suddenly, he gave a loud squeak and leapt to the floor.

'Get him!' Charlie cried.

Billy ran out and Charlie followed, closing Paton's door behind him. He could see Rembrandt hurrying along, close to the wall. Billy had almost reached him, when a door opened between him and the rat.

Grandma Bone came out of her room and stood facing Billy. 'Oh?' She raised a long black eyebrow. 'Has Charlie brought a little friend home?'

Billy blinked up at her.

Charlie said, 'It's Billy Raven, Grandma. He's staying the weekend.'

'I'm not blind. I can see it's Billy Raven,' said his grandmother. 'I'm glad you've come to your senses, Charlie. Billy's a nice boy. A great improvement on that

smelly Benjamin, not to mention fiddling Fidelio and that drip Gabriel.'

Charlie hated her talking about his friends like that, but he was too worried about the rat to argue. For some reason Rembrandt had stopped right behind his grandmother, and was now sitting up and watching them.

Billy didn't know what to do. He stared at Rembrandt with his mouth hanging open.

'Why are you looking at my shoes, little boy?' said Grandma Bone. 'Look me in the eye. I don't bite.'

Not half, thought Charlie.

As Billy tore his gaze away from the rat, Charlie was relieved to see it scamper downstairs.

'Grandma . . .' Charlie began.

'What was that?' Grandma Bone leaned over the banisters, but the rat had disappeared.

'Well now, Billy,' she said. 'The person who usually does the cooking in the house has gone on holiday.'

'Hardly,' said Charlie. 'Grandma, do you . . .?'

'Be quiet,' she snapped. 'As I said, we haven't got a cook, but I'll do my best to find some nice titbits for you. Charlie should be on bread and water, since he *stole my*

goose liver pâté!'

Charlie pointed to his uncle's door and shouted, 'Grandma, do you realise Uncle Paton's lying in there half-dead?'

'I'm perfectly well aware of my brother's state,' she said coldly. 'He deserved everything he got. Meddling, that's what he was doing. Well he bit off more than he could chew this time, didn't he? Met his match. Ha! Ha!' She gave a nasty snigger and swept downstairs. 'I'm going to get some prunes,' she called, and, putting on her hat and coat, she left the house.

'I don't like prunes,' said Billy with a nervous frown.

'You won't have to eat them,' said Charlie. 'Come on, let's find something better.'

Billy thought they should look for Rembrandt first, but although they searched every room on the ground floor, the black rat couldn't be found.

'He's probably curled up asleep somewhere,' said Charlie. 'I'm going to put some chips in the oven.'

Before he could do this, his mother walked in with an armful of carrots. She showed no surprise on seeing a small white-haired boy sitting at the kichen table. She was used

to Benjamin's visits, and was glad that Charlie would have a friend around at the weekend. She had guessed that Paton had come home because she'd heard strange noises very late the previous night, but she hadn't had time to pop in and see him before she left for work.

'He's ill, Mum,' said Charlie. 'Really, really ill. His hair's gone grey, and he can't speak.'

'Oh dear, perhaps I'd better go and see.' Mrs Bone ran upstairs.

A few minutes later she came down looking very worried. 'I'll ring the doctor. Does your grandmother know about Paton?'

'She said he deserved it for meddling,' Charlie told her.

Mrs Bone shook her head. 'That family!' she muttered.

While Charlie got the supper ready, Amy Bone rang the doctor. She was on the phone for quite some time, trying to describe Paton's symptoms. It wasn't easy explaining that someone had gone grey overnight.

'I don't think the doctor believed me,' said Amy, replacing the receiver. 'But he's coming round in an hour, just to check.'

At that moment Grandma Bone came back with her

prunes. As soon as she heard that a doctor had been called, she went to the phone and cancelled his visit.

'How could you do that?' said Amy. 'Paton needs a doctor.'

'No he doesn't,' Grandma Bone retorted. 'There's nothing a doctor can do. It's a waste of his precious time.'

'Honestly! Your own brother,' cried Amy. 'Suppose . . . suppose he dies? How would you feel then?'

'We all die – in time,' said Grandma Bone, rinsing her prunes.

Watching the arguments in wide-eyed silence, Billy decided that family life wasn't all that it was cracked up to be.

Supper was an uncomfortable affair. Refusing ham and chips, Grandma Bone worked her way through a bowl of prunes, making a horrible sucking noise in the process.

After supper, while Mrs Bone made up a bed for Billy, the boys told her about Rembrandt.

'Oh, Charlie, not another animal,' sighed Mrs Bone.

'He's very clean,' said Billy, 'and not a biter.'

'But a rat . . .'

'Just look out for him, please, Mum,' begged Charlie.

'We don't want Grandma to find him first.'

'I should think not,' said his mother with a grin. 'I'll do my best, but don't blame me if I scream when I see him.' She left the bedroom, saying, 'Rats, whatever next?'

Billy wanted to continue the search for Rembrandt, but Charlie was afraid Grandma Bone would become suspicious. Besides, Uncle Paton, who could always be relied on in a crisis, was now lying in some terrible stupor, unable to tell anyone what had happened to him. Perhaps he would never be quite himself again.

'Your uncle breaks light bulbs, doesn't he?' said Billy.

'He's a power-booster,' said Charlie. 'Something happens when he looks at a light – it just kind of explodes. That's why he doesn't go out until after midnight. Someone might see one of his "accidents".'

'There was a light on in his room,' said Billy.

'What?' Charlie hadn't noticed. He had to find out if it was true.

When he looked into his uncle's room, there it was – a bright light hanging from the ceiling, right above his uncle's desk.

'It's gone, Charlie,' came a faint voice from the bed.

Paton's dark eyes were now open. He was gazing at the light with an expression of horror.

'Uncle, you're awake!' cried Charlie.

'If you can call it that,' croaked Paton. 'He's done for me, Charlie. I'm cleaned out, whipped. He's stronger than anyone could imagine.'

'Who?' said Charlie.

Paton closed his eyes again. 'Your grandmother put the light on to test me. She wanted to make sure I'd lost the power. Well – I have.'

'But who did this to you?' Charlie asked.

Paton's grey head tossed from side to side. 'I thought he was dead – gone. But he never will be.'

'*Who?*' begged Charlie.

'I can't say his name. Perhaps tomorrow . . .' Paton turned his face to the wall.

Charlie realised that he couldn't press his uncle any further. He was about to leave the room when the wand caught his eye, and the beginning of an idea crept into his mind. He picked up the ruined wand and slipped back to his room.

Billy was sitting on Charlie's bed, looking very

despondent.

'Don't worry about Rembrandt,' said Charlie. 'He's a clever rat, and you're his friend. He'll turn up soon, I bet.' He saw that Billy wasn't really listening to him, he was gazing at Charlie's hands with an expression of awe.

When Charlie looked down he saw that the burnt wand was changing. He could feel it moving gently under his fingers, as slippery as silk and warm as sunlight. The silver tip began to sparkle and the blackened wood gradually faded until it was a pure white.

'How did that happen?' breathed Billy.

Charlie shook his head. 'Don't know.' He sat beside Billy and ran his fingers over the smooth white wood.

'It's a wand, isn't it?' said Billy. 'It was all black and broken and now it's like brand new. Is it your uncle's?'

'No,' said Charlie slowly. 'I borrowed it from a person who had stolen it from someone else.'

'Looks like it really wanted to be with you,' observed Billy. 'Like it belonged to you.'

'It can't,' said Charlie. 'It's impossible. I'm not a wizard, or a sorcerer.'

'But you're endowed, like me.'

'Not in that way,' Charlie muttered. He decided to tell Billy the truth about the wand.

Reaching under the bed, Charlie pulled out a small painting. It showed a man in a long black robe, with silver-black hair, and a beard the same colour. He was standing in a room lit by candles in a tall iron stand. With a piece of chalk he was drawing a star on a stone wall already covered in strange symbols.

'You brought that picture to school last term, didn't you?' said Billy.

'Yes. The man's a sorcerer called Skarpo. I stole the wand from him.'

Billy's jaw dropped. He turned to Charlie and gave him one of his long dark-red stares. 'You . . .?' he said huskily.

'I went into the picture,' said Charlie. 'I'd never done that before, I'd only heard voices.' He caught a sudden glint in the sorcerer's eye and quickly turned the painting over. 'I mustn't look at him too long or he'll drag me in again.'

Billy shook his head in wonder. 'How did you get out?'

'That was a bit tricky. Lysander helped me.' Charlie glanced at Billy, wondering again if he could really trust

him. He decided he would have to chance it. 'The thing is, Billy, I thought I might go in again. That sorcerer is very powerful. He had loads of stuff in his room, did you notice? Herbs and feathers and things.'

'He had a dagger, I saw that.'

Charlie held the painting up to Billy. 'What else do you see?'

'Bowls and books and jars of coloured water, and big candles and signs on the wall – oh, and a mouse looking out of his pocket, and loads of junk on the table.'

'He might have a cure for my uncle,' said Charlie. 'If I give him back the wand, maybe he'll give me something in return. And I could ask him about Ollie. He may know a cure for invisibility.'

'Lysander's not here today,' said Billy dubiously. 'Suppose you can't get out?'

'That's where you come in, Billy. Just cling on to my arm, will you? And if I'm acting a bit funny, give me a tug. I don't go right in, you see, it's just my mind. But he can see my face, and he'll probably see the wand. I won't go in as far as I did last time. I'll keep to the edge and just talk to him.'

Charlie propped the painting against his bedside lamp, then he got up and held the wand in front of him. 'Are you ready?'

Billy slid off the bed and clutched Charlie's arm. 'Ready.'

Charlie looked at the sorcerer. It didn't take long for Skarpo to see him. 'You're back,' said a husky sing-song voice.

Charlie felt himself sliding forwards, through a drifting white mist. All he could see was the sorcerer's bony face, and he quickly lowered his eyes to avoid Skarpo's magnetic yellow gaze. A rich smell of burning herbs filled his nostrils and he sneezed violently.

'Stop that!' said the voice.

'S-s-atichoo! Sorry, couldn't help it,' said Charlie. He looked past the dark robed figure and scanned the objects on the table.

'What d'you want this time, you thief?' said Skarpo.

'I've brought back your wand,' said Charlie. 'And I was just wondering . . .'

'What?' Skarpo seemed to be looking at the wand. 'Take it away,' he said in a low voice.

'But I thought you wanted it,' said Charlie. 'You were so angry when I took it. I came back to exchange it for – well, just a bit of advice really, you being so experienced in magic and everything. I thought you might be able to help me.'

'It's not mine, boy, I see that now.' The sorcerer seemed unable to drag his eyes away from the wand. 'Well, I never. It was yours all along.'

'I don't understand,' said Charlie. 'It's not mine. But anyway, the thing is, my uncle's very ill, so ill he's lost the power he used to have. It was him that first told me about you, actually, so have you got anything for endowed people that have sort of become unendowed?'

'I'd have to see your uncle.' Skarpo took a step towards Charlie.

'You can't do that.' Charlie took a step backwards.

Skarpo moved closer. 'I'll have to, my wee fellow. How can I help a man I don't see? Besides, I've a mind to peep into your century.'

'That's impossible,' said Charlie firmly. 'You belong in your picture.'

'I'll hitch a ride with you.' The sorcerer's pale hand

stretched out towards Charlie, and Charlie felt something tug his sweater. He stepped backwards, very fast, saying, 'No! No! No! I'm going now. Now! Now!' And again he stepped back. This time he tripped and found himself falling. It was like tumbling through air, down, down and down.

Charlie had to close his eyes against the horrible pitching and tossing that was happening to his body. And then the back of his head hit something hard, with a loud bang.

Charlie opened his eyes. He was lying on his bedroom floor, not quite on the floor, but on something small and bumpy.

A muffled voice beneath him said, 'Charlie, you're squashing me.'

Charlie rolled over and found Billy stretched out beside him. His glasses had fallen off and his eyes were wide with fright.

'Sorry,' said Charlie. 'What happened?'

'Wee-i-erd,' said Billy, sitting up. He found his spectacles and put them on. 'I held on to you, like you said, but you kept moving backwards, and saying, 'Now!

Now!' and then you tripped over my foot and we both fell down. I couldn't see anything 'cos you were on top of me, but there was an almighty wind and someone trod on my hand, and the door blew open.'

At that moment the front door slammed. The boys were silent, waiting to hear footsteps in the hall. There were none. Charlie got up and looked out of the window. There were several people in the street, and a few passing cars. And then, in the distance, he saw a dark shadow travelling very fast against the evening light.

Charlie felt slightly queasy. Whether it was from banging his head, or the feeling that somehow things had gone a little bit wrong, he wasn't sure.

'What happened in there?' asked Billy, pointing at the picture.

Charlie noticed that the sorcerer was still in the painting. That was reassuring. He laid it face down on the bedside table. 'He wanted to come out,' he said.

'Perhaps he did come out,' said Billy.

'No. Couldn't have. Let's get ready for bed. You can use the bathroom first.'

The two boys changed into their pyjamas and Billy took

his washbag to the bathroom. In a few minutes he was back, with toothpaste round his mouth and a black rat in his hands. 'Look what I've found!' he cried.

'Rembrandt! Where was he?'

'In the bathroom, under the bath.' Billy put Rembrandt on Charlie's bed. 'It's so good to see you, Rem!'

'I don't think I fancy Rem in my bed tonight,' said Charlie, and he ran down to the kitchen to look for a box.

Unfortunately Grandma Bone was in the kitchen, slurping up another bowl of prunes. 'What are you looking for?' she demanded, as Charlie rummaged about in the larder.

'A box,' he said.

'What for (*slurp*)?'

'To put something in.' Charlie emerged with a box in his hands, and six biscuits in his dressing-gown pocket.

'What sort of thing? Drat!' Grandma Bone missed her mouth and a prune fell on to the tablecloth.

'Whoops!' said Charlie.

'What are you putting in that box?'

'A monster with six eyes, four tails and bad breath,' said Charlie, running out of the room.

'Don't be insolent!' screeched Grandma Bone. She came into the hall and was about to shout something else when she suddenly changed her mind, and said sweetly, 'Say goodnight to that little boy for me.'

Charlie was so unnerved by her tone he almost dropped the box. Did his grandmother think she could use Billy against him?

'Phew, Grandma certainly likes you,' he said, handing Billy the box. 'This is for Rembrandt. And I've got some biscuits for his supper. Billy? Billy!'

Billy's white eyebrows were drawn together in an odd frown.

'What's up?' said Charlie.

'I've been talking to Rembrandt,' Billy said in a puzzled voice.

'He gave you some bad news by the look of it,' Charlie remarked.

'He said there was a bad smell in the bathroom.'

'There's always a bad smell,' said Charlie. 'It's Grandma.'

'No, Charlie. This is different,' Billy said gravely. 'Rembrandt says it smells of bad magic and things that

should be dead.'

Charlie resisted the temptation to say 'Like I said', and marched along to the bathroom, followed by Billy who was still clutching Rembrandt.

'Can't smell a thing,' said Charlie, opening the door.

'Look!' Billy whispered. 'Under the basin.'

Charlie looked. Sitting under the basin was a brown mouse. It began to squeak, almost hysterically, and while it squeaked, Rembrandt joined in, squealing even louder than the mouse.

Billy began to translate Rembrandt's shrill words, if they could be called words. 'He says . . . the mouse is very scared . . . because it doesn't know . . . where it is . . . or how it got here. Rembrandt says its smell is from a long time ago, so long it's messing up his brain.'

'A long time ago?' Charlie looked at Billy, who returned his gaze with a mixture of disbelief and bewilderment.

'Skarpo had a mouse in his pocket,' Charlie said slowly.

'So, where's Skarpo?' Billy whispered.

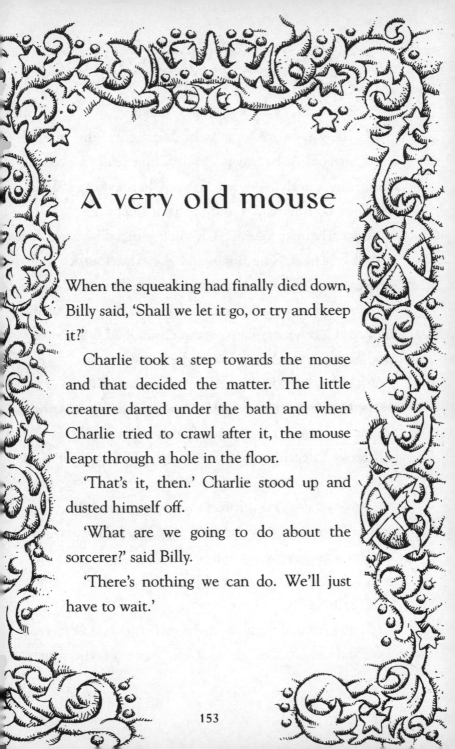

A very old mouse

When the squeaking had finally died down, Billy said, 'Shall we let it go, or try and keep it?'

Charlie took a step towards the mouse and that decided the matter. The little creature darted under the bath and when Charlie tried to crawl after it, the mouse leapt through a hole in the floor.

'That's it, then.' Charlie stood up and dusted himself off.

'What are we going to do about the sorcerer?' said Billy.

'There's nothing we can do. We'll just have to wait.'

Charlie was awake for most of that night. Billy grunted and chattered in his sleep while the rat made a peculiar twittering sound. Now and again Charlie would shout, 'Shut up, both of you!' but his visitors slept on.

Very early next morning Charlie tiptoed downstairs for a bowl of cereal. The house and the street outside were eerily quiet. And Rembrandt was right, there was a very strange smell about the place. Was that how bad magic smelled? Charlie wondered if the mouse had brought bad luck, as well as bad magic, into the house.

When he'd finished his cereal, Charlie took a cup of tea and a biscuit up to his uncle's room. Paton was sitting propped up against a mound of cushions and pillows. He still looked deathly white, but a bit of life appeared to have seeped back into his grey hair.

'Morning, dear boy,' Paton's voice was very faint.

'You're looking a bit better, Uncle,' said Charlie. 'Your hair – it was all grey yesterday.'

'Ash,' Paton said hoarsely. He touched his throat. 'Can't talk much.'

Charlie noticed that the light was still on. It flickered now and again, but there were none of the bright

explosions that Paton usually managed to generate.

'Maybe it's a good thing that you've lost your . . .' Charlie hesitated. 'Well, I mean, now that lights don't explode all around you.'

'It crossed my mind,' Paton whispered, 'but only for a moment. I've realised that it's never a good thing to lose your talent; you lose a bit of yourself along with it.'

'I suppose so,' said Charlie solemnly. 'Uncle Paton, what *happened* to you?'

Paton closed his eyes. 'Can't talk now, Charlie. If you see Miss Ingledew, tell her . . . tell her . . .'

'Yes,' said Charlie eagerly. 'Tell her what?'

'Tell her I wish –' Paton shook his head. 'No, I'm afraid it's too late.'

'Too late?' cried Charlie. His uncle's expression scared him. 'What d'you mean, too late?'

'Never mind. I'd like to be alone now, Charlie.'

Whatever it was that had happened to his uncle, Charlie was afraid that the effects might be permanent, or fatal. He quietly closed the door and went back to his room. Billy was sitting on the edge of Charlie's bed with Rembrandt on his knee. 'I thought it was all a bad dream,'

he said, rubbing his eyes. 'But it really happened, didn't it? The mouse and the sorcerer.'

''Fraid so,' said Charlie.

'What d'you think Skarpo will do, if he's here – somewhere?'

'We'll just have to wait and see. Billy, you won't tell anyone about this, will you?'

Billy shook his head. 'I won't tell about Skarpo, but I think they already know about you going into pictures and that. I heard them talking once, about the painting, old Mr Ezekiel and Matron. They said, "D'you think Charlie will go in?" I didn't understand what they were on about then.'

Charlie perched beside the small albino. 'I know you couldn't help being a spy,' he said, 'but it's time you chose sides, Billy. I've got to know if I can trust you.'

Billy hung his head. 'Mr Ezekiel said he'd found some really kind people who wanted to be my parents, but it was a lie. I'll never trust him again.'

'The Bloors lie about everything,' said Charlie. 'But when this is all over, I'm sure someone will find some parents for you.'

'Cook said she would, but when all what's over?'

Charlie wasn't sure himself. Perhaps he meant when Ollie Sparks had been rescued, and Belle, or Yolanda, had disappeared. When Uncle Paton was himself again, and Lyell, Charlie's father, had been found. Or perhaps he meant the struggle between those who ruined lives if they didn't get what they wanted, and others who couldn't help trying to stop them. 'The children of the Red King,' Charlie murmured. 'It's a battle between all of us. I meant when that was over.'

Billy looked dubious. 'Perhaps it will never be over. Or maybe it will be a long, long time. I think I could wait quite a long time. Maybe a year. But I don't want to be grown up before I get parents. I wish I could remember my real parents. I wish I knew how they really died. No one would ever explain it to me.'

Charlie thought of his own father. Everyone pretended that he was dead, but Charlie knew it was a lie. At least Billy had a photo. Charlie didn't even have that. 'You showed me a photo of your parents once,' he said. 'They looked nice.'

'Yes,' said Billy sadly.

'Come on, let's get dressed,' said Charlie on a brighter note.

They found Mrs Bone in the kitchen, cooking two large breakfasts. 'I'm sorry, I've got to leave you on your own,' she said, 'but there's plenty of food in the fridge and I'll be back before teatime. Thank goodness Paton is better.' Charlie wasn't so sure about Paton.

'We're not exactly on our own,' said Charlie as a door slammed upstairs. Grandma Bone was on the move.

Amy glanced up at the ceiling and said, 'You know what I mean. Enjoy your breakfasts. Bye now.' And she was off.

By the time Grandma Bone came marching into the kitchen, Charlie and Billy had eaten their breakfasts, and Billy had managed to slip some toast and bacon into his pocket.

'A bit of starving wouldn't hurt you,' she said, glaring at Charlie, 'after eating all my specials.'

Charlie almost told her that Runner Bean had eaten the pâté, but he thought better of it. He wanted a peaceful weekend.

'Sorry,' he mumbled. 'I made a mistake. We're going to the park now, Grandma.' He took his plate to the sink, but

when he turned round his grandmother gave him one of her mean smiles.

'No, you're not,' she said. 'Someone very important is coming to visit us.'

'Who?' asked Charlie.

'That's for me to know,' she retorted. 'Clean yourselves up and look nice; they'll be here in half an hour.'

Billy scuttled nervously to the sink with his plate.

'Wash it up, dear,' said Grandma Bone.

Charlie waited while Billy dutifully cleaned his plate and put it in the rack.

Back in the bedroom, Billy fed the hungry rat and then began to grunt to it. Rembrandt squeaked back.

'He says the mouse ought to go home,' Billy told Charlie. 'It's not good for him here.'

'It's not good for us either,' said Charlie. 'But even if we found the mouse, I wouldn't know how to get it back into the painting. Unless I took it myself, and I don't want to go in again. I don't trust Skarpo. He might make it impossible for me to get out.'

'If he's still in there,' said Billy.

'He must be,' said Charlie desperately. 'I mean, if he was

out, we'd know by now. He's dangerous. He only deals in destruction. He told me once that he liked to maim, poison, burn, shrink, drive people mad.'

Billy's mouth had fallen open. He uttered a soft 'Oooo' of horror.

The two boys waited anxiously for their important visitor to arrive. Occasionally they looked down into the street, but no one grand or imposing walked up to their door. No flashy or expensive car stopped close by.

And then Billy suddenly shivered and said, 'There it is. It's *him*.'

Charlie saw a black car with smoked glass windows gliding to a halt in front of the house. He recognised the car immediately. It had come once before, when Billy had stayed with him. Charlie had never seen the passenger. When he had gone to look in the car, a long cane had whipped through the open door and whacked him on the knees – something he wasn't likely to forget.

A powerful-looking man in a black suit got out of the driver's seat and walked round to the passenger's door. A black chauffeur's hat hid the cropped head, but Charlie knew the broad nose, red face and small slanting eyes. It

was Weedon, the gardener-cum-handyman.

Weedon opened the passenger door very wide, and then leant into the car. After a moment of manoeuvring, he stood up with a weird bundle in his arms. Most of it was covered by a tartan blanket, but Charlie could see a hideously wizened face under a black skull cap, and two scrawny legs in white socks, with red velvet slippers on the feet.

'Is that who I think it is?' said Charlie.

Billy nodded miserably. 'Mr Ezekiel. He's come for me.'

'Maybe not. Let's wait and see.' As Charlie said this a third person got out of the car, slammed all the open doors and followed Weedon and his bundle.

'I should have known she'd come too,' said Charlie as he watched his great-aunt Lucretia mount the steps.

'Charlie! Billy! You're wanted,' shouted Grandma Bone.

Billy put Rembrandt in his box and followed Charlie downstairs. Grandma Bone was waiting for them outside the sitting room door. 'Come in, boys. Come in,' she said, smiling as though they'd won tickets for a football match.

Charlie went in first, and found himself facing the

oldest-looking man he'd ever seen. He was sitting in the biggest armchair, still wrapped in his tartan blanket. His face was so wizened it looked like a skull, and his thin white hair hung to his shoulders in waxy strands. His mouth had all but disappeared beneath a long, knobbly nose, but his black eyes glittered with a frightening intensity.

'Charlie Bone – at last.' The old man held out a stringy, mottled hand.

Charlie looked at the hand, wondering if it ate things. He decided he'd better shake it but, before he knew it, his fingers were being pulverised by something that felt like a nutcracker. He retrieved his hand with a gasp of pain, and Mr Weedon, who was sitting in an upright chair beside the old man, gave a malicious grin.

'We know Billy,' said Mr Ezekiel. 'In fact we know each other very well, don't we, Billy?' He picked up a cane propped against his chair, and tapped the floor by Billy's feet.

Billy gave a silent nod.

'Sit down, boys!' Mr Ezekiel's voice sounded rather like a rusty saw.

Charlie and Billy made for the nearest chair and shared it, both perching on the edge. Grandma Bone sat beside Lucretia on the sofa, and Lucretia said, 'Well, isn't this nice?'

Charlie thought: hardly.

'Now,' Mr Ezekiel rubbed his hands together. 'To begin with, I'm very pleased to see you two boys have made friends. We've all got to work together, haven't we? The more of us the better. Isn't that so?'

Charlie said, 'It depends.'

Mr Ezekiel frowned, and Grandma Bone and her sister muttered, 'Insolence! Behave yourself.'

'You're not going to be like your father, are you?' said Mr Ezekiel, raising his voice and glaring at Charlie. 'I expect you've noticed I can't walk. D'you know who's responsible? Your father, damn him. He did this to me. He deserved to die.'

Charlie gritted his teeth. He was so angry he was afraid he might do something violent. Instead he muttered, 'He isn't dead.'

'What?' cried the old man. 'What did you say?'

'I said my father isn't dead!' Charlie shouted.

The old man's black eyes flashed. He stared at Charlie for several seconds and then he gave a shrill cackle. 'Prove it,' he sniggered.

Charlie said nothing.

'No, you can't, can you?' said Mr Ezekiel. He was suddenly overcome by a bout of coughing and Grandma Bone rushed out to fetch him a cup of tea. While she was gone, Aunt Lucretia snarled, 'You're a very stupid boy, Charlie Bone. Why can't you see sense? Why can't you do the right thing?'

Charlie remained silent and Billy squashed himself further back into the chair.

Grandma Bone returned with three cups of tea and a plate of biscuits. She handed the tea and biscuits to Ezekiel, Lucretia and Mr Weedon, but when Charlie put a hand towards the plate, Lucretia gave him a hard slap.

'Ouch!' Charlie withdrew his stinging hand.

Mr Ezekiel said, 'Aw, we mustn't hit Charlie. We want him on our side, don't we?'

'I sometimes wonder if he's worth the trouble,' sniffed Grandma Bone.

Charlie couldn't stop himself. 'If you want me on your

side, you've got a funny way of going about it.'

Grandma Bone raised her eyebrows. Ezekiel slurped his tea. Lucretia stirred hers. At last the old man said, 'We never meant to do you any harm, Charlie. Not permanent harm. We just had to teach you a lesson, now and again. You have to be shown the way.'

'And what way is that?' asked Charlie.

Ezekiel shook his head. 'I want us all to be on the same side, Charlie. Think how powerful we could be. All you bright, gifted children – children of the Red King. Think what you could do. Billy understands, don't you, Billy?'

Billy squirmed in his seat.

'Billy's a good boy,' said Grandma Bone. 'Billy does what he's told. He doesn't break the rules.'

'Rules?' said Charlie. 'My father broke your rules and you did something horrible to him. And my uncle, Paton, went where you didn't want him to go, and now he's all – ruined. That's not fair!'

Mr Weedon leant forward. 'All's fair in love and war,' he anounced in a commanding voice.

The other three adults looked at him in surprise, and Charlie had an odd feeling that, of all the people in the

room, Mr Weedon was the one he should fear most.

Ezekiel gave an exasperated sigh. 'I'm tired of this. I don't like arguing with little boys. Just behave yourself, Charlie Bone. You know what I can do to people who don't.'

Charlie was trying to think of a clever reply when a mouse suddenly appeared on the mantelpiece. Everyone watched it scuttling round the candlesticks and china ornaments. And then it stood on its hind legs beside the clock and started to squeak.

Grandma Bone and Aunt Lucretia had already begun to shriek when Ezekiel shouted, 'What's it saying, Billy? Tell us.'

'It says it's lost,' said Billy, although the mouse was actually saying, *'I'm going out of my mind with worry. Where am I? I don't understand how I got here.'*

Billy was about to say something reassuring to the little creature when Mr Weedon brought his hat down, bang, over the mouse. 'Got the little blighter,' he said.

Billy and Charlie watched in dismay as the big man turned his hat over, and put his hand on top of the mouse. But then he gave a grunt of fury and dropped both hat and

mouse. 'Blighter bit me!' he yelled.

Charlie whispered to Billy, 'With any luck he'll get the plague.'

The mouse leapt out of the hat and raced under the sofa.

'Get me out of here!' shrieked Ezekiel. 'Weedon, leave the damn mouse. Billy, fetch your bag, you're coming home with me!'

'But I'm staying with Charlie,' said Billy, 'for the weekend. I don't want to come back to Bloor's.'

'Don't argue,' shouted Ezekiel. 'He's a bad influence. Go and get your stuff.'

Billy wriggled out of the chair and left the room with a look of despair.

'It's not fair,' said Charlie. 'Billy's alone every weekend.'

'Not fair! Not fair!' mimicked Grandma Bone. 'Nothing's fair with you, is it?'

'No.' Charlie was so disgusted with everyone he walked out of the room, growling softly, 'And it's not fair to keep invisible boys locked up.'

'What did you say, you insolent boy?' his grandmother shouted.

Billy came downstairs with his bag and Rembrandt in the box. Charlie was about to advise him to hide the box when Mr Weedon burst out of the sitting room carrying the old man.

'What's in there?' said Ezekiel, tapping the box with his cane.

'A – a rat!' said Billy, too frightened to lie.

'What? Get rid of it.'

'But it's a friend,' said Billy faintly.

'It's not coming into my house,' declared Ezekiel.

'But it belonged to Mr Boldova,' said Billy, making things worse for himself. 'And now he's gone, there's no one else to look after it.'

Grandma Bone and Aunt Lucretia had come into the hall, and both began shouting at once, 'In the house?' 'A rat?' 'Someone kill it!'

Billy's eyes began to fill with tears. 'You c-can't . . .' he sobbed.

'I'll look after it,' cried Charlie, seizing the box. 'Don't worry, Billy.'

'You will *not*!' roared Grandma Bone. 'I won't have it in the house. Weedon, bang it on the head!'

But Weedon had his hands full with Mr Ezekiel and before anyone else could make a move, Charlie had opened the front door.

'Bye, Billy,' he shouted, as he raced down the steps. 'I'm taking Rembrandt somewhere where he'll be safe.'

'Come back!' called Grandma Bone.

'That boy's out of control,' bellowed Aunt Lucretia.

'Not for long!' said Ezekiel.

Charlie didn't hear this. He ran up Filbert Street, and on into the city, stopping only once to look into the box. Rembrandt stared out fearfully, his nose twitching at least a hundred times a second.

'Sorry, Rem,' Charlie panted. 'I hate to do this to you, but you didn't stand a chance back there.' He raced up Frog Street, and sped down the alley to the Pets' Café.

'Hullo, Charlie. You look puffed,' said Norton, the bouncer, as Charlie leapt through the door.

'I've got to see Mr Onimous,' said Charlie. 'Is he about?' He held up the box. 'Rat,' he said. 'In a bit of trouble.'

'Orvil's in the kitchen,' said Norton. 'Just go round the counter.'

Leaping over a birdcage and two dachshunds, Charlie

hastily made his way round the counter and through the door at the back. Mr and Mrs Onimous were having a cup of tea at the long kitchen table. Several large saucepans were bubbling away on the stove and they both looked very flushed.

'Well, if it isn't Charlie,' said Mr Onimous, dabbing his face with a red handkerchief. 'Sit down, mate, and have a cuppa.'

'Thanks, but I'm in a bit of a rush,' said Charlie.

There was a joyful bark and Runner Bean erupted from under the table. Charlie put his box on the table and allowed his face to be licked while he rubbed the big dog's rough hair. When he looked round Rembrandt was sitting beside Mrs Onimous's cup of tea.

'Well, this is a nice surprise,' she said. 'A very pretty rat indeed.'

Runner Bean growled and Charlie asked him if he would please be quiet as the rat was already in quite a state.

'I brought him here, because Grandma Bone would have killed him,' Charlie explained. 'I thought he'd be safe with you. Can you look after him, Mrs

Onimous, please?'

'You'd better tell us what all this is about, young Charlie,' said Mr Onimous.

'And have some cake while you do it,' said Mrs Onimous. 'Sit down, Charlie, and make yourself at home.'

Charlie hadn't intended to stay. He was worried that his mother would get home from work and find Grandma Bone in a fury. But the smell of freshly baked cakes and the Onimouses' welcoming smiles were too hard to resist. So he sat between them at the table and munched his way through an enormous slice of chocolate cake, while he told his friends everything about Ollie Sparks, the blue boa and the terrible loneliness of Ollie's invisibility. And then the final dreadful scene with Mr Ezekiel and poor Billy.

'Billy wanted to keep the rat,' said Charlie, feeding Rembrandt a crumb. 'It's a friend, you see. It can understand what Billy says. But that revolting old man said he couldn't have it, and Grandma Bone told Mr Weedon to bang it on the head.'

'The poor, dear creature.' Mrs Onimous clutched her chest. 'Come to me, my love!'

Rembrandt leapt over a plate and landed in Mrs Onimous's lap. Obviously, Billy wasn't the only person he could understand.

'You say your uncle has a mystery illness,' said Mr Onimous, who had great respect for Paton Yewbeam. 'And you have no idea what caused this strange affliction?'

'All I know is that he met someone in Yewbeam Castle,' said Charlie. 'And this person did something to him.'

The Onimouses stared at Charlie, equally horrified.

'That's a terrible place,' said Mr Onimous at last.

'Have you been there?' asked Charlie.

'Never,' Mr Onimous shook his head. 'Wild horses wouldn't drag me there. It's an evil place, Charlie. Your uncle was lucky to get out alive.'

'But maybe he won't stay alive,' said Charlie fearfully.

'We must live in hope, dear,' said Mrs Onimous, who looked anything but hopeful.

The wand

On his way home, Charlie called in at the bookshop. Emma was on duty at the counter, while her aunt wrapped books in the back room.

'Tell Miss Ingledew that my uncle's home,' said Charlie. 'But he's not very well.'

'What's the matter with him?' asked Emma.

'It's hard to explain. But it's scary, Em. I'm afraid he might not get better – ever.'

'Why?' asked Emma with a worried frown. 'How did it happen? Is it a mystery bug or something?'

'Can't really say. Got to go now, Em.

There was a bit of trouble before I left.' Charlie hurried off, leaving Emma looking baffled.

There was a not-quite-peaceful silence inside number nine.

Billy had obviously been taken back to Bloor's and there was no sign of Grandma Bone. It was lunchtime so Charlie began to help himself from the fridge: cheese, cucumber, salami and peanut butter all sandwiched between two thick slices of bread. He was about to sit at the table when he remembered his uncle. He made another identical sandwich and put them both on a tray with a glass of water.

Paton called, 'Come in! Come in!' immediately Charlie knocked.

'Praise be, refreshments,' said Uncle Paton when he saw the tray. He heaved himself up on his pillows and patted the bed.

Charlie put the tray in front of his uncle. He was glad to see that Paton had managed to change into his pyjamas. Hopefully this meant that he'd had a wash, though there was still a funny smell in the room.

'Scorched socks!' said Paton, who had noticed Charlie's

discreet sniff.

'Uncle, what happened?' asked Charlie. 'Can you talk about it now?'

Paton took a long drink of water, cleared his throat rather loudly and said, 'Ahem. You'll have to know something of our past, Charlie. It all began when I was seven. You'll remember I discovered my gift on my seventh birthday.'

Charlie nodded. 'The lights exploded and all the other children went home, and you ate all their ice-cream and were sick.'

'Good memory,' Paton remarked. 'Well, shortly after this we all went to visit my great-aunt, Yolanda, at Yewbeam Castle.'

Charlie waited breathlessly, while his uncle massaged his throat.

'My mother was French,' Paton went on. 'A very beautiful woman. She'd been an actress but when she married my father she found that she loved children. So she had five and gave up the stage. She was very proud of my gift. There'd been a few "unusual talents" in her own family.

'She told Yolanda about me on our very first night there. We were having supper in a long, dark room on the ground floor. There were eight of us, and Lyell, your father, who was two. His own father, a pilot, had already been killed – crashed his plane in the desert. Well, my mother said, "Guess what, Aunt Yolanda, Paton is endowed." I can see Yolanda's face now. The way her eyes lit up.' Paton bit into his sandwich.

'And then my sister, Venetia, who was twelve, said, "Like me. And like Eustacia, she's a clairvoyant. But Lucretia and Grizelda aren't endowed, poor things." The two eldest were very put out, as you can imagine, but then Grizelda said, "Who knows? Baby Lyell may have a gift one day."

'Yolanda gazed round at us. She looked so hungry. A real predator.' Paton paused and took another bite of his sandwich. 'This is uncommonly good, Charlie,' he said. 'What's in it?'

'I've forgotten. Please go on, Uncle Paton,' begged Charlie.

His uncle looked suddenly very grave. 'Yewbeam Castle is a terrible place. It's built of rock that seems to attract the

night. It's a sooty grey, inside and out. And they still haven't put in electricity. The stairs are narrow, steep and dark. On our second day my mother fell and broke her neck.' Paton gave a frown of pain and touched his throat again.

'We were all in the garden, if you can call it that. It's just a field of wild grass that grows right up to the castle walls. I heard my mother cry out, but my father reached her first – I was just two steps behind him. She was lying at the bottom of a treacherous stairway leading out of the hall. I heard her say, "Don't let her . . ." and then she was gone.' Paton pulled a handkerchief from under his pillow and vigorously blew his nose.

'Yolanda pushed her, didn't she?' Charlie said grimly.

Paton gave a huge sigh. 'I'm sure she did. But who could prove it? Besides, my sisters were already under her spell. They wouldn't hear a word against her. In fact they wouldn't even leave the castle after my mother died. Yolanda tried to keep me, too. She begged and wheedled, she screamed and threw things. She turned into a wild dog, a bat, a serpent – she's a shape-shifter, you know. She tried to hypnotise my father but he escaped with me and

he never let me out of his sight until he was sure I could take care of myself.'

'You went to Yewbeam Castle to stop Yolanda coming *here*, didn't you?' said Charlie.

Paton nodded. 'I heard my sisters plotting the night before I left. So I decided to pay Yolanda a visit. But I was too late. She wasn't there –'

'Uncle Paton,' Charlie interrupted, 'she's here.'

'What?' Paton sagged against the pillows. 'I was afraid of that. Is she . . .? What shape has she taken?'

'She's a girl, quite a pretty one. But her eyes keep changing, as if they can't remember what colour they're supposed to be. I knew, right away, there was something wrong. She's living with the aunts in Darkly Wynd. But why has she come here, Uncle, after all this time?'

'I only caught snatches of my sisters' conversation,' said Paton. 'I was in the kitchen having a midnight snack when they arrived. I don't care for their chatter, so I hid in the larder. Very undignified, but luckily they only had a cup of tea. They discussed Yolanda and then moved off into the sitting room. From what I could gather, Yolanda was called in to help the old man – Ezekiel – in some

nefarious plan to disappear.'

Charlie gasped. 'The boa!' he exclaimed. 'Ezekiel's got a blue boa that can make things invisible. He's done it to a boy called Ollie Sparks.'

'Ah, well it seems it's just a one-way ticket at the moment. You can go, but you can't come back, if you take my meaning. Ezekiel wants it both ways, naturally. But as he's an incompetent magician, he can't do it.'

'So he's practising on Ollie,' Charlie murmured. 'He's kept in the attics.'

'Dear lord, whatever next?' sighed Paton.

Charlie was still desperate to know about his uncle's visit to the castle. 'Uncle, what happened?' he said gently. 'Why have you lost your power?'

Paton closed his eyes. His face had a closed look, shuttered and blank. It seemed that he couldn't speak of his ordeal just yet. It had been too terrible.

The doorbell rang.

Grandma Bone must have been in the house all the time, because the front door opened and Charlie could hear her voice.

'You're not welcome here. Please leave!'

Charlie opened the window and looked down at the steps. 'It's Miss Ingledew,' he told his uncle. 'And Emma. Hi, Emma!' he called.

'*Julia?*' Paton's eyes flew open. 'She wants to see me then!'

'Hi!' said Emma, waving a bunch of roses at Charlie.

Miss Ingledew looked up. 'Hullo, Charlie, I've come to . . .'

She was cut short by Grandma Bone who stepped out of the house and growled, 'I asked you to leave.'

'But I've come to see Mr Yewbeam. I heard he wasn't well.' Miss Ingledew held up a yellow paper bag. 'We've brought flowers and bananas. They're so good for –'

'We've got our own bananas!' barked Grandma Bone, advancing on her unwelcome visitors. 'Mr Yewbeam is far too ill to have company.'

'He's not!' cried Charlie.

'Be quiet!' Grandma Bone glared up at Charlie, while Emma and Miss Ingledew were forced to step down on to the pavement.

'Really, Mrs Bone,' said Julia. 'I'm sure it wouldn't do Paton any harm to see me. I'm concerned about him.

Don't you understand?'

Paton's face turned from white to pink, then back to white again as he struggled out of bed. 'Julia!' he said breathlessly. 'Don't let her go, Charlie!'

'Stop stalking my brother,' Grandma Bone followed Miss Ingledew down the steps. 'You're not welcome here.'

'I am *not* stalking him. I have never stalked anyone in my life.' Clearly upset by Grandma Bone's insinuation, Miss Ingledew threw back her head of magnificent chestnut hair and marched away up the street. Emma waved bleakly at Charlie and ran after her.

'Has she gone?' croaked Paton.

''Fraid so, Uncle,' said Charlie. 'I think Grandma Bone offended her.'

Paton put his head in his hands. 'I'm scuppered,' he moaned. 'I might as well be dead.'

'Don't say that!' Charlie couldn't bear to see his normally vigorous uncle in such a pitiful state. 'I'll try and get her back,' he said.

Grandma Bone met Charlie in the hall. 'Where d'you think you're going?' she said.

'Out,' said Charlie.

'Oh no, you're not. You've got work to do. Revision, I believe. You've got tests coming up on Monday. Lots of them. Get upstairs and take out your books. Right now!'

Charlie almost exploded with indignation. 'How could you do that to Uncle Paton?' he demanded. 'He really wanted to see Miss Ingledew.'

'That woman's no good for him,' said Grandma Bone. 'Now if you don't get to work this minute, I'll tell them to give you detention next Saturday. In fact, after your disgraceful behaviour this morning, I'll be surprised if you don't get it, anyway.'

'I . . . You're just a . . .' Charlie struggled to contain himself and then rushed to his room before he said something so rude his grandmother would make sure he had detention for years to come.

For several hours Charlie wrestled with history dates, geographical locations, English grammar and French verbs. He began to get a headache and found he was forgetting things more than remembering them. Occasionally he looked out of his window, longing to see Benjamin and Runner Bean racing across the street. But no friendly face appeared, and nothing interesting

occurred to break the monotony of Charlie's awful afternoon . . . until he noticed the wand.

It was lying under his bed, caught in a thin beam of sunlight. Charlie picked it up. The wand felt warm and silky. It was very comforting to hold, almost like tasting something exceptionally delicious or lying on a bed of feathers.

Charlie had an idea. Skarpo had stolen the wand from a Welsh wizard so, reaching for the Welsh dictionary his uncle had given him, Charlie looked for the words 'help me'. He found 'helpu fi' and remembered the 'u' was pronounced 'i', and the 'f' like a 'v'.

Charlie sat at his table and, holding the wand in his lap, he stared at a column of French verbs and their English equivalents. 'Helpi vee,' he said. 'Helpi vee! Helpi vee!'

For a few moments nothing happened, and then Charlie had the strangest sensation. It was as if the word 'Look' was whispered into his brain. He tightened his grip on the wand, and looked at the words in front of him. A few minutes later he tested himself. Miraculously, he had learnt every verb and its meaning.

Charlie was so excited he dashed into his uncle's room

without knocking.

Paton's eyes were closed, but his face was distorted by a terrible frown. Charlie had forgotten Miss Ingledew's unfortunate visit.

'I'm sorry to disturb you, Uncle,' Charlie said in a quietly urgent voice, 'but something amazing has happened.'

'What?' Paton said wearily.

'You know you took the wand when you went to Yewbeam Castle and it got all burnt by something? Well, it got better, somehow. It's as good as new, and I just tried using it to memorise my French, and – *it's amazing* – it worked!'

Paton's eyes opened. He looked at Charlie with interest, and then his gaze was drawn to the wand. 'Curious,' he murmured. 'Very curious.'

Charlie said, 'I know this sounds silly, but d'you think the wand might really be mine?'

'How could that be possible, dear boy? You got it from an ancient painting.'

'Yes, but . . .' Charlie was reluctant to tell his uncle that Skarpo had refused to take the wand back. Paton had

warned him, more than once, not to go into the painting
again.

Paton was now staring at Charlie's feet, and Charlie
had a horrible feeling he knew exactly what his uncle was
looking at. He had forgotten to shut the door and
something had crept into the room. Yes, there it was, right
beside his left foot. It began to squeak.

'That is a very singular mouse,' Paton observed. 'I've
always known we had mice in the house, but that one
looks abnormally old. I can't say why.'

'Actually it is,' Charlie confessed.

Paton eyed his great-nephew suspiciously. 'Explain!'

Charlie explained, as best he could, how he had taken
a step, just a fraction of a step really, into the painting of
Skarpo. 'I did it for you, Uncle,' he said. 'I thought he
might have something to cure you. That's when he said
the wand belonged to me. He wanted to meet you, but I
wouldn't let him. As you see, I got out all right, but the
mouse that was in his pocket came with me.'

'What!' Paton's head dropped back on to the pillows.
'Then the sorcerer's out too!'

'Maybe not,' said Charlie hopefully. 'I mean, he'd have

done some damage by now, wouldn't he?'

'If the mouse is out, then *he* is out, you stupid boy,' Paton snapped.

'But he's still in the picture.'

'That's just his image, Charlie. The essence of the man, the living, breathing being, with all its mischief, its magic and mayhem is OUT!'

After a moment of humble silence, Charlie said, 'What shall I do with the mouse, then?'

The mouse ran under the bed.

'It hardly matters,' Paton muttered. 'What have you done, Charlie? I thought that life couldn't get worse, but now here I am, done for, and that *person* is on the loose.' He closed his eyes.

Charlie would have liked to bring up the subject of the wand again, but clearly his uncle would rather he left the room.

'Sorry,' Charlie murmured. He tiptoed out and closed the door on his uncle and, presumably, the mouse.

Amy Bone had just come back from work and Charlie could hear her laying the table for tea. He ran down to the kitchen.

'Where's Billy?' asked Mrs Bone.

Charlie told her about Ezekiel's visit.

'That poor boy,' said his mother. 'He must be so lonely. Something should be done about it. I'm sure someone would adopt him, he seems such a nice little fellow.'

'The Bloors will never let him go,' said Charlie. 'They like to own people.'

'That they do,' his mother said quietly. 'Take your uncle some tea, will you, Charlie?'

'Erm . . . I don't think that would be a good idea,' said Charlie.

'Why ever not?'

'Him and me . . . well, I think he's a bit cross with me.'

One of the many good things about Amy Bone, from Charlie's point of view, was that she never reproached him for any quarrels he might have had with other members of the family.

'Ah well,' she sighed. 'I'll do it then.' She put some tea and cakes on a tray and took it upstairs. In a few minutes she came back looking very worried.

'I'm really concerned about your uncle,' she told Charlie. 'He's just lying there, looking grey and ill, and so

melancholy. Whatever is the matter with him?'

'He went to Yewbeam Castle,' Charlie said.

His mother gasped. 'Where that awful Yolanda lives? Has she done this to Paton?'

'No, Mum. It was something else. He won't say what. Yolanda's *here*. She's staying with the aunts, only she isn't old. She looks my age. She came here once when you were out. Her name's Belle.'

Mrs Bone clapped a hand over her forehead. 'Stay out of her way, Charlie. She tried to keep your father up there, you know. When he was young. Luckily, it turned out that Lyell wasn't endowed, so she lost interest in him.'

'Maybe not so lucky,' said Charlie. 'If Dad had been endowed he might have been able to save himself.'

'Who knows?' Mrs Bone looked thoughtful. 'I wish you weren't part of that awful family.'

'Well, I am,' said Charlie. 'And I don't care. If they try to mess with me, they'll regret it.'

His mother gave him an encouraging smile.

On Sunday, Charlie decided to visit the Pets' Café. With the wand's help he had managed to finish all his revision.

'Runner Bean's waiting for you!' said Norton, the bouncer, as Charlie stepped into the café. 'Going to take him for a run, then?'

Charlie felt guilty. He'd almost forgotten about Runner Bean. 'The park's a bit far away,' he said.

'Take him on the heath,' said Norton. 'He's really missed you, he has.'

Charlie was about to go round the counter when he noticed Lysander and Olivia, sitting at a table in the corner. As soon as she saw Charlie, Olivia jumped out of her seat and waved frantically at him. She looked surprisingly normal. Her hair was mouse-brown and her face free of any make-up or decoration.

Charlie made his way over to their table. It took him some time as a gang of lop-eared rabbits kept bouncing round his feet.

'No warpaint today, then?' he said, leaping over Olivia's white rabbit and grabbing a chair.

'I'm preparing my face for the end-of-term play,' said Olivia. 'I thought if I looked normal for a while, my transformation would be all the more dramatic.'

'I can't wait,' said Charlie. 'I didn't think any of you

were coming here today.'

'I got bored,' said Olivia, 'but I think Sander's here for another reason.'

Charlie noticed that the normally cheerful African looked extremely agitated. He kept darting wild, anxious glances round the room, and his grey parrot, Homer, fluttered from his head to his shoulder and back again, every time he moved.

'Where's Tancred?' Charlie asked Lysander.

'His dad made him stay in to revise. I've done my work. I just *had* to come out.'

'What's the trouble?'

Lysander shook his head. 'My ancestors are angry,' he muttered. 'I couldn't sleep. All night I heard their drums in my head, their loud voices, their furious wailing.'

All at once, Homer cried, 'Catastrophe! Catastrophe!'

'He knows when things are wrong,' said Lysander. 'He feels their rage through me.'

'Why don't they tell you what's upsetting them?' asked Olivia.

Lysander frowned at her. 'I have to find out myself,' he said.

Lysander's spirit ancestors were very powerful. They were more than ghosts. Charlie had seen their strong brown hands, their spears and shields. More than once, they had helped to save him. If they were angry, then it was for a very good reason.

'Let's go for a walk,' Charlie suggested, hoping fresh air would clear Lysander's head.

'Good idea!' said Olivia, scooping up her rabbit.

Charlie was about to go and fetch Runner Bean when Mr Onimous appeared with the dog. Runner Bean rushed up to Charlie, while cats and rabbits scattered in all directions.

'Oh, he has missed you, Charlie,' said Mr Onimous as the big dog leapt up and began licking Charlie's face and hair.

'And is the rat OK?' asked Charlie.

'Right as rain,' said the little man. 'Very popular with Mrs Onimous. And the flames adore him.'

'How unusual,' Olivia remarked. 'I mean cats liking a rat.'

'*They're* unusual, miss,' said Mr Onimous solemnly. 'Off you go now. Charlie, give that dog a nice long run. My legs

can't keep up with him.'

The three friends left the café and headed towards the heath at the edge of the city. Olivia carried her rabbit in a basket, but Lysander's parrot travelled on his shoulder, its head bobbing up and down in rhythm with its master's stride.

When they reached the heath, Charlie let Runner Bean off the lead and he tore across the grass, barking joyfully. Homer the parrot left Lysander's shoulder and flew over the big dog's head, crying, 'What a to-do. Dog ahoy!'

'Ship ahoy, if you don't mind,' called Olivia.

'He's confused,' said Lysander.

'I'd say he'd lost the plot,' said Olivia, giggling.

'It's not a joke,' barked Lysander. 'He gets muddled when he's upset. Like me. I'm muddled.'

'Sorr-e-e-e!' said Olivia.

Charlie glanced at her. She might almost have been laughing at Lysander. It was all very well for her, Charlie thought. Olivia could be a good friend when she chose to be, but she didn't really understand what it was like to be endowed, what a burden and a puzzle it could be.

'Cool it,' he said.

Olivia raised her eyebrows, but she seemed to understand the warning look in Charlie's eyes.

'I don't think I'll go to school tomorrow,' Lysander murmured.

'Why?' asked Charlie.

'Don't really know, I think there's trouble for me there.' Lysander's voice had sunk so low they could hardly hear him.

'But you've got to,' Charlie said desperately. 'What about the carving? What about Ollie Sparks?'

'Why do you care so much?' said Lysander, surprised by Charlie's vehemence.

'I just do,' said Charlie. 'I can't help it. I feel bad about Ollie because I haven't tried to rescue him again. There's been so much else going on. But think how awful it must be for him, alone in those dark attics, not knowing if he'll ever get out. We've got to rescue him soon, Sander. We've just got to. Please say you'll come to school on Monday. *Please!*'

'I'll think about it,' said Lysander. He whistled to his parrot, and the grey bird wheeled about and flew back to

perch on his shoulder.

'See you,' said Lysander. He turned and strode away across the heath.

The parrot looked back at Charlie and Olivia, and called, 'Watch it!'

Bull, bells and golden bats

As he made his way up the steep hill to his home, Lysander began to feel breathless. This had never happened before. He was a strong boy, tall for his age, a great runner and champion hurdler.

It was the drums that took away his breath. That's what it was. Their angry beats echoed in his head like distant thunder, making him shudder.

'Trouble!' called Homer from his master's shoulder.

'Yeah, trouble,' Lysander agreed.

He had just climbed the steepest part of the hill road, a long curving ascent that

ended in a welcome stretch of even ground. Here he stopped and looked out across the city. The cathedral, with its great domed roof, dwarfed all the other buildings in the city. Only the shadowy mansion to the north was anywhere near as tall.

'Bloor's,' Lysander muttered.

Beyond the grey roof of the academy, and just at the edge of the wood that covered the castle ruin, there issued a thin plume of smoke.

When he saw it, Lysander's eyes began to smart, his skin burned, his throat felt raw. Tearing at his collar, he ran the last few metres home. He reached a pair of tall iron gates and, pulling one open, he tore up the path to an imposing white house, set behind lawns as green and smooth as billiard tables.

Mrs Jessamine Sage was watching a quiz show on TV when her son went pounding up to his room. Mrs Sage knew her son's trouble immediately. She could hear the drums accompanying his footsteps. It was from her that Lysander had inherited his power. At certain times, she too heard the drums speak and the ancestors clamouring for attention.

Mrs Sage levered herself up from her comfortable chair. She was a well-rounded woman of considerable strength, but she'd been feeling heavy and listless of late. She didn't need drums to tell her that another baby was on its way. There were other, very obvious signs.

The beautiful and stately woman climbed the stairs to the first floor. Behind the two doors on either side of her son's room, her daughters, aged ten and fourteen, were playing loud unmelodic music; guitars and voices. It was all squeaky shouting and rap, rap, rap. Not a drum beat between them.

'Hortense! Alexandra! Reduce!' barked Mrs Sage, in such a commanding tone that both girls immediately obeyed.

When Mrs Sage opened her son's door she was met by another barrage of sound, this one so tumultuous it almost knocked her back on to the landing.

'Lysander! Calm!' called Mrs Sage across the room. She never used two words, or even five for that matter, where one would do.

Lysander was lying on his bed with his eyes tight shut and his hands over his ears. Even so, he heard his mother's

powerful voice. He opened his eyes.

'Think of a tree,' sang Mrs Sage.

'Roots, leaves, branches.

'Holding, lifting . . .

'Sky . . .

'Think of the king.'

Lysander removed his hands from his ears.

'There,' said his mother, lowering herself on to the bed. 'Better?'

It worked every time. As soon as Lysander thought of a tree, as soon as he saw, in his mind's eye, the mysterious painting in the King's Room, he felt calmer. He sat up and rubbed his eyes. The drum beats were still there, in his head, but now quiet enough for him to think.

'Tell,' said his mother.

'Trouble!' cried Homer from his perch by the window.

'She didn't ask you,' said Lysander with a rueful grin. 'There is trouble, though,' he told his mother. 'I don't know what. But it's at Bloor's. I saw smoke and I felt my skin burn. The ancestors are angry, Mum.'

'They always have a reason,' said Mrs Sage.

'I don't want to go to school on Monday. I don't want

to face whatever it is. I never felt like this before.'

'You must face it.' Mrs Sage patted her son's hand. 'You must go to school.'

'That's what Charlie Bone said.'

'Charlie?'

'Yes. You know, the kid with rough hair. His uncle had a party last term, remember? He's smaller than most of us, but he pushes his way into trouble and somehow we find ourselves following; Tancred, me and Gabriel. He's doing it again, trying to rescue a boy from invisibility.'

'Invisibility?' Mrs Sage frowned.

'I'm making a carving,' Lysander went on. 'It's really good, Mum. The best I've ever done. I thought the ancestors would be able to bring the boy back. But the drums say no, I've done the wrong thing.'

Mrs Sage stood up. 'Not you, Lysander. Someone else has done wrong. Go to school and put it right.' She swept out of her son's room, her long, flowered skirt whispering round her ankles like the sea.

'What a picnic!' shrieked Homer.

'For you, maybe,' said Mrs Sage, closing the door.

* * *

On Monday morning, the reason for Lysander's terrible foreboding soon became clear.

After their history test, Charlie and Fidelio, emerging into the garden, saw a group of their friends clustered round the remains of a fire. Weedon was always burning rubbish in the grounds, so this wasn't too unusual – it was the attitude of the group that alerted Charlie. Lysander was standing in stony disbelief, while Tancred's stiff yellow hair sparked with electricity.

Olivia, standing next to Lysander, caught Charlie's eye and gestured wildly. Charlie and Fidelio rushed over to them.

Among a pile of scorched twigs and burnt paper, two blue eyes stared out at them. The eyes were all that remained of Lysander's beautiful carving.

'How could they?' whispered Emma.

Lysander was shuddering. He held his arms stiffly at his sides and his hands were clenched. He seemed unable to speak.

Charlie noticed a group of sixth formers watching them. Asa Pike had a satisfied smile on his face, while Zelda Dobinski's long features were twisted in a horrible

smirk. Manfred, however, was staring straight at Lysander, as if he were outraged by the African's clever attempt to rescue Ollie.

'No one else knew . . .' Lysander muttered. 'Who would . . .?'

'Obviously someone in Art,' said Olivia.

Silence fell over the little group and then, almost as one, they looked over to the walls of the ruin, where Belle and Dorcas were standing watching them.

'But why?' said Lysander.

'Because your carving was too good,' said Olivia grimly. 'And because someone doesn't want us to rescue Ollie Sparks.'

'Don't give up, Sander,' said Charlie.

'You don't know what it's like for him,' said Tancred. 'He can *feel* the injury, can't you, Sander? It's like he put a bit of his own heart into that piece of wood. D'you know what that's like, Charlie?'

'No,' said Charlie in a small voice. 'I'm sorry.'

'What's that?' said Fidelio, rubbing his head. 'I can hear drums.'

'What d'you expect?' said Tancred, almost angrily.

'Come on, Sander, let's get out of here.' He grabbed his friend's arm and steered him away from the fire. Lysander seemed hardly aware of his surroundings. He allowed Tancred to lead him back towards the school, but not before Charlie, too, heard the faint throb of a drum, almost like a heartbeat, following Lysander across the grass.

'I didn't ask him to do it,' Charlie murmured, gazing at the accusing blue eyes. 'He wanted to. It was his idea.'

'It wasn't your fault,' Fidelio said cheerfully. 'Sander will get over it. We'll just have to think of something else.'

'It's so awful,' murmured Emma. 'I feel I'm looking at a real boy, or what *was* a real boy.'

'Let's get away from here,' said Olivia, glancing at Belle and Dorcas. 'We don't want them to enjoy our misery for too long, do we?'

As they turned away from the fire, Gabriel came leaping up to them. 'I've had a really weird piano lesson,' he panted. 'It went on for ages and . . .' He stopped in mid-sentence. 'Oh, no,' he said, staring at the blue eyes. 'Is that . . .?'

'Lysander's carving,' said Charlie. 'And we've got a

good idea who did it.'

In an effort to cheer them up, Olivia announced that she'd brought a frisbee to school. 'Let's have a game,' she suggested.

While they tossed the red frisbee from one to the other, Gabriel told them about his strange piano lesson.

Mr Pilgrim, the piano teacher, was an odd person at the best of times. A tall, dark, morose man, he was seldom seen outside the music room at the top of the west tower. He hardly ever spoke and it was so difficult to get any advice from him, he had lost most of his students. During Gabriel's extended piano lesson, however, Mr Pilgrim had said quite a lot – for him.

'So come on, tell us what he said.' Olivia leapt for the frisbee, losing a yellow shoe mid-leap.

'It was weird,' said Gabriel. 'He said, "I don't know how he got up here, but I couldn't help him." So I said, "Who, Mr Pilgrim?" And he said, "It's all too much, he can't take it in – lights, traffic, plastic things. He doesn't like them, they confuse him. He'll do away with them, and who can blame him . . .?" and then Mr P looked very hard at me, and said, "I can't see how he'll do it, though, can you?"

I said . . .' Gabriel caught the frisbee and yelped with pain. 'Ouch! That was a hard one, Charlie!'

'Come on, come on,' cried Olivia. 'So what did *you* say?'

'I just said, "No, sir." I mean, what else could I say?'

'You could have said, "Do *what?*"' said Fidelio.

A nasty thought suddenly occurred to Charlie. He stood stock-still, with the frisbee clutched in both hands.

'Come on! Come on! Throw it, Charlie!' called the others.

'Hold on,' said Charlie. 'Did Mr P describe this mysterious visitor?'

Gabriel shook his head. 'I couldn't get a name out of him, either. He just said, "He can, you know. He's quite exceptional. Look what he did to the music!" So I looked, and d'you know, all the notes on one of the music sheets had turned to gold. It was Beethoven's Sonata No. 27, as a matter of fact. And then I noticed that the bats in the corner – Mr Pilgrim's always had bats in his room, but he doesn't mind, nor do I, they're just like flying gerbils really . . .'

'So what had happened to the bats?' asked Fidelio

impatiently.

'They were gold too,' said Gabriel.

'Oh.' Charlie felt queasy.

Emma looked at him. 'What is it, Charlie?'

'Er, nothing,' Charlie mumbled.

'So were the spiders,' Gabriel went on blithely, 'and their webs. They looked really pretty, like Christmas decorations.'

Charlie was glad to hear the hunting horn. He was beginning to wonder when the next nasty surprise would hit him. For once, all he wanted to do was to bury himself in a complicated maths test.

'I've got a feeling you know who it is,' said Fidelio, racing Charlie across the grass. 'Mr P's visitor, I mean.'

'Ssssh!' hissed Charlie.

'Tell us, Charlie, go on!' cried Olivia.

They piled into the hall, where Charlie was grateful for the rule of silence. He walked off to the maths room with Fidelio in tow, while the girls went to their cloakrooms and Gabriel dragged himself up the stairs to a dreaded theory test.

Charlie might have longed to bury himself in fractions,

but he found he couldn't. His thoughts kept returning to Mr Pilgrim's mysterious visitor. Who else would turn spiders into gold? Who else would be confused by lights and traffic? At the end of the test, Charlie knew he'd done badly. He wished he'd put the wand to work on mathematics instead of French.

There was more bad news waiting for him in the canteen. One of the dinner ladies was in quite a state, having only that morning witnessed a large bull charging out of the butcher's, where before there had only been two large sides of beef, hanging at the back.

'Beef one minute, bull the next,' Mrs Gill kept muttering, as she handed out plates of cottage pie. 'What's happening to the world?'

'What indeed, Mrs Gill?' said Fidelio, with his usual charming smile.

'I don't think you believed her, did you?' whispered Charlie, as they made their way to a table.

'Well, did you?' said Fidelio. 'Poor old thing, she's a real fruit cake!'

'Actually, I did believe her,' said Charlie.

At that moment, Gabriel joined them, saying, 'Have

you heard what Mrs Gill's been . . . ?'

'Yes, we have,' said Fidelio. 'And Charlie believes her, because he knows why or who or what . . . well, why, Charlie?'

'You know that painting?' Charlie said. 'The one I brought to school last term?'

Fidelio and Gabriel, with forks halfway to their mouths, stared at Charlie.

'You mean the one with the sorcerer?' asked Gabriel in a squeaky whisper.

Charlie looked round the canteen. No one was paying them any attention, and the noise of scraping knives and forks and chattering voices was so loud, not a soul beyond their table could have heard him. All the same, Charlie lowered his voice as he told his two friends about his visit to Skarpo, and the escaped mouse.

'You mean, you think he got out too?' said Fidelio.

'Must have,' said Charlie. 'At first I thought it was impossible, because he was still in the painting. But my uncle says that's only his image, not his essence. I'd convinced myself that Skarpo couldn't get out because I desperately didn't want to believe it.'

'You mean the golden bats and the bull and stuff are him . . .?' said Fidelio.

'Must be,' said Charlie. 'And I've a horrible feeling he's only just begun. It could get worse.'

It did.

The pupils in Bloor's Academy were about to go out for their afternoon break when a cloud passed over the sun. And then another, and another. The sky was filled with a lurid, purple glow. It darkened to deep indigo, which gradually turned black. Pitch black.

A crowd of children gathered round the garden door, reluctant to be the first to step into the eerie darkness.

'For goodness' sake, you ninnies,' sneered Zelda Dobinsky. 'Get out! Go on! You're not afraid of a few clouds, are you?'

To show her contempt for the younger children, she pushed through the crowd and took several steps into the dark garden.

A toad fell on her head. And then another. When the first toad plonked on to Zelda's head, she opened her mouth. When the second one came, she gave a loud shriek and leapt back into the crowd.

Then it began to rain frogs.

Some of the children screamed and retreated into the hall. Others put out their hands to catch the frogs, but the slimy creatures were falling with such force, there were cries of 'Ouch!' 'Help!' 'Ow!' and hands were quickly withdrawn.

In the distance, they could hear police sirens, ambulances and fire engines wailing round the city.

Standing at the back of the crowd, Charlie's heart sank. Where *was* Skarpo? How on earth could he be caught and taken back to where he belonged?

It was obviously too dangerous to play outside in complete darkness. The lights came on in the building, and the children were sent back to their classrooms. In Charlie's case this was Mr Carp's English room. Mr Carp was broad and red-faced. He kept a slim wicked-looking cane, propped beside his desk, and had been known, accidentally, of course, to flick children on the ears when he was irritated. Charlie had become rather good at ducking these attacks, but he could tell from the malicious gleam in Mr Carp's small eyes that he was determined to get Charlie one day. Charlie thought it might be today.

From the desk beside Charlie's, Fidelio whispered, 'What's he going to do next, Charlie? Got any ideas?'

Charlie shook his head.

In a high-pitched screech, Mr Carp cried, 'You've got half an hour to revise your Wordsworth before the test.'

Mindful of their ears, twenty children got out their Wordsworths and silently bent their heads.

Outside, the dark clouds lifted and the sun came out. Mr Weedon and several sixth formers could soon be observed collecting frogs in nets, boxes and bags. Charlie wondered if frogs had fallen all over the city, or had Bloor's been singled out for the favour? Through the window, he saw Manfred wiping his slimy hands on his trousers, and he smiled to himself. His smile didn't last long.

Nobody thought it unusual when the cathedral bells began to ring. But when the bells in five smaller chuches joined in, people began to worry. Soon the sound of pealing bells resounded throughout the city. And they didn't stop. On and on and on they went. Vicars, curates, vergers, wardens and bell-ringers rushed into the churches to find the bell-ropes mysteriously rising and falling, all by themselves.

Fidelio looked at Charlie. Charlie rolled his eyes and shrugged. And then one of the girls in the front row put up her hand. When Mr Carp, who had his hands over his ears, took no notice, the girl – Rosie Stubbs – shouted, 'Excuse me, sir, but there's an elephant in the garden.'

Everyone turned to look. There was.

Mr Carp, a livid glow spreading over his cheeks, lifted his cane. Rosie put her hands over her ears.

The noise from the bells increased.

'SHUT UP! SHUT UP! SHUT UP, ALL OF YOU!' screeched Mr Carp, although the class was completely silent. 'I can't stand this. Who is doing it? They should be shot!'

Everyone gasped.

Recollecting himself, Mr Carp shouted, 'Put away your books. It's no good. We can't continue. Class dismissed.'

The class gratefully slipped their books into their desks and filed out of the classroom into the hall. Other classrooms were emptying. Harassed-looking teachers were rushing down the hall to the staffroom, black capes flapping, papers flying, books tumbling out of their arms.

The children who had gathered in the hall, finding it

almost impossible to observe the rule of silence, whispered and muttered their way down to the canteens where an early tea was hoped for.

Charlie and Fidelio had just managed to grab a biscuit and a glass of orange juice, when Billy Raven rushed up to Charlie, saying, 'You're wanted in Dr Bloor's study.'

'Me?' said Charlie, turning pale.

'All of us. You too, Gabriel.'

'All of us?' said Gabriel. 'That's unusual. What on earth's going on?'

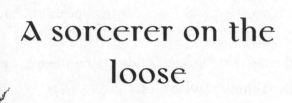

A sorcerer on the loose

Charlie had never been to Dr Bloor's study. Nervous as he was, he couldn't help feeling curious.

'I've been there,' said Gabriel as the two boys followed Billy up to the hall. 'It was when I first came here. I had to go and explain about my clothes problem. It's the sort of room that makes you feel as though you've done something wrong; I don't know why.'

Manfred and Zelda were waiting for them in the hall, and gradually the other endowed children began to arrive: Dorcas and Belle, with Asa close behind, wearing a

silly smile, Tancred, whose hair was crackling with nervous electricity, and Emma with a pencil behind her ear.

'Take that out!' barked Zelda. 'Tidy youself up, girl. What d'you think you look like?'

Emma seemed bewildered, until Charlie pointed to the pencil, which she pulled out and stuck in her pocket, smoothing her blonde hair as best she could.

'Ah, here comes the great sculptor!' Manfred announced as Lysander slouched gloomily into the hall. 'Cheer up, boy! What's the trouble, eh?'

'You know very well,' Lysander said grimly.

Dorcas giggled and Belle's awful eyes turned from blue, through grey, to violet. Manfred look momentarily uneasy, and then said, 'Billy, lead the way. You know where it is.'

'Yes, Manfred.' Billy crossed the hall to the door into the west wing. The old door creaked open and Charlie, close behind Billy, found himself in the dark, musty passage that led to the music tower.

They reached the round room at the base of the tower and were about to ascend the staircase up to the first floor, when they saw Mr Pilgrim sitting on the second step.

'Excuse me, sir,' said Billy, but Mr Pilgrim didn't move. He appeared not to have heard Billy.

'We've got to go to Dr Bloor's study, sir,' said Charlie.

Mr Pilgrim stared at Charlie with a puzzled expression. 'So many bells,' he said. 'Why so many? Who died? Was it – me?'

Charlie was about to reply when Manfred suddenly pushed past him and, glaring down at the music teacher, said, 'Please move, Mr Pilgrim. Now. We're in a hurry!'

Mr Pilgrim pushed a thick lock of black hair away from his eyes. 'Is that so?' he said in a surprisingly stubborn voice.

'Yes, it is. Move!' Manfred demanded rudely. 'Come on. NOW!' His narrow eyes took on an intense, chilling look as he stared at Mr Pilgrim.

Charlie glanced at Manfred's coal-black eyes and remembered how it felt to be hypnotised. He longed to warn Mr Pilgrim, to make him fight that horrible disabling stare. It was possible to resist Manfred's power. Charlie, himself, had done it once.

But it seemed that Mr Pilgrim had neither the strength, nor the will, to oppose Manfred. With a groan of dismay

the music teacher stood and whirled away, up the narrow, curving steps. His footsteps could be heard clattering to the top of the tower as Manfred led the way to the first floor.

They went through a low door and into a thickly carpeted corridor, where Manfred stopped outside another door, this one panelled in dark oak. He knocked twice, and a deep voice said, 'Enter.'

Manfred opened the door and herded the others into the room.

Behind a large, highly, polished desk sat Dr Bloor, his broad, greyish face illuminated by a green desk-lamp. The curtains behind him had been drawn against the sunlight, and the booklined room was plunged in gloomy shadows. Dr Bloor beckoned and the children shuffled forward until they stood in a row before his desk.

The headmaster scanned their faces with steely grey eyes, and then his gaze came to rest on Charlie. 'I want to know who is responsible,' he demanded in a cold voice.

Charlie's legs felt weak. He hated the way Dr Bloor could do this to him. He knew the headmaster wasn't endowed, but he gave the impression that he had

enormous power, that he could do anything he wanted and that his will was so strong he could overcome anything, or anyone.

'Children of the Red King!' Dr Bloor sneered. 'Look at you! Freaks! That's what you are.'

Manfred shifted uncomfortably and Charlie wondered how it felt to have your father calling you a freak.

'All of you!' shouted Dr Bloor, and then, glancing at Belle, he muttered, 'Almost all of you.'

'Excuse me, sir,' said Zelda, rather boldly. 'But do you mean who's responsible for the bells and the frogs, et cetera? Because it certainly wasn't me. I got one on the head. Actually, it was a toad and there were two.'

Charlie knew he was in serious trouble but he still had an urge to giggle.

'I didn't think it was you, Zelda,' the headmaster said coldly. 'I'm well aware that that kind of thing is quite beyond you.'

Zelda reddened. She glared down at the line of younger children and said, 'I think it's Tancred, sir.'

'I do storms,' Tancred retorted angrily. 'Weather.'

'Wind can make bells ring, sky darken, frogs rain,' said

Manfred.

'Not elephants!' cried Tancred, whose hair crackled violently. His green cape lifted and a blast of cold air blew a pile of papers off the desk.

'CONTROL YOURSELF!' roared Dr Bloor.

Tancred gritted his teeth and Dorcas Loom began to gather the papers, putting them, one by one, on to the desk.

'I know who is capable and who is not,' said Dr Bloor. 'But I want a confession. Do you understand my position?' He got up and began to pace behind his desk. 'The people of this city know that I harbour children with unusual, and in some cases,' he glanced at Asa Pike, 'undesirable talents. They tolerate *you* because they respect *me*. We are the oldest family in this city. We can trace our ancestry back for nearly a thousand years.' He gestured towards the bookcases. 'These walls have witnessed alchemy, hypnotism, divination, metamorphosis, magic of unimaginable splendour, shape-shifting, even,' he coughed and lowered his voice, 'apparitions.'

All at once Dr Bloor stopped pacing and swung round to face his victims, 'But never, never, never,' he raised his

voice, 'NEVER have the events in this building impinged upon the city. Never have the citizens had to suffer for our – peculiarities. But now,' he banged his fist on the desk and bellowed, 'all at once day has turned to night, bulls have run rampant, bells have gone berserk. Can you imagine what it's like out there, in the city?' He flung a hand towards the window. 'The danger, the chaos. There have been more traffic accidents in ten minutes than in a whole year. The mayor was on the phone to me immediately. Oh, he knows very well where the trouble is coming from.'

'I think we know too, sir,' said a voice.

Everyone turned to look at Belle. She gave a wide smile and her eyes changed to a brilliant emerald green. She said, 'It's Charlie Bone. Isn't it, Charlie?'

Charlie's mouth went dry. He felt slightly queasy. 'I don't know,' he mumbled.

'Liar,' said Manfred.

'Coward,' hissed Zelda.

Asa gave an unpleasant snort.

'You can go,' said Dr Bloor, dismissing them all with a wave of his hand.

Surprised by the sudden turn of events the eleven children turned to the door, but before Charlie could reach it, the headmaster added, 'Not you, Charlie Bone.'

Gabriel threw Charlie a look of sympathy as Manfred pushed him through the door after the others. And then Charlie was alone with Dr Bloor. The headmaster paced again, finally sinking into his large leather chair, and clasping his hands together on a sheaf of papers lying on the desk. He gave a sigh of exasperation and declared, 'You are very stupid, Charlie Bone. I had my doubts, but when I saw you all, standing there, it didn't take me long to identify the culprit. I gave you a chance to confess. You should have taken it.'

'Yes, well . . . but I didn't . . .' began Charlie.

'You idiot!' roared Dr Bloor. 'D'you think I don't know what you can do? I'm well aware of the painting you can . . . enter. I know about the "person" whom you have so carelessly let out. Who else could cause this mayhem? There's obviously a sorcerer on the loose, and I want to know what you intend to do about it?'

'Um – find him?' Charlie suggested.

'And how are you going to do that?'

'Er – look for him?' said Charlie.

'Oh, brilliant!' said Dr Bloor sarcastically. 'Well done!'
He raised his voice. 'If this nonsense hasn't stopped by
nine o'clock tomorrow, then it will be very much the
worse for you.'

'In what way, sir?' asked Charlie, clearing his throat.

'I'll let you know,' said the headmaster. 'Your famous
relations assured me that you would be an asset to this
school, but so far you've been nothing but trouble. They're
very disappointed and I'm sure they'll approve of any
punishment I choose – even if they have to lose you
forever.'

Charlie shuddered. He thought of his father,
permanently lost, unreachable, unknown. 'Yes, sir,' he
said. 'Can I go now, and start looking?'

'You'd better. You haven't got long,' came the grim
reply.

Charlie whisked himself through the door as speedily as
he could. Once in the corridor, however, he decided not
to return the way he had come, but to walk further into
the Bloors' intriguing quarters. Eventually, he hoped, he
would find a staircase leading to the attics. For that was

surely where Skarpo must be hiding, amongst the cobwebs and eerie, empty rooms.

Charlie trod softly over the rich carpeting in the corridor. He passed dark oak-panelled doors, portraits in gilt frames (these he avoided looking at), shelves crammed with dusty books, a collection of small skeletons in a glass case, the head of a bear mounted on a wooden shield. 'Gruesome,' Charlie muttered and hastened on, beneath the stuffed birds and bunches of dried herbs suspended from hooks in the ceiling.

He reached the end of the corridor and climbed a narrow stairway to the second floor. Here, a brief glimpse showed him a shadowy passage where, in the distance, something horribly like a coffin stood upright against the wall.

Charlie hurried up the next staircase, this one uncarpeted and creaky. At the top he found himself entering the airless, gas-lit passage that he and Emma had passed through on their way to find Ollie. The steps to the attic were halfway down, he remembered.

A sound drifted towards him: music. Not Mr Pilgrim's fine piano-playing, but a brass band, accompanied by a

harsh, quavering voice. Charlie stopped and listened. There was no mistaking the voice. Old Ezekiel obviously lived in this gloomy region of the house.

Charlie cautiously crept forward until he reached the stairs that led to the attic. He had climbed several steps when something made him glance upward. There, at the top, something gleamed: a coil of thick, silvery-blue rope. But, of course, it wasn't rope. Charlie could now make out a faint pattern of scales.

Sensing Charlie's presence, a head lifted from the coil, a flattish triangle with black eyes and strange markings across the top. Strangest of all were the thin blue feathers sprouting from its neck. All at once a hiss, like a gas explosion, errupted from the creature's wide mouth.

Charlie backed away, missed his footing and tumbled down into the passage, landing on all fours. As the hissing snake began to glide down the steps, Charlie picked himself up and tore to the end of the passage. He had just begun to descend to the second floor when Ezekiel's shrill voice called, 'Who's there? Who's upset my treasure? You'd better watch out, whoever you are, or you'll be DUST!'

'Dust?' Charlie murmured under his breath as he leapt

down spirally steps and creaking stairways. 'Nothingness more like. Zero. Zilch. No more Charlie.'

He had just reached the landing above the entrance hall, when he ran straight into Mr Weedon.

'What are you doing in the west wing?' grunted the handyman. 'It's out of bounds.'

'I was given permission,' Charlie panted.

Mr Weedon raised his eyebrows. 'Oh? And who gave you permission?'

'Dr Bloor,' said Charlie. After all, Dr Bloor had commanded him to find Skarpo. 'I'm looking for someone. I suppose you haven't seen him? He's got kind of silvery hair and a beard and he's wearing a dark robe and a little cap on . . .'

'It's *you*. Of course. You little squirt. You're responsible for all the mess outside that *I've* got to clear up. Not to mention the elephant. Damn near killed me when I tried to move it.'

'What happened to it?' asked Charlie, who couldn't help being curious.

'Vanished, didn't it? But its dung didn't vanish – nor its blasted footprints on my lawn. If I do see that wretched

sorcerer, I'll damn well wring his neck.'

'Oh, I wouldn't try to . . .' began Charlie.

'Get out of my way,' growled Mr Weedon. 'I'm sick of the lot of you. Endowed, my foot!' And he marched off towards the west wing, leaving Charlie anxious and relieved all at the same time.

Below him, the hall began to fill with children making for the garden door. The afternoon break had begun and Charlie decided to continue his search outside.

'What happened to you?' said Fidelio as Charlie ran up to his friends.

Charlie explained. 'I've got to find the sorcerer before nine o'clock tomorrow, or I'm dead meat. Worse than dead meat – I'm . . .' he ran his hand across his throat.

Fidelio and Gabriel offered to help.

'The woods,' suggested Gabriel.

They waded through the thick undergrowth beneath the trees that surrounded the grounds. But the deeper they went, the harder it was to know if the dark forms sliding round the tree trunks were solid, or merely shadows of moving branches. So many resembled a tall man in a long robe.

When the hunting horn called them in for the last lesson, Charlie wasn't sure what to do. Dr Bloor had set him a task. He would have to risk getting detention from the other teachers if he was to continue his search for Skarpo.

He decided to inspect the dormitories. There were twenty-five of these, scattered over three floors, and Charlie had only searched ten before the dinner bell went. What should he do now? Surely he wasn't expected to miss his supper? He began the long journey from the third floor down to the dining hall. As he approached the hall he could hear raised voices. He was very late and hoped he hadn't missed the first course. When he opened the door and stepped inside, the noise was deafening. And then someone shouted, 'There he is! It's all his fault.'

Charlie ducked his head, hoping to look inconspicuous. But everyone was watching him now. Someone had spread the news. Charlie Bone was responsible for frog rain, for darkness, mad bulls, golden bats and vanishing elephants. Worst of all, he was responsible for tonight's supper.

As Charlie slid on to the bench beside Fidelio, he saw a heap of cabbage and a slice of stale-looking bread on his

plate. Everyone else had a similar meal.

'What's this?' Charlie murmured to Fidelio.

'Trouble in the kitchens,' Fidelio explained in a low voice. 'We were going to have scrambled eggs, but one of Cook's assistants found the larder full of chickens instead of eggs. You can hear them if you listen.'

Charlie could, indeed, hear clucking from behind the door into the kitchen. His heart sank.

After watching Charlie take his place, the rest of the table began to chew their bread and cabbage. There were mutters of disgust and sounds of 'Uurgh!' 'Yuk!' 'Blurgh!' all round Charlie, but Billy Raven, sitting opposite, whispered, 'Actually, I don't mind cabbage.'

And then, from the drama table, Damian Smerk piped, 'This food is disgusting. I'd like to stuff my foot down Charlie Bone's throat.'

'Shut up, Fatso,' came Olivia's voice. 'It's not his fault.'

''Tis, you wet cabbage . . .'

The rest of Damian's rude remark was drowned by Dorcas Loom's shout of 'Charlie Bone should be made to eat slugs for the rest of his life.' She followed this with a loud titter and several of her cronies on the art table

joined in.

In Charlie's defence, Tancred made a remark that Charlie couldn't quite hear, but it was evidently so rude that it caused loud gasps of horror and astonishment.

Dr Bloor stood up and glared down the room. He was about to speak when Tancred's anger got the better of him. Plates and crockery began to slide across the tables as a violent wind rushed round the dining hall.

Suppers crashed to the floor and members of staff leapt to their feet in dismay.

'Enough!' roared Dr Bloor. 'Tancred Torsson, CONTROL yourself!'

The headmaster stood at the edge of the dais, his hands behind his back, glowering at Tancred while the stormy boy calmed down, and the supper tables gradually returned to normal. 'Now, go and get a dustpan and a cloth,' Dr Bloor shouted at Tancred. 'You can clean up the mess you've caused.'

'Yes, sir.' Tancred slouched out of the hall, only just managing to keep his green cape under control.

Charlie felt guilty. It was all his fault. Tancred was paying for his terrible carelessness in letting the sorcerer

out. He was almost relieved when Dr Bloor said, 'Charlie Bone, stand up.'

Charlie stood, knees shaking slightly, hands clinging to the table.

'You know where you should be, don't you?' said the headmaster in a steely voice.

'Erm, I'm not sure, sir,' said Charlie.

'Searching, boy. Searching!'

'I have been, sir. I can't find – it – er, him.'

'I'm sure there's one place where you haven't looked, isn't there?' He waited for an answer, but when Charlie failed to give him one, he repeated, 'ISN'T THERE?'

In a small shred of a voice, Charlie croaked, 'Yes, sir.'

'And where is that?'

'The ruin, sir.'

Every knife and fork was still. Every mouth was motionless. Every eye was on Charlie, and every person in the room felt glad to be themselves and not Charlie Bone.

'Then you'd better get out there, hadn't you?' Dr Bloor's voice was now a menacing hiss.

'Yes, sir.' Charlie took one look at his pile of cabbage and left the dining hall.

The bright, sunny day had turned dull and damp, and Charlie shivered as he ran towards the castle ruin. It was one thing to go into the castle with a friend, in daylight. It was quite another to go alone when dusk was approaching.

The tall, red walls were half-buried in the woods and when Charlie stepped through the great arched entrance, he paused to catch his breath, and to make a decision. He was in a paved courtyard facing five stone arches, each one a different entrance into the castle. Which one to choose? Charlie eventually made for the middle arch because he knew where it led.

He stepped into a dark passage where small creatures scurried round his feet and wet, slimy things moved under his fingers as he put out a hand to steady himself. At last he emerged into the light, and crossing yet another courtyard, he descended a flight of stone steps into a glade ringed by broken statues. In the centre of the glade stood a large stone tomb and, climbing on to its mossy lid, Charlie stood up and listened.

He hoped that from this position he would hear any unusual creaks or rustles that might give Skarpo's position

away. But it was hopeless. Sounds came from all directions: the stirring of leaves and rubble, the sighing of the wind and the continuous patter and scrabble of tiny feet.

Charlie jumped down from the tomb and walked through the ring of statues to a gap in the wall behind them. He waded through brambles and nettles, he stumbled over fallen walls and tumbled down hidden steps, and then he began to call, 'Skarpo! Skarpo! Are you there? Please, please tell me. I'll do anything for you if you help me now.' Charlie realised this was a bit rash, but he was desperate.

Shadows moved across the walls, trees murmured and birds scattered, shrieking into the wind.

Charlie looked at his watch. Nine o'clock. Homework was over. His friends would all be in bed. Dr Bloor hadn't told him when to come back. Was he expected to stay in the ruin all night?

'No way,' Charlie muttered to himself. He knew what sometimes stalked the ruins after dark: a boy that wasn't a boy, Asa Pike on four feet, furred and fanged, his eyes glowing a wild yellow, his spiteful snigger turned to a snarl.

A running, hunting, deadly beast.

Charlie began to retrace his steps. Plunging through the undergrowth he reached the ring of statues quicker than he had hoped. He was about to cross the glade when he saw a movement on the courtyard above him. Charlie shrank into the bushes behind a statue. In the dying rays of the sun he saw something that made his flesh creep. A woman was standing at the top of the steps; an ancient woman in a long white dress, grey-faced, her flesh lined like a spider's web, her white hair hanging in thin strands over her bony shoulders.

'Yolanda,' breathed Charlie. 'Belle.'

He wished he hadn't seen her. And he wished he hadn't seen the grey beast crouching in her shadow.

The woman's eyes narrowed; she seemed to be looking straight at Charlie, and then she walked away. As she moved, the beast followed, close at her heels, like a dog. Only it wasn't a dog, or a wolf, or a hyena. It was a grey thing with a crooked back, a long, drooping tail, yellow eyes and a snout like a boar.

Charlie closed his eyes and held his breath. They're the same, he thought. Asa and Belle. Both shape-shifters. No

wonder Asa can't keep away from her.

It was dark when he felt safe enough to come out of his hiding place. Even so, he crept every inch of the way. But once he was beyond the castle walls, he tore across the grass and flung himself through the garden door, tumbling on to the flagstones of the hall, as if he'd been pole-axed.

The building was silent. Charlie dragged himself up to his dormitory and fell on to his bed.

'Any luck?' Fidelio whispered sleepily.

'No,' murmured Charlie. He thought, dismally, of the punishment awaiting him. There was no question, now, that he would be punished. How could he possibly find Skarpo before nine o'clock? He thought he was too worried to sleep, but exhaustion overcame him as soon as he closed his eyes.

When he woke up he thought he'd been having a nightmare. It was still dark and at the other end of the dormitory, Billy Raven seemed to be muttering to himself. There was an awful smell in the room.

Damian Smerk moaned, 'Billy Raven, get that ruddy dog out of here. It stinks to high heaven.'

More muttering. A pattering of claws across the floor,

and then the door banged shut.

Charlie closed his eyes again, but all at once a voice beside his ear whispered, 'Charlie? Charlie, are you awake?'

'Uh?' grunted Charlie.

'It's me, Billy. Blessed was here. He says Cook wants to see you. Now. It's very urgent.'

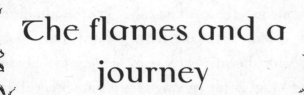

The flames and a journey

At the back of the blue kitchen there was a broom cupboard. The contents of this cupboard – mops, dustpans, brushes and dusters – hid a low door with a handle that looked like a small wooden peg. A duster hung on it permanently, as a disguise. If the handle was turned, however, the door opened into a softly lit corridor.

When Cook came to Bloor's Academy, she had been given a cold room in the east wing, but she had no intention of staying there. The Bloors had no idea of her true identity; they never imagined that Cook knew more about the ancient building than

they did themselves. She had very soon moved into a secret underground apartment they knew nothing about.

How could the Bloors have guessed that Cook had arrived with the sole purpose of helping the children of the Red King? Being endowed herself (another thing the Bloors had no inkling of), Cook had always had a powerful urge to protect children who might suffer for their talents. And she had a strong suspicion that of all the endowed children at Bloor's Academy, it was Charlie Bone, with his eager and often clumsy attempts to help people, who was most in need of her watchful eye.

Charlie had a tendency to rush at things without thinking them through, and now he had made his most foolish move yet. With Cook's help he would have to put it right.

Blessed led Charlie as far as the kitchen but would go no further. He lay in front of the door, with his head resting on his paws. Obviously he was in the habit of guarding Cook's quarters at night.

Charlie made his way over to the broom cupboard. He had been to Cook's underground rooms twice before but, as far as he knew, Gabriel was the only other person in the

school who knew about them, and he had been sworn to secrecy.

Charlie clambered over bottles of polish, tins, brooms and piles of rags. He turned the handle in the small door and it creaked open. Charlie stepped into the corridor behind it and ran towards a flight of steps. He entered another cupboard and knocked on a panel at the back.

'Is that you, Charlie Bone?' came Cook's voice.

'Yes,' said Charlie softly.

'You'd better come in then.'

Charlie stepped into a low-ceilinged room with worn, comfortable armchairs, and darkly glinting wooden furniture. In winter, Cook's stove glowed with bright coals, but today the fire was out and the room had an indoor, summer stuffiness.

One of the armchairs had been turned to face the cold stove and in the lamplight, Charlie could see a long black shoe and the hem of a dark robe. Someone else was in the room.

Cook put a finger to her lips. 'Sssh!'

Charlie tiptoed round the chair and almost jumped out of his skin. There, fast asleep, was Skarpo the sorcerer.

'How did he get here?' whispered Charlie.

'I might ask you the same thing. What have you done, Charlie Bone?'

'It's not my fault, honestly. I didn't think it was possible. You see . . .' Charlie felt slightly embarrassed. 'I went into this painting where he was. And he must have come out with me. But I didn't see him.'

'Tch! Tch!' Cook shook her head. 'The poor man was in a terrible state when I found him. He was crouching in my broom cupboard, weeping, begging me to let him go home. He can't stand it here – the noise, the lights, so many people. He's terrified.'

'He's done some pretty terrifying things himself,' said Charlie, forgetting to whisper.

Skarpo's eyes suddenly flew open. 'You!' he cried, glaring at Charlie.

'Yes, me,' said Charlie.

The sorcerer uttered a string of words that were quite unintelligible to Charlie. 'What's he talking about?' he asked Cook.

Cook gave a grim smile. 'He speaks in an ancient jargon, but luckily we come from the same part of the

world, so I can just understand him. The poor man is asking you to take him home.'

'How can I do that?' said Charlie. 'The painting's at home, and I won't get out of here till Friday.'

Skarpo, who'd been watching Charlie's lips, turned to Cook with a frown. In a strange sing-song voice, Cook explained Charlie's problem.

Skarpo groaned.

'I'm already in trouble over this,' said Charlie. 'Dr Bloor guessed it was my fault – all the bells, and the frogs and chickens and stuff. I'm dead meat if it doesn't stop. So you'd better quit putting spells on things or I won't be around to help you.'

Skarpo scowled and muttered something.

'I think he understands,' said Cook. She heaved a sigh. 'I suppose I'd better keep him here until Friday, although I can tell you, I don't fancy sharing my quarters with a sorcerer. Imagine! His father sailed over from Italy with Rizzio, Mary Queen of Scots' great chum.'

'Wasn't he murdered?' said Charlie.

'Horribly,' said Cook in an undertone. 'You'd better pop back to bed now, Charlie, or you'll never wake up

in the morning.'

Charlie was about to leave when a problem occurred to him. 'How's *he* going to get out of here without being seen?'

'The same way he got in,' said Cook mysteriously. 'Goodnight, Charlie.'

Charlie didn't trust Skarpo. Next morning he waited for something awful to happen. But no more elephants or frogs arrived. The sky was clear and blue, the sausages remained sausages and nothing happened to the evening cottage pie.

'More's the pity,' muttered Fidelio, the vegetarian.

All through supper, Charlie could feel Dr Bloor's cold eyes on him, and he had a feeling that the headmaster was almost disappointed. He had probably enjoyed thinking up some awful punishment for him.

In the King's Room after supper, there was an atmosphere you could cut with a knife, as Grandma Bone would have put it. Charlie heard Zelda whisper, 'Bone's Mayhem Monday,' and Asa gave one of his horrible snorts.

It was a very uncomfortable hour, with Lysander's drums still throbbing in the background, and Tancred's angry breeze blowing paper off the table. Just to put him in his

place, Zelda started moving books and pens out of their owners' reach. Worst of all was Manfred's hypnotising stare which seemed to be constantly aimed at Charlie.

Belle was watching Charlie, too. But her face wore a spiteful, bitter look. What was she up to? Charlie wondered.

He told no one of his night-time visit to Cook, but when he, Gabriel and Fidelio were on their way to bed, Fidelio said, 'Come on, Charlie, what's happened? Did you find the old fellow?'

'Yes,' said Charlie. He looked over his shoulder. There was no one within earshot so he described his meeting with the sorcerer.

His friends stood motionless in the passage and listened with rapt attention.

'So that's why the bats aren't gold any more,' murmured Gabriel.

Matron came striding towards them, shouting, 'Why are you three lurking there? Bed. Come on, now.' She clapped her hands aggressively.

To Charlie's great relief, the rest of the week passed without more unpleasant or magical incidents. People

stopped giving him funny looks and whispering behind his back, and by Friday afternoon most of the school were so occupied in the end-of-term play, they had forgotten about Charlie Bone's Mayhem Monday.

Charlie had often wished he could take part in the play. All his friends were involved; if they weren't acting, they were painting scenery, making costumes or playing an instrument. Even Billy Raven had been roped in to play an elvish drummer. But Charlie was considered useless when it came to entertainment.

Today, however, Charlie was glad to get out of school while so many of the others had to stay behind for rehearsals. But as the school bus approached Filbert Street his stomach began to lurch uncomfortably. If Skarpo had managed to get into the house without Grandma Bone seeing him, where would he be? And what would he be doing?

Charlie got off the bus and walked very slowly down Filbert Steet. He was thinking of a bargain he wanted to make with Skarpo. He would agree to take him back into the painting, only if he could advise Charlie how to make Ollie Sparks visible again. Surely a sorcerer would know

how to do that?

Charlie climbed the steps of number nine and was about to let himself in, when the door suddenly opened and there stood Skarpo.

'AAAH!' shrieked Charlie.

The sorcerer gave a black-toothed smile and Charlie quickly looked round to see if anyone was watching. But no one in the street paid any attention. They were used to the strange goings-on at number nine.

The sorcerer said something that sounded like 'Whisht!' and pulled Charlie over the threshold.

'Has anyone seen you?' Charlie whispered. 'A woman? An old woman?'

'Nae woman,' said Skarpo. He grabbed Charlie's arm and dragged him into the kitchen where the painting sat propped against a bowl of fruit on the table. Skarpo nodded at the painting, and said, 'Now!'

'Not here,' said Charlie. 'Someone might come in. Upstairs.' He pointed at the ceiling.

Skarpo grabbed the painting and shoved Charlie through the door. He was gabbling away but Charlie could hardly recognise a single word. Still muttering, the

sorcerer pushed him up the stairs and along the landing to his bedroom. Once inside, Skarpo sat on the bed with the painting on his knee, facing Charlie.

It was rather odd, seeing him sitting there with his silver beard bobbing up and down as he spoke, while the painted Skarpo stood perfectly still in a candlelit room.

'Now!' thundered Skarpo. 'We go!'

'Actually, it's not going to work like that,' said Charlie. 'You've got to do something for me, first.'

'Ach!' Skarpo flung down the painting.

'And you'd better not break that or you'll *never* get back.'

The sorcerer glowered at Charlie.

Choosing his words very carefully, Charlie explained Ollie's predicament.

Skarpo frowned. 'What the snake hath done, the snake must undo.'

There was no mistaking his words this time, but just to make sure, Charlie asked, 'The snake? The *snake* must do it?'

'Aye, aye. The snake,' said Skarpo. He beckoned Charlie. 'Thou maun tak me awa frae here.'

'Hold on,' said Charlie. 'There's another thing . . .'

'Nae mooa!' shouted Skarpo.

Charlie stood his ground. 'Yes, more. You said you could help my uncle if you saw him. Well, he's in the room next door.'

'Ach!' grumbled Skarpo, but without more ado, he jumped up and walked out of the room.

'Wait!' cried Charlie, fearing Skarpo would meet Grandma Bone. But the sorcerer had already marched through Paton's door. Charlie found him nosily examining the objects on the bedside table while Paton gaped at him from the bed.

Without moving his lips, Paton muttered, 'Charlie, is this who I think it is?'

'Er – yes,' said Charlie. 'He might be able to help you.'

'And how's he going to do that?' Paton nervously enquired.

All at once, Skarpo leapt to the door and locked it, then, reaching into his voluminous robes, he brought out a chain. He smiled at Paton and twirled the chain in the air.

'Ye gods! You are not going to chain me to the bed!' yelled Paton.

Skarpo's smile grew wider. He put the chain back, and

brought out a small silver bell which he rang just above Paton's feet. It tinkled pleasantly as the sorcerer began to chant.

'What's that? My death knell?' groaned Paton.

'I don't think so, Uncle,' said Charlie. 'You know, it's funny, but when I was in the painting I knew what he was talking about, but now I can hardly understand a thing he says.'

'Nor can I. I imagine that when you "go in", as you put it, you acclimatise to where you've gone; bound to happen when you think about it.'

'I see,' said Charlie thoughtfully.

Skarpo was now walking round the room, ringing his bell and chanting in a deep sing-song voice. All at once, he came to rest beside Paton and commanded, 'Show thy tongue!'

Paton scowled up at him and obliged.

The sorcerer recoiled, saying, 'Wha hast thou been?'

'If you mean what I think you mean, I've been to Yewbeam Castle,' said Paton.

'God's teeth!' the sorcerer exclaimed. 'A dritful family – rogues, scoundrels, murderers. Woe to ye!'

'Woe indeed,' Paton murmured.

'Vervain!' said the sorcerer. 'The sacred herb. Bathe, wash thy heed, drink, tak it on thy breath.'

At that moment the door handle turned and before Charlie could stop him, Skarpo sprang to unlock it. The door swung open, revealing Grandma Bone. For a brief second, she stared wordlessly at the sorcerer and then she closed her eyes and slowly sank to the ground.

'A swoon!' Skarpo declared.

'What's happening?' asked Paton, who couldn't see beyond the door.

'Grandma Bone,' said Charlie. 'She's fainted. Seeing Skarpo in the flesh must have been a shock!'

'Put her on her bed,' said Paton. 'She'll think she's had a nightmare.'

Skarpo was one step ahead of them. He had already thrown Grandma Bone over his shoulder and, while Charlie led the way, he carried the unconscious woman to her room, where he flung her on the bed.

'Watch it!' said Charlie. 'Old bones, you know.'

Skarpo gave a loud cackle and then demanded, 'Now. Tak me hame!'

'OK,' said Charlie.

When they were back in his bedroom, however, he began to have doubts. 'You will let me come out again, won't you?' he asked the sorcerer. 'I don't want to be stuck with you forever.'

'Nae mooa do I,' said the sorcerer. 'I will give thee a poosh.'

'Right,' said Charlie doubtfully.

He put the painting against his bedside light and stared into the painted eyes of the sorcerer. Nothing happened. But then, how could it? Charlie realised that the real Skarpo was here, beside him, clinging to his arm. Beyond those painted eyes there was no soul, no will to draw him into the painting.

'I think you'll have to *want* me to go in,' Charlie said.

'Aye.' Two bony hands sank into Charlie's shoulder blades. He took a step nearer the painting, and then another.

'Poosh, thou wretch, thou mean beastie,' said a voice behind Charlie's ear.

'Do you mind, I'm trying to hel –' Charlie suddenly found himself flying forwards. It was the oddest sensation, for the hands at his back seemed to reach right through his

body, so that they were pulling as well as pushing. Charlie was travelling so fast he couldn't get his breath. He began to choke on the clouds of dust that streamed into his face. He closed his eyes and sneezed violently.

The familiar mixture of candle-grease and decay filled Charlie's nostrils. He wiped his eyes and saw, far ahead, the flicker of candlelight. Closer now and there was the sorcerer's room, the long table, the symbols on the wall, the skull on the floor. And in the centre, Skarpo himself, with a blank stare in his dark yellow eyes.

Expecting to fall into the sorcerer's room, Charlie was surprised to find it suddenly receding. He reached out, trying to grab the man in the painting, but his hands met empty air. He thrust his feet forward in an effort to touch the ground, but with a sickening jolt, he was turned upside down and bowled backwards.

He landed with a painful thud, face-down on the floor of his own room. Beside him, the sorcerer was kneeling on all fours, with his outer black robe right over his head. From beneath this came a muffled moan.

'What happened?' gasped Charlie.

The sorcerer pulled his robe away from his face and sat

back. He shook his head for a while, and then said, 'Moosie!'

'What?' Rather unsteadily Charlie got to his feet. 'What d'you mean? We were almost there. What happened?'

'Nae moosie,' said Skarpo pointing angrily at Charlie. 'Thou hast stolen the moos.'

'Moos?' For a moment Charlie stared stupidly at the sorcerer, trying to make sense of his speech, and then at last, it came to him. 'Oh, the *mouse*. Of course, you can't get back without your mouse. I suppose things have to be exactly the same as they were when you came out.'

'Aye,' groaned Skarpo.

'The last time I saw it was in my uncle's room. Won't be a sec.'

Skarpo leapt to his feet, anxious not to let Charlie out of his sight. They burst into Paton's room both talking at once about the lost mouse and the unsuccessful travelling.

'Do be quiet,' groaned Paton. 'My head is splitting. Why is that man still here?'

Charlie explained. 'We have to find the mouse or he won't be able to get back.'

'Ridiculous,' said Paton. 'That mouse is long gone. You won't find it in here. It's somewhere under the floorboards.

250

There are probably enough crumbs down there to keep it going for months.'

Skarpo dropped into a chair, put his head in his hands and began to rock back and forth, wailing like a siren.

'For pity's sake.' Paton clamped his hands over his ears. 'Charlie, find my phone.'

Paton had bought himself a mail-order mobile phone which he used, primarily, for ordering books, although, now and again, ill-fitting garments would arrive, only to be hastily sent back.

Charlie eventually found his uncle's mobile buried under a mound of paper on the desk. 'What are you going to do?' he asked, handing his uncle the phone.

'I'm going to call Mr Onimous,' he said, dialling a number. 'The cats will sort this out.'

'The cats? They'll kill it,' said Charlie.

His uncle took no notice. 'Ah, Mr Onimous,' he said. 'Paton Yewbeam here. We have a problem, Charlie and I, and ah – someone else. I should be very gateful if you could bring the famous flames to see us. If they are available, of course.' He paused, while a light, musical voice came leaking out of the mobile. 'They are?

Splendid.' Paton glanced at the sorcerer. 'Speed would be appreciated. Thank you!'

Skarpo had stopped wailing and was now watching Paton with interest. 'Thy fingers have a magic touch,' he said, wagging his own finger at the mobile.

'Yes, you could say that,' Paton agreed, avoiding Charlie's eye. 'Now then, Mr – Skarpo? Patience is required. Very soon a good friend of ours will arrive – with help. In the meantime, I would be very obliged if you would keep quiet. As you are aware, I am none too well, and any more noise might finish me off. Thank you!'

The sorcerer listened attentively to Paton's speech. He was obviously impressed. Now and again he hummed under his breath, but apart from that the room was so quiet you could hear a clock Paton had mislaid ticking from the inside of a cupboard.

The house was quiet too, until Amy Bone came home from work. Charlie went down to the kitchen to let his mother know what was going on. He spoke so fast it all came out in rather a muddled rush, but Mrs Bone soon got the gist of what Charlie was trying to say. She dropped her shopping bag and sat down, saying, 'How amazing,

Charlie. D'you mean to say a medieval sorcerer is actually
– in the flesh – sitting in Paton's room?'

'I think he's probably more Tudor than medieval,' said
Charlie. 'His father had something to do with Mary
Queen of Scots.'

'I can't get over it. I mean, I'd no idea your talent would
lead to this. Does your grandmother know?'

'Yes. But she fainted when she saw him.'

'I'm not surprised.'

The bell rang and Charlie ran to open the door.

'Here we are, Charlie. At your service.' Mr Onimous
leapt into the hall, followed by the three cats. 'Afternoon,
ma'am,' he said, when Amy Bone popped her head round
the door.

'I'll leave you to it,' she said, retreating into the
kitchen.

The presence of the cats always made Charlie feel
unaccountably happy. It was like watching the sun come
out after a grey, rainy day. They paced round his legs,
rubbing their heads against his knees and filling the hall
with their loud purring, while Charlie explained the
situation to Mr Onimous. 'Uncle Paton thought the

flames would find the mouse,' said Charlie. 'But surely they'll kill it, won't they?'

'Of course they won't. Not if they know what's wanted,' said Mr Onimous. 'Upstairs with you, my beauties!'

The cats bounded up the stairs, Aries leading, with orange Leo close behind and yellow Sagittarius bringing up the rear like a bolt of brilliant light.

Unfortunately, Grandma Bone chose that moment to open her door. 'Cats!' she screamed.

Aries spat at her, Leo hissed and Sagittarius growled.

Grandma Bone stepped back into her room and slammed the door. 'I'm not coming out until those creatures have left the house,' she shouted.

'That's fine by me,' muttered Charlie.

He led Mr Onimous and the cats into Paton's bedroom, where Mr Onimous bent over the invalid's bed and said, 'I heard of your affliction, Mr Yewbeam. Rest assured we'll do all we can to help.'

'Thank you, Orvil,' said Paton, 'but it is that man whose needs are most pressing.' He pointed at Skarpo.

Mr Onimous gave a little jump. He hadn't noticed the sorcerer, hunched in an armchair beyond Paton's desk.

'Mercy! Forgive me, sir. What an honour. Orvil Onimous.'
He held out a paw-like hand.

The sorcerer allowed his own hand to be shaken, but he
seemed hardly aware of Mr Onimous. His gaze was fixed
on the three bright cats. 'Beautiful beasties,' he murmured.
'Ancient creatures. Leopards, nae doot. Thine, sir?'

'They belong to no one,' said Mr Onimous. 'Though,
once, they were the king's. I'm speaking of the Red King,
of course.'

'The Red King. Aye.' Skarpo nodded, his eyes still on
the cats, watching them hungrily.

'You can't take them back with you,' said Charlie
sternly.

Skarpo's beard quivered. 'I am not a thief, boy.'

'Actually . . .' Charlie just stopped himself from
mentioning the stolen wand. The situation was delicate
enough.

'Where's this painting then, Charlie?' asked Mr
Onimous.

Charlie fetched the painting from his room and Mr
Onimous, putting a finger on the painted mouse, said, 'See
that, Flames? That mouse there, peeping out of a pocket?'

The cats watched Mr Onimous's finger, and then turned their earnest gaze towards Skarpo. Their bright eyes travelled from his face to a dark pleat on the side of his robe, where there was, now, no mouse. Their quick understanding was astonishing. In a second they had darted round the room, under the bed and out of the door.

Charlie looked into the passage to see what the cats would do. The house was filled with golden light and a soft pattering, a gentle scratching, a mewing and a purring could be heard. Clever paws turned handles, opened cupboards, lifted carpets, papers, curtains, covers; pulled out drawers, boxes, shoes, clothing. And then the trio stopped and sniffed and listened.

Charlie held his breath and listened with them. Not for long. There was a sudden thump, a squeak and a yowl. And then up the stairs they came, Sagittarius first, holding a mouse in his jaws.

The flames ran into Paton's room and Sagittarius, miaowing loudly, laid the terrified but unharmed mouse in the sorcerer's lap.

'Moosie!' cried Skarpo, grabbing the mouse. ''Tis well done, brave creature.' He stroked the yellow cat's head. 'I

thank thee.' Putting the mouse in his pocket he stood up and made a little bow to Paton and Mr Onimous. 'Gentlemen, fare thee well!' Then he propped the painting against a stack of books on Paton's desk and turned Charlie to face it. 'Now!' he commanded.

'OK.' Charlie looked at his uncle and Mr Onimous. 'Could you help me back – if I get stuck?'

'The flames will keep you safe,' said Mr Onimous. And the cats moved closer to Charlie as the whole uncomfortable business of being pushed and pulled began all over again.

But this time, while Charlie travelled, he felt a comforting warmth enfolding him, and as he watched the blank eyes of the sorcerer, he kept glimpsing flashes of red and gold beside him. When the sorcerer's eyes began to glow with life, Charlie knew he had succeeded in bringing him home. Now he must retreat before Skarpo started playing tricks.

However, it seemed that Skarpo had no intention of tricking Charlie. 'Go now, Charlie Bone,' he said, waving his hand. 'And mind the herb for thine uncle's affliction.'

What happened next was certainly not Skarpo's fault.

Behind the sorcerer's table there was a window and Charlie's gaze was drawn to a stretch of glittering sea beyond. Before he could tug himself away, he found himself flying through the window.

As he sailed over the moonlit water, Charlie sensed again the warm presence of bright creatures, and he wasn't afraid. The dark mass of a forest loomed in the distance and he felt breathless with anticipation as he drew closer. Now he was floating above the trees to a place where the topmost leaves were touched with firelight.

He looked down into a glade where a man stood tending a fire. The man wore a red cloak and his skin was the colour of warm, brown earth. Charlie felt him to be the saddest man in the world.

Sparks from the fire began to float up to the sky, and when the man followed them with his eyes, he saw Charlie. Sadness left the man's face and he gave a sudden, joyful smile. In a deep, melodious voice, he called three names and three creatures stepped out of the shadows. The firelight danced on their pale, spotted coats, and they looked up at Charlie with eyes of gold.

The garden in Darkly Wynd

'Flames,' Charlie murmured.

'Are you back, Charlie?' asked a voice.

A silvery mist surrounded Charlie and when he blinked, he found himself caught in the gaze of six golden eyes. 'Oh,' he said.

The loud purring that had filled his ears began to fade, and he bent to stroke the three bright heads.

'That was quite something, Charlie. I won't forget it for the rest of my life.'

The mist receded and Charlie could see Mr Onimous in the chair that Skarpo had recently vacated.

'What happened?' asked Charlie.

'There you were, and there was the sorcerer,' said Mr Onimous, leaning forward excitedly. 'And the sorcerer – well, he went right through you. He faded first, like, until he was just a bit of shadow, and then he vanished. Phew!'

'And what happened to me?'

'You? You just stayed where you were, Charlie. Standing like a stone, and staring at that picture. But the cats, now that's a different story. Never stopped moving. Round and round your legs they went, purring and singing like I never heard before.'

'I think they came with me,' said Charlie. 'Came with my mind, I mean, when it travelled.'

'Did they now? Well, I wouldn't put it past them.'

Charlie didn't mention his encounter with the leopards and the man in the red cloak. It was so intimate and precious he didn't have the words for it. Instead he turned to his uncle, and found he was asleep.

'Didn't Uncle Paton see what happened?' he asked.

'Poor man, he dropped off before the sorcerer had left us,' said Mr Onimous. 'Your uncle is a very sick man, Charlie. It's a tragedy to see such a bold and clever person brought to this.'

'I want to help him,' said Charlie, 'and I'm going to. Skarpo says he has to bathe in something called vervain. Where d'you think I can find it?'

'Hmm.' Mr Onimous rubbed his furry chin with his forefinger. 'I'll ask around, Charlie. Better be off now. Good luck!'

In his usual speedy way, Mr Onimous leapt from the chair and was out of the room and down the stairs before Charlie could think of another question.

'Bye, Mrs Bones both,' he called as he left the house, with the bright cats bounding behind him.

'Have they gone?' shouted Grandma Bone.

'Yes, Grandma,' said Charlie with a sigh.

She appeared in her doorway. '*All* gone?' she said. 'You know who I mean?'

'Yes, he's gone too.'

'Praise be!' She went back into her room, slamming the door behind her.

Charlie joined his mother for tea, but throughout the meal he kept thinking of his journey beyond the sorcerer's window. I've seen the Red King, he thought. And he has seen me. I've seen the leopards and the forest where they

lived. And Charlie became more and more convinced that Aries, Leo and Sagittarius had taken him to that distant forest. But why? And how?

'Penny for your thoughts, Charlie,' said his mother.

Charlie hesitated. 'I was just wondering where I could get vervain.'

'Vervain? It's a weed, or a herb, but I've never seen it. What d'you want it for, Charlie?'

'To help Uncle Paton.'

'Oh.' His mother raised her eyebrows, but said no more.

Later that evening, Charlie took a tray of supper to his uncle's room. But Paton wouldn't touch it. The room was in darkness so Charlie lit a candle that stood on Paton's desk. 'Please try and eat,' he begged. 'I thought you were getting better.'

Paton turned his head away. 'Sorry, Charlie. I think I'm done for. It's in my head, my bones, my guts. He's finished me off.'

'But what did he do?' cried Charlie. 'And who is he?'

His uncle wouldn't say. In a soft, ragged voice, he asked, 'Has Julia been here again?'

'Don't think so,' said Charlie.

'Oh,' said Paton sadly.

'She might have come while I was at school,' Charlie suggested, regretting his thoughtlessness. 'In fact I expect she did. But Grandma Bone probably wouldn't let her in.'

'No,' sighed Paton, 'She's forgotten me.'

Charlie couldn't think what to say. He wondered if he should tell his uncle that he'd seen the Red King. Perhaps it would cheer him up. But he still couldn't find the words to talk about it. 'You could try vervain,' he said. 'I think the sorcerer really meant to help you.'

'Vervain,' muttered Paton. 'The sacred herb.'

'D'you know where it grows?'

'In Eustacia's garden probably. She grows everything you've ever heard of. But I advise you not to go there, Charlie. It's a dangerous place.'

'I'm not afraid,' said Charlie. 'I've been there before.'

His uncle groaned, 'No, Charlie,' and then he fell into another agitated sleep, muttering and mumbling, with his eyes closed, his mouth twisting and his teeth grinding.

Charlie's mind was made up. Somehow he would find a way into Eustacia's garden. But first he had to know what vervain looked like. He didn't want to pick something

dangerous and deadly, and he was sure Eustacia would have plenty of those sorts of plants about.

On Saturday morning, after his mother had left for the greengrocer's, Charlie went to see Miss Ingledew. There was a surprising buzz of activity in the bookshop. It was usually a quiet place, but today Charlie found Olivia, Tancred and Lysander prancing about behind the counter in strange feathered headgear.

Emma and Tancred had been asked to design hats for the play, and Tancred had brought Lysander along to cheer him up. It certainly seemed to have worked. The eerie beat of drums could no longer be heard following Lysander, and he even managed to laugh when Tancred sent his yellow-feathered hat flying up to the ceiling.

'You look serious, Charlie,' Tancred remarked. 'Don't worry, we haven't forgotten Ollie. We're working on a plan, but the play kind of got in the way.'

'What exactly is the play about?' asked Charlie, puzzled by the gaudy hats.

'It's a kind of mixture of *The Tinder Box* and *The Twelve Dancing Princesses*,' said Olivia. 'I'm one of the princesses.'

'So, who's got the biggest part?'

'They haven't decided,' said Olivia. 'Manfred wants Lydia Pieman to be the lead. I reckon he's got a thing about her. Zelda's insanely jealous.'

Emma's aunt appeared and asked the children if they would please try their hats on in the back room. 'I wouldn't like customers to think this place had turned into a clothes shop,' she said with a smile.

Charlie explained that he hadn't come to try on hats, he had a rather urgent mission. 'It's for my uncle,' he said.

'I see.' Miss Ingledew tried not to look interested but Charlie could see that she was. 'Your grandmother believes I was stalking Paton, and I'd like to make it quite clear that I absolutely was not.'

'Course not,' said Charlie. 'The thing is, Uncle Paton's getting worse. He won't even eat now.'

'Oh, Charlie, I didn't realise. Poor Paton. I must . . . I'm so sorry.' Miss Ingledew seemed suddenly very agitated.

'I sort of heard that a plant called vervain might cure him,' said Charlie.

Miss Ingledew frowned. 'Where did you hear that?'

'I bet it was the sorcerer,' said Olivia.

'Was it?' asked Emma. 'Was it, Charlie?'

'Tell us,' urged Tancred, 'or I'll blow your pants off.'

Charlie clutched his belt. 'Yes, it was,' he admitted with a grin.

'I don't know what you're talking about,' said Emma's aunt. 'And I'm not sure I want to.'

'The thing is, I don't know what vervain looks like,' said Charlie. 'And I thought there might be a picture of it in one of your amazing books.'

At that moment two customers came into the shop and Miss Ingledew told the children to search the books in the back room. 'Look under H,' she said. 'Herb to Horticulture.'

It was Lysander who found it, partly because he was the tallest and all the Hs were on the top shelf. 'Here it is,' he said, laying the open book on a table and pointing to a photograph. Vervain appeared to be a bushy plant with yellowy-green leaves and tiny mauve flowers at the tip of each shoot. 'It says people used to believe it cured everything, even witchcraft.'

'The sacred herb,' Olivia read over his shoulder, 'said by the Romans to cure the plague and to avert sorcery

and witchcraft.'

'And I know where to find it,' murmured Charlie, gazing at the picture.

'WHERE?' Four pairs of eyes were trained on Charlie.

'In my great-aunt's garden,' he said. 'In Darkly Wynd.'

'We'll come with you,' said Olivia.

'There's no need . . .' Charlie began.

'Course there's a need. We're coming,' Lysander insisted. 'I've got to do *something* that works, or I'll blow my top.'

Charlie had to agree that it would be good to have company in Darkly Wynd, though he worried that five children might attract too much attention in such a quiet and gloomy place.

'You're stuck with us,' said Tancred.

The five friends left the bookshop, telling Miss Ingledew they were off to find vervain. She gave a cautious nod, but was so involved with an elderly couple searching for a cookery book, she failed to ask the children any more questions. When her customers had gone, however, she found the book the children had been looking at and brought it into the shop. Placing it on her

counter, she studied the picture of the leafy plant with its tiny mauve flowers. 'A sacred herb,' she murmured, 'sorcery . . . witchcraft . . .'

The door opened with a loud tinkle, and two girls stepped down into the shop.

'Can I help you?' asked Miss Ingledew.

'We don't want a book,' said the rather pretty blonde girl. 'We're looking for our friends.'

'We thought we saw them come out of your shop,' said the other girl, who was shorter and plumper than her companion.

'Oh, you mean Emma, my niece,' said Miss Ingledew.

Her two visitors had by now reached the counter, and the blonde girl turned the open book round to read it. 'Vervain. How interesting.'

'Yes.' Emma's aunt closed the book.

'So, could you tell us where Emma and the others have gone?' asked the plump girl.

'I've no idea.'

'Aww! We were going to meet up,' said the girl.

'What a pity,' said Miss Ingledew. She had the distinct impression that the girls were lying. She disliked them,

especially the pretty one. Her eyes kept changing colour; it was most unnerving.

'Oh, well,' sighed the blonde girl. 'We'll see if we can catch up with them.' She gave a broad smile, showing immaculate white teeth.

'Goodbye!' Miss Ingledew put the book under her arm and watched the girls leave the shop.

'And what were *they* up to?' she muttered.

Charlie and his friends had just reached Greybank Crescent, when a figure emerged from a dark alley leading off the crescent.

'Aunt Venetia!' Charlie whispered to the others. 'Quick! Before she sees us.'

They leapt over the road and hid behind the large fir tree in the centre of the crescent, while Venetia Yewbeam walked on towards the main road. She carried a large leather shopping bag with a gold Y printed on the side. As she drew closer, Charlie pulled the others further back under the tree. His great-aunt stopped and, for a moment, Charlie thought she was going to cross the road and investigate. After a few seconds, however, Venetia walked on.

When his aunt had turned the corner into the main road, Charlie led the others over to the gloomy alley named Darkly Wynd.

'What a gruesome place,' said Olivia. 'Who would want to live here?'

'My great-aunts,' said Charlie.

They walked past the derelict houses where rats scuttled out of bins and tramps grumbled from damp basement steps, and then they were facing the three thirteens.

'Which one?' said Lysander.

'Well, Venetia lives in the last one, so if it goes by age, Eustacia must be in the middle,' said Charlie.

'D'you think she's at home?' asked Olivia.

'Don't know,' said Charlie. 'But I'm not going to knock on the door and ask.'

'So how do we get into the garden?' said Emma.

Charlie hadn't thought about that. Luckily, Tancred had. 'Over here,' he called, beckoning them from a small iron-barred gate. Beyond the gate, a narrow passage ran between number twelve and number thirteen. Obviously a way to the gardens at the back.

The gate gave a loud squeal as they hurried through, and Charlie glanced nervously at the side of number thirteen. But there was only one window, high in the wall, and that had a curtain drawn across it.

At the back of the houses, yards and gardens were clearly defined by high grey-stone walls. An alley ran between the gardens of Darkly Wynd and those of the houses in the crescent. But, unlike the others, there were no gates in the walls of the number thirteens.

'You'll just have to climb over,' Lysander told Charlie. 'You can stand on my back.'

'We'll keep watch,' said Emma.

'I'm going with Charlie,' said Tancred.

'No, me!' cried Olivia. 'PLEASE!'

'Ssshhh!' hissed Charlie. 'You can both come.'

As soon as he'd climbed on to Lysander's back and looked over the wall, he realised he would need two more pairs of eyes to help him search. The garden was a mass of plants. Herbs, flowers, shrubs and weeds crowded together between the walls; a veritable carpet of vegetation.

'Wow!' said Olivia when she saw the garden. 'Where do we start?'

They decided to keep in a line, working their way from the wall to the house. Charlie could see it wouldn't be easy. The plants were so tightly packed it was difficult not to tread on them. Olivia, in her clumpy mauve shoes, made more mess than the boys. She kept tripping and crashing into the tallest and most delicate-looking blooms. Charlie tried not to look at her, and kept his eyes trained on the plants in front of him.

Now and then, one of them would call softly, 'I see it,' and then, 'No, that's not it.'

They had almost reached the house when Charlie heard something drop on to the wall between Eustacia's garden and the yard next door. He jumped over the last clump of plants to see what it was.

A smooth grey pebble sat on top of the wall. It looked strangely familiar. And then it came to Charlie. 'Mr Boldova,' he murmured. 'The sparks!' But had the stone come from Eustacia's house, or Venetia's next door?

'Have you found it, Charlie?' Tancred called in a harsh whisper.

'No, I . . .'

There was a loud whistle from the wall and Lysander

called, 'Watch out, Charlie. Something's happening inside.'

Charlie looked up at the gaunt soot-stained building. He could hear voices. A top window clanged shut, and then they all heard footsteps running down a staircase.

'Let's get out,' said Olivia.

'But I haven't found the vervain,' said Charlie.

'Forget it,' said Tancred. 'Come on, we'll try another day.'

But there might not be another day. Charlie wouldn't give up. He whirled round, screwing up his eyes and staring at the plants, while the others raced for the wall.

'Look out!' yelled Tancred as the back door opened.

And then Charlie saw it, almost at his feet. There was no time to tear off a sprig. He bent down and yanked the plant right out of the ground, roots and all.

'What d'you think you're doing?' screeched Great-Aunt Eustacia from the doorway.

She ran down the steps as Charlie bounded over the garden, trampling plants as he went. Olivia was already scrambling on to the wall when there was a loud crack under Charlie's right foot and before he could stop himself

he was sliding through the earth.

'Eeee-er-ooo-ow!' yelled Charlie, trying to cling to a spindly shrub. It was no use; he was tumbling deeper and deeper into a dark pit.

'You didn't see my trap, did you, you stupid boy?' cackled Eustacia.

'Charlie, where are you?' called Olivia.

'Help!' Charlie clawed at the sides of the pit, but the black earth was slimy with slugs and rotting weeds.

Of all the great-aunts, Eustacia had the worst laugh. It crackled with spite. 'Ha! Ha! Ha!' She stood right above Charlie, and he had a nasty view of brown tights and black underwear.

He closed his eyes and murmured feebly, 'Help!'

'It's too late for help,' sneered Eustacia. 'You're caught like a rat in a trap, Charlie Bone. Now, what shall I do with you?'

Charlie looked up. 'Old women can't do this to children,' he said defiantly.

'*Can't*? But I just have,' sniggered his great-aunt. 'And if you . . .' All at once, in mid-sentence, Eustacia flew into the air. It was quite astonishing. As Charlie squinted up at

the large figure in the sky, it disappeared in a cloud of leaves. He could hear a wind roaring above him now, gathering twigs, earth, stalks and plants in a great whirlwind.

'Tancred,' breathed Charlie, as four hands stretched down towards him.

'Climb up, Charlie,' came Tancred's voice, though Charlie couldn't see him through the flying debris.

'Tancred's fixed the old bat,' said Olivia, 'so come on up.'

But Charlie couldn't even touch the waving hands. 'I can't! I can't!' he cried.

Two more hands appeared, strong brown hands that could stretch further down into the pit. 'Get a move on, Charlie,' said Lysander's voice. 'Push it, man. Come out of there!'

This time, Charlie clamped the vervain between his teeth and leapt as he reached for the brown hands. They caught him and slowly he began to climb.

Tancred and Olivia grabbed one arm, while Lysander pulled the other and gradually Charlie was dragged towards the mouth of the pit. He could hear a muffled

screaming in the distance, and when he crawled out into the wind, he saw what must have been his great-aunt, covered in greenery, fighting the gale that roared through her garden.

'Stop!' shrieked the green mound as Charlie and the others raced for the wall.

Lysander gave Charlie a shove from behind, and they all fell into the alley overcome with helpless laughter.

'What happened?' asked Emma, who was too small to see over the wall.

'Tancred did his thing, and now Charlie's aunt looks like a compost heap!' said Olivia.

'She'll take it out on you, Charlie,' said Emma, too worried to see the funny side.

Preferring not to think about this, Charlie took the vervain from his mouth, spat out mud and dusted himself down as they all began to run down the narrow passage into Darkly Wynd. When they got there, Emma, the only one to have thought ahead, took a plastic bag from her pocket and held it out to Charlie.

'What would we do without you?' said Charlie, dropping the muddy vervain into the bag.

'It's got roots,' Emma observed. 'You could plant it again.'

'I'll have to find out if it works first,' said Charlie.

They hurried down Darkly Wynd and out into the sunshine of Greybank Crescent. The change in temperature was dramatic. Behind them lay a place the sun had never touched. An empty, forgotten place of cold stone and gloomy shadows. They all gave an involuntary shiver and turned their faces up to the sun.

And then Tancred said, 'By the way, Charlie, what were you looking at when your aunt came through the door?'

Charlie had almost forgotten the pebble. He pulled it out of his pocket. 'This,' he said.

They looked at the smooth grey stone lying in Charlie's palm.

'Looks familiar,' said Lysander.

'I'm sure it belonged to Mr Boldova,' said Charlie. 'The stones that sparkled in his hand looked just like this.'

'You're right,' said Olivia. 'But how did it get into your aunt's garden?'

'It was dropped from a window,' said Charlie. 'I think she stole it.'

Everyone agreed that this was a possibility. And yet who had dropped the pebble? And why? It was a puzzle.

'There are too many puzzles,' said Lysander. 'We'll meet up tomorrow, right? And discuss the Ollie problem.'

'What about Charlie's uncle?' said Emma. 'Suppose the vervain doesn't work?'

'I'll come whatever,' said Charlie.

When they reached the main road, the five friends parted, and Charlie ran home with the prized vervain. He could hardly wait to see if it worked. First he would chop some into tea leaves, and take his uncle a cup of vervain tea. He leapt up the steps of number nine, opened the door – and walked straight into Grandma Bone.

'What's that you've got?' she said, eyeing the plastic bag.

'Nothing – er, some fruit from Mum's shop,' said Charlie.

'Liar! I know what you've been doing. Eustacia rang me. You're a thief!'

'No.' Charlie backed out of the open door.

'Give me that bag!' she demanded.

'No!' yelled Charlie.

Grandma Bone made a grab for the bag, but at that very

moment a large yellow dog bounded up the steps and leapt on Charlie's grandmother, knocking her back into the house.

'Runner!' cried Charlie. He ran down the steps with Runner Bean at his heels, while Grandma Bone roared from the house, 'Stop! Come here! You wait, Charlie Bone! You won't get away with this.'

Charlie raced up the street, panting, 'Runner, where did you come from? You saved my life!' And then he saw Fidelio, speeding towards him.

'Hi, Charlie!' called Fidelio. 'Runner got away from me. I guess he couldn't wait to see you.'

The two boys met halfway up Filbert Street, and Fidelio explained that he had gone to the Pets' Café hoping to find Charlie, but instead he had run into Norton Cross, who insisted he take Runner Bean for a walk.

'I forgot,' said Charlie. 'In fact, I keep forgetting. I'm sorry, Runner.' He patted the dog's shaggy head.

'So where were you? And what's going on?' asked Fidelio.

Charlie described his visit to Darkly Wynd, and the reason for stealing his great-aunt's vervain.

'Wish I'd been there,' said Fidelio, a little aggrieved at being left out of things. 'You'd better come home with me while your grandma cools down.'

Charlie thought this a very good idea.

Runner Bean didn't, but he was so pleased to see Charlie, he was prepared to put up with a place he considered to be the noisiest in the world.

Fidelio's seven brothers and sisters all played different musical instruments, and at any one time at least five of them would be practising. Add to this the rich bass and shrill soprano of Mr and Mrs Gunn, and you had a sound resembling the work of the most daring experimental composer.

'Let's go to the top,' shouted Fidelio as soon as they got inside. 'It's a bit quieter up there.'

Runner Bean dragged himself up the stairs behind the boys, flinching every time he passed a room where a drum or a trumpet, a horn or a cello was being beaten, blown or scraped.

At the top of the house, there was a shady attic where the Gunns kept their broken instruments. The two boys made themselves comfortable on a large crate and Charlie

gave Fidelio a more detailed account of his dealings with Skarpo. But he found that he wasn't yet ready to tell even his best friend about his mysterious journey over the sea.

Fidelio listened thoughtfully to Charlie's story, and then he said, 'You'd better stay out of your grandma's way today. And let's put that plant in water before it dies.'

Down they went again, passing children with freckled faces and brown curly hair who all patted Runner Bean and greeted Charlie like a long-lost brother. Into the kitchen, where a singing Mrs Gunn was making banana sandwiches and real lemonade.

'That looks a powerful weed!' she exclaimed when Charlie drew the vervain out of its bag. 'D'you want me to put it in a pot?'

'Actually, Mum, Charlie needs to hide it from his grandma,' said Fidelio. 'So it wouldn't be any good in a pot. And it's not a weed, it's a special herb.'

'Aha!' sang Mrs Gunn. 'We can still plant the roots. I'll snip off some leaves and you can hide them under your T-shirt when you go, Charlie. The rest of the plant will be here when you need it.'

Charlie handed over the vervain, accepted two banana

sandwiches (one for himself and one for Runner Bean), and then he and Fidelio took the yellow dog for a run in the park.

At four o'clock, after several more sandwiches (Stilton and peanut butter, and egg and blackcurrant), Charlie left Gunn House and took Runner Bean back to the Pets' Café. He promised Norton he would call again next day, but he was anxious to get home before his mother ran into an angry Grandma Bone.

When Charlie reached number nine, however, Grandma Bone had left the house, and his mother was about to take Uncle Paton a cup of tea.

'Can I do it?' begged Charlie. He pulled the sprigs of vervain from under his T-shirt and put them on the table. 'I want Uncle Paton to try some of this.'

Mrs Bone frowned. 'Where did you get it, Charlie?'

'From Aunt Eustacia,' he confessed. 'Actually I stole it, and there may be a bit of trouble.'

His mother gave him one of her anxious smiles. 'There's bound to be,' she said. 'Let's hope it works before your grandmother comes back.' She snipped off a few leaves, put them in a tea-cup and filled it up with boiling water.

Charlie watched the water turn bright green. It looked dangerous. Was Skarpo tricking them?

'I hope it doesn't do more harm than good,' said Mrs Bone. 'It looks very powerful.'

'It may be Uncle Paton's last chance, Mum,' said Charlie desperately.

He waited until the vervain tea had cooled and then took it up to his uncle, with the rest of the herb tucked under his arm.

Paton was lying in semi-darkness. The curtains were closed and from the thin light trickling into the room, you would never have guessed that outside there was a bright summer afternoon.

Charlie put the tea on his uncle's bedside table and whispered, 'Uncle Paton, I've brought you a drink.'

Paton groaned.

'Please take a sip. It'll make you feel better.'

Paton raised himself on one elbow.

'Here.' Charlie held out the cup.

Paton's eyes were still half-closed and his hand trembled when he grasped the cup. Charlie watched intently as his uncle raised the tea to his lips.

'Go on,' said Charlie. 'Drink it.'

'Anyone would think you were trying to poison me.' Paton made a funny, choking noise that was probably a laugh.

'I'm trying to help you,' Charlie whispered earnestly.

His uncle opened his eyes properly and looked at Charlie. 'Very well,' he said, and took a sip. 'Urgh! What *is* this?'

'Vervain,' said Charlie. 'You remember the sorcerer said it would cure you. And I've brought the rest.' He laid the leafy stems on his uncle's bed.

'Looks like a weed,' Paton observed. 'I can guess where you've been, Charlie.' He gave a real chuckle and took another sip, and then another.

Charlie waited while his uncle drained the cup.

'Not bad,' said Paton. 'Not bad at all. Bless you, Charlie.' He lay back on the pillows and closed his eyes.

Charlie took the empty cup from his uncle's hands and tiptoed out of the room.

'Did it work?' asked Mrs Bone when Charlie came back into the kitchen.

'I don't know, Mum. But he looked kind of peaceful.

It'll probably take a while.'

They found themselves talking softly and moving as quietly as they could. TV was out of the question. It seemed as though the air in the house had become charged with mysterious and delicate spirits that could be disturbed by the slightest breath of wind, the tiniest sound.

It grew dark but Grandma Bone didn't come home. Charlie imagined that a meeting was taking place in Darkly Wynd. They would be plotting to put him in his place, once and for all. He glanced at his mother, reading at the kitchen table, and hoped that whatever might be coming his way wouldn't hurt her as well.

Suddenly Mrs Bone looked up from her book. 'Did you hear that?'

Charlie did hear it. Upstairs a door was opening. The floorboards creaked. A moment later the sound of running water could be heard. A bath was filling up.

When the tap stopped running, the silence was so profound Charlie could hear the beat of his own heart. And then a strange perfume stole through the house, a perfume laced with magic.

Lysander's plan

Charlie opened his eyes and looked at the kitchen clock. It was midnight. His mother was washing a milk pan in the sink.

'I've only just woken up,' she said, putting two mugs of cocoa on the table. 'I don't know what came over us, Charlie.'

'Uncle Paton had a bath,' Charlie muttered. 'I remember hearing the water running, and then I fell asleep.'

'Me too,' said Mrs Bone. 'Your grandmother is still out. Let's get to bed before she comes home.'

They drank their cocoa and slipped upstairs. As Charlie passed his uncle's door

he stopped and listened. Not a sound came from Paton's room. Not even a snore. Charlie crept into his own room with a worried frown.

Just as he was getting into bed, he heard a car pull up outside. A door slammed and Grandma Bone called out, 'Goodnight, Eustacia. I'll fix the little brute, don't you worry.'

Charlie pulled the bedclothes over his head and tried not to think about meeting Grandma Bone in the morning.

He woke up very early, tiptoed down to the kitchen and ate a bowl of cereal. He thought of leaving his mother a note explaining he'd be out for the day, though he hadn't decided where he would go. Anything would be better than facing Grandma Bone.

But it was already too late for a note. Too late to run out of the house. Charlie froze as a pair of large feet thumped down the stairs. They crossed the hall and the kitchen door opened.

'Caught you!' Grandma Bone stood on the threshold in her evil-looking grey dressing-gown.

'Morning, Grandma,' said Charlie, as casually as he could.

'I suppose you thought you'd get away before I woke up.'

'N-no.'

'Don't lie. You're in big trouble, Charlie Bone.' His grandmother marched into the kitchen and glared down at Charlie. 'What were you doing in my sister's garden? No, don't bother to answer. You were stealing. And those friends of yours were no better. Eustacia's in a terrible state. She almost had a heart attack.'

'Sorry,' mumbled Charlie.

'Sorry's not good enough. You'll have to pay!' screeched Grandma Bone. 'Dr Bloor will be notified, and you'll stay here till we've decided what to do with you.'

'Not go out?' asked Charlie. 'Not even to school?'

'NO! Not for a month at least.'

This wouldn't normally have worried Charlie. But in the circumstances he *had* to go to school. There was a blue boa to be tamed, there was Ollie Sparks to rescue. 'But . . .' he said.

'And that confounded woman's in it too,' growled Grandma Bone. 'A book was seen lying on her counter, with a picture of the herb you stole openly displayed.'

Charlie couldn't be sure, but he thought he heard the faint tinkle of broken glass while his grandmother was

shouting. He was just wondering who had seen the book at Ingledew's and passed on the information, when his grandmother suddenly thumped the table and shouted, 'WE WON'T HAVE IT! THIS CONTINUAL MEDDLING, THIS DISOBEDIENCE, THIS ... WHY CAN'T YOU TOE THE LINE?'

Charlie was about to give a feeble answer when a voice from the doorway said, 'Aha!'

There stood Uncle Paton, in a shirt so white it was almost blinding. His hair was two shades blacker than it had ever been, and he looked at least three inches taller. So tall, in fact, that he had to duck his head to get under the doorframe.

Grandma Bone looked as if she'd seen a ghost. 'You're better,' she croaked.

'Aren't you pleased?' said Paton.

Grandma Bone nervously licked her lips. 'But ... but ...'

'Thought he'd done for me, didn't you?' said Paton, advancing on his sister. 'Thought he'd turned me into a flabby, fluttering, half-baked yes-man?'

'I don't know what you're talking about,' she said.

'Of course you do!' Paton thundered. 'You set it up. You

planned it all. You brought that evil, shape-shifting hag into our midst. What were you up to, *eh*?'

'Stop it!' cried Grandma Bone. 'I – I could ask you to leave this house!'

'And I could ask you to do the same thing,' roared Paton, towering over her.

Charlie watched in fascination as his grandmother gave a strangled gasp and ran out of the kitchen with both hands over her heart.

Paton gave Charlie a beaming smile and began to make himself a cup of coffee.

'It worked!' said Charlie. 'The vervain. It really worked!'

'Something worked. I feel as bright as a button,' said Paton, who looked nothing like a button.

'I was afraid Skarpo might have tricked us,' said Charlie. 'But maybe I should trust him now. Wow, Uncle Paton! It's brilliant to see you well again.'

'It feels brilliant, Charlie. Thank you.' Paton made a little bow and brought his cup to the table. 'So, are you going to tell me how things stand at Bloor's Academy?'

Charlie did his best to bring his uncle up to date with everything that had been going on while he lay on his

sickbed. He was just describing events in Eustacia's garden when someone stumped downstairs and walked out of the house, slamming the front door behind them.

Through the window they saw Grandma Bone marching up the street in her new straw hat – black with purple cherries on it.

'She's off to Darkly Wynd, no doubt,' said Paton, 'to hatch another plot. I bet my recovery will give them a nasty shock, especially that hag Yolanda.' He chuckled.

'Uncle Paton, d'you think you could talk about what happened in the castle now?' Charlie asked tentatively.

Paton scratched his chin and said, 'Yes, Charlie. It's about time.' He drained his cup and set it back on the table. For a moment he stared into space, and then he began. 'Imagine the castle as I described it, dark without and dark within. I arrived at dawn but there's never a sunrise at Yewbeam Castle. The sky turns a dull yellow and no birds sing. The wind shrieks over the stones. There are no trees, no leaves or flowers, only the dead grass.

'The road ends at a narrow footbridge, so I left the car and walked the half mile to the castle. Thirteen steps carved into the rock lead up to a door that is never locked.

After all, who would want to enter a place like that?'
Paton paused and hunched his shoulders.

'And then?' said Charlie.

'It all came back to me, Charlie: my mother's horrible fall, and my father rushing away with me. I almost turned and ran, but I had to find out if Yolanda had left, and why she was coming south after all these years. I called, but there was no reply. The place seemed deserted. And then it began. First laughter like I had never heard. More like howling, it was. And then a roar, and the screams of a thousand animals that you could never name. And out of this awful noise a voice called, "What do you want, Paton Yewbeam?"

'I stood my ground, but I can tell you, Charlie, my stomach was churning. And I said, "Is that Yolanda's voice?" "No," came the reply. "Yolanda's had an invitation she couldn't refuse." And then the awful laugh came again.

'I ran for the door but something pushed me back. I brought out the wand and tried to strike the invisible being in front of me, but the wand hissed like a thing on fire and burnt my hand. After that . . .' Paton sighed and shook his head, 'I don't know how long I was there. I lay

on the stone floor, blind and never knowing if I was awake or dreaming. My body was either burning or freezing. Sometimes I would see him but he never looked the same. One minute he'd be a child, then an old man. One day there'd be a great black dog beside me, then a bear. There'd be a raven tearing my head, a wolf gnawing my bones. But every time, as soon as he'd gone, I'd crawl a little closer to the door.

'Eventually I reached it. I pulled myself up by the great iron handle, turned it and fell through the door. I stumbled down the thirteen steps, and then I ran. Don't ask me how. I could feel him behind me, burning my neck, scorching my shoes. I got to the car and tumbled in. The nightmare had only begun. He jumped on the roof and smashed the windscreen with his fists. I don't know what shape he was – a monster by the sound of it. He rolled off and ran in front of me, hurling rocks at the headlights. He threw flames at the tyres and the way ahead was lit by a thousand sparks.

'We reached another bridge, and when I drove over it, he fell away. Perhaps his power couldn't survive beyond the borders of his land. But I heard him call after me, and

I'll never forget that awful, wailing voice.' Paton shivered and closed his eyes.

Charlie waited expectantly, but then he could wait no longer and begged, 'What did he say?'

Paton gave a droll smile. 'He said, "If you harm my dear one, you'll pay for it with your life." '

'And who *is* he?'

'Oh, didn't I say?' Paton grimaced. 'He's Yolanda's father, Yorath, a shape-shifter so old he can't keep his own shape but has to borrow from other – beings.' Paton looked at the burn marks on his right hand and repeated, 'Yes, other beings.'

'Wow, Uncle Paton,' Charlie said gravely. 'It's amazing that you didn't end up dead.'

Paton nodded. 'Amazing indeed. I don't know what kept me alive, Charlie, unless it was the memory of my mother and . . . and a certain other person.' He cleared his throat. 'Yolanda may have come to help Ezekiel, but now she knows what you can do, she'll want to take you back, you know.'

'To Yewbeam Castle?' squeaked Charlie.

'We won't let it happen,' said Paton firmly. 'And now,

on a brighter note, you've got things to do, Charlie. Plans to make for rescuing the invisible boy. If you ask me, Billy Raven is the key.'

'Billy? How?'

'He can talk to creatures, can't he? Get him to talk to that boa. It can't be all bad.'

Charlie sat thinking about this, while his uncle went to the cooker and made himself an enormous breakfast, to make up for all the days he'd been without. A little later Mrs Bone came downstairs from her room on the top floor. She'd heard none of the shouting and slamming that had gone on earlier, and was so astonished to see Paton up and about and better than ever, she almost fainted.

Grabbing a chair, Amy Bone sat down heavily and muttered, 'That strange gentleman from the painting can't have been so bad after all, Oh Paton, I'm so glad you're well. We'll all sleep easier in our beds now you're back on form.'

Charlie wondered why Skarpo had stopped being a bad-tempered trickster and decided to be helpful. Was it when he saw the wand in Charlie's hands? And if so, why?

At one o'clock, Charlie politely declined Paton's offer

of a special lunch, ordered by phone from the grandest store in town, and set off for the Pets' Café. He had too much on his mind to enjoy a rich meal. Orange juice and cookies would do nicely.

All his friends were there, sitting round the largest table in the room, with birds, gerbils, rabbits and Fidelio's deaf cat, sitting on shoulders, heads and laps. Runner Bean greeted Charlie in the usual rough, wet manner, pawing, licking and barking, until Charlie bought him a large chocolate brownie and threw it under the table.

'Is everyone ready?' said Lysander, rather severely. 'We've got urgent matters to discuss. Tancred and I have made a list, and we'd like some input from the rest of you.' He placed a sheet of lined paper in the middle of the table. It said:

1 The blue boa to be found.
2 The blue boa to be tamed.
3 The blue boa to be taken out of Bloor's Academy, to a place where it can cure Ollie.
4 Ollie Sparks to be found.
5 Ollie Sparks must leave Bloor's Academy

while still invisible. (Easier that way.)
6 The blue boa to make Ollie visible.
7 Ollie must be taken home to Sparkling
Castle.

Everyone stared at the list, written in Lysander's admirable calligraphy. They passed the paper round the table until they had all read it thoroughly. When this had been done their faces looked either doubtful or downright gloomy.

'It's not that bad,' said Charlie. 'For one thing, I know where the boa is, and I can find it again.'

'But how do we tame it?' asked Emma.

'Billy,' said Charlie. 'He can talk to animals.'

'So how do we persuade Billy to do that?' asked Olivia. 'I mean, would you like to have a conversation with an outsized, invisible-making snake?'

'I trust Billy now,' said Charlie. 'I really think he wants to help us.'

'Rembrandt,' Gabriel said thoughtfully. 'We'll tell Billy if he helps us, he can have Rembrandt. He'd do anything to see that rat again – he loves it.'

'Good idea, Gabriel,' said Lysander, 'but with Weedon

and Manfred on the lookout – not to mention that awful Belle – where on earth is Billy going to keep the rat?'

Charlie thought of Cook. 'I know somewhere,' he said, but when they all looked at him for more information, he said, 'Trust me.'

'OK,' said Lysander. 'Now we have to find a way of getting the boa out of the academy.'

'I've got an idea,' said Charlie. 'I'm working on it.'

His friends stared at him with questions forming on their lips, but Charlie added quickly, 'I can't tell you anything yet, but I know I'll be able to work it out.' Once again, he was thinking of Cook.

'Now, we come to Ollie.' Tancred pointed to number five on the sheet.

'Actually, I've thought of that,' said Emma. Reddening slightly as everyone turned to look at her, she put an enormous spider on the table.

There were several loud gasps, and a wild blast of air blew the paper off the table as Tancred yelled, 'Yikes! How's that going to help?'

'Give her a chance,' said Olivia, retrieving the paper.

'It's not real,' said Emma, slipping her finger into the

spider's body. 'It's like a finger puppet, only Ollie can put it on his toe. Then he can walk through the main doors whenever one of the staff goes out, and they'll just see a spider instead of a toe.'

'Brilliant!' said everyone, except Tancred who obviously had a thing about spiders. 'A leaping spider,' he muttered. 'I mean, it's hardly going to walk like a real spider, if it's on the end of a great leaping foot.'

There were shouts of 'Don't be so picky!' 'It's a great idea!' 'Got a better one?' 'It'll work!' and '*You* haven't got to wear it, Tanc!'

'What about Ollie, then?' said Tancred. 'Where's he going to go when he's out? We won't be around to help him. We can't get out dressed as spiders.'

Olivia said, 'We've thought of that, Emma and me. He can go to the bookshop. It's easy to find because it's right beside the cathedral, and you can see that from anywhere in the city.'

'I've told my aunt if someone rings her doorbell after hours, but there's no one there . . .'

'Except a spider,' muttered Tancred.

'Anyway,' Emma went on. 'She'll look after him until

we can get him – visible.'

Charlie's mind was racing. His uncle would soon have to buy a new car. Suppose he bought a people-carrier? Half-term was coming up. Would a journey to Sparkling Castle be possible, for eight children – and a dog?

'I think we've got enough sorted out to start our little operation,' said Lysander. 'Let's begin on Monday night, with numbers one and two, the finding and taming of the boa.'

Charlie had a problem: how to get Billy up to the west wing attics without being seen.

'Distraction,' said Tancred, who seemed to have recovered his composure. 'Leave it to us. Lysander and me. We can do it, can't we, Sander?'

Lysander nodded.

They left the Pets' Café in very good spirits, each one of them eager to begin the week ahead. At that moment, none of the seven children wanted to consider the pitfalls of their mission. They could only imagine the visible Ollie Sparks reunited, at last, with his grieving parents.

While the others went home to feed their pets or work on the end-of-term play, Charlie took Runner Bean for a

walk. When he returned the dog to the Pets' Café, Mr Onimous popped out from behind the counter.

'Something's going on,' said the little man. 'If you need a hand, Charlie, you know where to come.'

Charlie thanked Mr Onimous and ran back to Filbert Street, eager to see if his uncle's amazing recovery had lasted.

It had.

When Charlie looked into the kitchen he was astonished to see his mother and Paton having tea with Grandma Bone. Perhaps it would be more accurate to say dessert, rather than tea. It was a hot afternoon and Paton had ordered several tubs of liqueur-laced ice-cream from the same grand store that had provided his lunch.

Charlie was invited to join them and he sat opposite Grandma Bone, who was guzzling a large bowl of green and brown striped ice-cream topped with almonds. She didn't so much as glance at Charlie, but kept spooning the ice-cream into her mouth at a rate of two spoonfuls a second, by Charlie's reckoning.

'Chocolate, cherry, rum and walnut? Toffee, apple, brandy and almonds? Or coffee, orange, whisky and

peanut?' Paton asked Charlie.

Charlie chose the chocolate, and began to tuck in. It was the most delicious ice-cream he'd ever tasted; he hoped Paton's recovery meant that more of the same would be arriving at number nine every weekend.

Grandma Bone's bowl was now empty. She stared at it, rather sadly, and wiped her mouth with the back of her hand. Charlie thought she looked tipsy. When she got up, she swayed a little as she moved to the sink. She had still not said a word, or even looked in Charlie's direction. What had happened to her?

Charlie's mother said, 'That was just about the best thing I've ever tasted. Thank you, Paton.'

'You're very welcome.' Paton winked at Charlie as Grandma Bone made slow and stately progress past the table and out of the room.

'What's happened to Grandma?' Charlie whispered.

His mother put a finger to her lips.

Charlie grinned. It was only then that he noticed the wicker basket sitting just inside the door. It gave him an idea. When his grandmother had finally tottered upstairs and closed her door, Charlie asked his uncle where the

basket had come from.

'It's a food hamper, Charlie,' said Paton. 'The store sent it round with my lunch.'

Charlie went to investigate. The hamper hadn't been entirely emptied. There were still several jars of jam, a fruit cake and two packets of biscuits left inside. Charlie picked out a jar of Best Strawberry Conserve.

'Whole strawberries,' Charlie murmured. 'Uncle Paton, could I have this jam?'

'Of course, Charlie. I think I can guess what it's for.'

'And the hamper,' said Charlie. 'Do you think you could get the store to send an even bigger one to Cook at Bloor's Academy? The very biggest they've got?'

'Charlie, whatever for?' said his mother.

'Charlie's got a plan,' said Paton. 'We'll just have to go along with it and not ask too many questions, Amy.'

Mrs Bone shook her head. 'I hope it won't stir things up again,' she said. 'Grandma Bone's settled down nicely this afternoon.'

'Too nicely,' Charlie muttered. 'And too quiet. Something's brewing, you can tell. I wonder what the aunts are up to.'

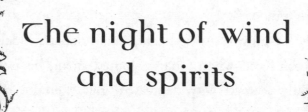

The night of wind and spirits

On Monday, Charlie took the first available opportunity to speak to Cook. In the middle of lunch, he slipped into the kitchen on the pretext of fetching a mop for a spilled glass of water.

Cook saw Charlie standing by the door and came over. Anyone observing them would have wondered why they appeared to be having such a deep discussion about mops. But the dinner ladies were too rushed off their feet to notice anything unusual. Charlie did most of the talking and Cook nodded now and again, eventually patting Charlie on the shoulder with a reassuring smile.

Charlie said, 'Thanks, Cook!' and left the kitchen – without a mop.

Billy Raven was sitting between Gabriel and Fidelio at their table, and when Charlie joined them, he noticed that Billy seemed very depressed. But then he hadn't looked happy since Rembrandt had gone.

It was Gabriel who brought up the subject of the black rat. 'Would you like to see Rembrandt again?' he asked Billy.

Billy gave a rueful nod. 'He was my best friend. I could talk to him about practically anything. He was so clever. But how can I see him? They won't let me out of here.' Billy's ruby eyes filled with tears.

'It could be arranged,' said Charlie. 'Cook says she would keep him for you, and you could see him every weekend. But you'd have to promise never, ever to tell anyone where he was.'

'I wouldn't!' said Billy, crossing his heart. 'I swear!'

'If we arranged this for you, you'd have to do something for us,' said Fidelio.

'What would I have to do?' Billy immediately looked anxious.

Charlie suggested they discuss things outside.

Olivia and Emma were sitting under a tree when they saw Charlie and his friends come through the garden door. The girls would have joined them but they noticed Billy was with them and decided to stay where they were, rather than intrude on what looked like a tense situation.

Billy was very pale – he kept shaking his head and nervously biting his nails. And then Gabriel said something and the little albino calmed down. He gave a resigned sort of smile, nodded and hung his head.

When the hunting horn sounded the girls rushed over to Charlie, just before he stepped into the hall.

'What happened with Billy?' said Olivia.

'He'll do it,' whispered Charlie. 'It'll be tonight. Don't leave the dormitory, and keep an eye on Belle.'

Emma quickly handed Charlie the spider. 'You'll need this,' she said.

For the rest of the day, Charlie found it hard to concentrate on anything but the night ahead. He knew he would have to wait until midnight at least, before he and Billy could set off to find the blue boa. And what if Billy failed to communicate with the snake? What if it hugged them both into invisibility? What then?

After homework, Charlie caught up with Tancred and Lysander before they went into their dormitory. 'Are you on for tonight?' he asked them. 'Billy's agreed.'

'We'll do our bit,' said Tancred. 'What time?'

'Midnight.'

'I hope we don't scare the kid,' said Lysander. 'The ancestors can look a bit awesome.'

'I'll tell Billy you're in control,' said Charlie.

'You wish!' Lysander gave a loud chuckle.

Zelda Dobinski happened to breeze past at that moment. She gave the trio a nasty look and sent one of Tancred's folders flying up to the ceiling. A cloud of loose paper fluttered out, as the folder flopped back on to the floor.

'She thinks she's so clever,' muttered Tancred, gathering up the paper.

'Wait till tonight,' Lysander said softly. 'She's in for a shock.'

'What are you lot doing?' This time it was Belle creeping up on them.

The boys stood aside and she marched over the paper, deliberately treading on every piece she could see.

'Watch it!' cried Tancred. 'That's my work.'

'So?' She glared back at him with blazing cherry-coloured eyes.

'So, just watch it,' Tancred retorted, his yellow hair sparking.

'Trouble?' said a voice, and Asa appeared, loping along in the gloom.

'Nothing I can't handle.' Belle gave Asa one of her brilliant smiles.

Asa smirked with pleasure. 'Pick up this stuff and get to your dormitories,' he told the boys.

Belle tossed her blonde curls and walked on, with Asa trotting in her shadow.

'I think they've guessed that something will be happening tonight,' Charlie whispered, as he helped the others to gather the paper.

'But they don't know what it is,' Lysander reassured him. 'Good luck, Charlie!'

'Thanks!' Charlie walked on to his own dormitory. He found Billy Raven sitting up in bed, looking horribly anxious.

'Are you OK, Billy?' Charlie asked.

Billy shook his head. 'I'm scared,' he whispered.

'Don't be. We've got a lot on our side. I'll wake you up when it's time.' Charlie went back to his own bed and changed into his pyjamas.

In the bed beside him, Fidelio was lying on his side reading a music score, in the same way that anyone else might read a book. 'Shall I come with you tonight?' he asked Charlie.

'No need,' Charlie replied. 'It'd be better if you stayed here to keep an eye on things.'

'You're on.' Fidelio returned to his music score, humming softly as he scanned the notes.

Gabriel came in just a few minutes before lights out. He was flushed and breathless, either from running or something that had taken him by surprise. He was carrying a rolled-up green cape.

'Are you changing to Art?' Charlie asked him, more as a joke than a serious question.

Gabriel took it very seriously. He sat down heavily on the bed on Charlie's other side. 'I found Mr Boldova's cape,' he said in a low voice. 'It was right at the back of the art cupboard. I've been looking for something that might give us a clue to his disappearance.'

'And did the cape . . . you know?'

'It certainly did,' said Gabriel.

Fidelio looked up. 'What's going on?' he said.

Gabriel glanced round the dormitory. Boys were coming and going from the bathroom, some were reading in bed, others chatting or arguing. No one appeared to be interested in Gabriel and the green cape.

'Mr B's quite close,' he said softly. 'He didn't go home. But he's kind of – lost. It's the same feeling I got about your father, Charlie, but Mr B's not quite as bad. Maybe it's because he's endowed. He can still fight.'

The mention of his father caught Charlie off-guard. Finding his father had been the last thing on his mind. Now, suddenly, he found himself wondering if his own family would ever be whole again. Where was Lyell Bone? Far, far away, or closer than anyone imagined? Close, yet lost.

Concerned by Charlie's frown, Gabriel said, 'I'm coming with you tonight, Charlie.'

'There's no need,' Charlie said slowly.

'I'm coming,' said Gabriel firmly. 'And I'm going to wear this.' He tucked the green cape under his pillow. 'Mr Boldova was a brave man. I think his cape will give me an

extra ounce of courage.'

On dangerous occasions, dreamy, slightly scatty Gabriel became someone calm and strangely powerful. Charlie was glad he would be with him on this risky boa hunt.

The children of Bloor's Academy still talk about the night of wind and spirits. It will never be forgotten.

On the stroke of midnight, that magical hour when Charlie always felt most alive and resolute, three boys left their dormitory and began to make their way towards the west wing. Billy walked between Charlie and Gabriel, the latter wearing Mr Boldova's green cape.

A light breeze came whispering in their wake. Gradually the breeze turned into a wind that sighed down the dark passages, rattling doors and windows, lifting carpets and tugging at the curtains. In the dormitories children pulled the bedclothes over their heads and tried not to hear the mysterious howling, creaking and rattling that was going on outside their doors.

Lucretia Yewbeam had been alerted by her clairvoyant sister Eustacia that something odd would be happening at Bloor's Academy that night. As soon as she heard the

unnatural wind Lucretia got out of bed intending to put a stop to any 'nonsense'. But when she opened her door, the wind threw her back on to her bed with such force, she could only lie there, breathless and terrified.

Others were also attempting to leave their rooms – in vain. Manfred Bloor tugged at his door handle, yelling with frustration. While, on the other side, two brown hands held it firm.

Old Ezekiel couldn't even manage to wheel himself to the door. An army of spears had invaded his room. They hung all around him, slicing the air with a violent hiss whenever he tried to move.

On the floor below, Dr Bloor was already marching along his brightly lit and thickly carpeted corridor. Halfway down he was met by the wind, but this was not enough to deter a man like Dr Bloor. He battled on, grunting with fury, until he came to a force too powerful to overcome. First the lights went out, and then three wraith-like shapes loomed before him. Their faces were hidden in mist but the dark hands that held their gleaming spears were clearly visible. And they made a strange sound, a distant rhythmic drumming.

At the top of the western tower, a man who rarely slept lifted his hands from the piano and laid them in his lap. Mr Pilgrim listened to the midnight chimes. There were other sounds in the air; distant drumbeats and a wind that moaned and sang. The music teacher frowned, trying to remember what his life might once have been.

Emma and Olivia hadn't closed their eyes all night. They'd been lying in bed, listening and watching. On the stroke of midnight Olivia saw a pale shape gliding towards the door. In a second she had jumped out of bed and raced towards the figure. It turned to face her, and in the dim light from the half-open door Olivia saw an old and hideous woman.

'Get away from me,' snarled the woman.

'No.' Olivia grabbed a bony wrist.

'Get off!' shrieked the hag.

'I know who you are, you old witch,' cried Olivia. 'Your name's Yolanda Yewbeam, and I'm not scared of you, not one bit.'

'Is that so?' The old woman gave a throaty cackle, and every other girl in the dormitory, but two, burrowed deeper under their bedclothes.

Olivia, still clinging to the hag, was dragged into the passage. As she kicked out desperately, her leg was clamped between jaws of iron. Olivia screamed as jagged teeth bit into her bone, and then she looked into the face of a beast so hideous and so terrifying she had to close her eyes. The scrawny wrist slipped from her grasp, and through half-closed eyes she saw the white-robed woman and the beast vanish into the shadows.

As she dragged herself back into the dormitory, Olivia almost fell over a body lying just inside the door. It was Emma, wrapped from head to foot in thick cord.

'Em!' breathed Olivia. 'What happened?'

'I was coming to help,' Emma gave a gasp of pain. 'I thought that being a bird would . . .'

Olivia saw the feathers at the tips of Emma's fingers, bound painfully tight with cord.

'Oh, Em. Who did this to you?' She began to tear at the cord.

'I can't be sure, but I think it was Dorcas.'

Olivia looked at the two rows of beds. Every girl had her head under the covers. 'I'll get you out of this, Emma,' she said fiercely and, finding a knot, she began to attack it

with her teeth.

Emma gave a sigh of relief, and the soft black feathers at the tips of her fingers started to fade.

Charlie, Gabriel and Billy had reached the dusty, gas-lit region where old Ezekiel had lived for a hundred years. Billy was now shivering with fright. Gabriel and Charlie held his hands and led him towards the staircase where Charlie had seen the blue boa. The snake was still there, a silvery blue coil at the top of the steps, gleaming softly in the dim light.

As the three boys mounted the stairs the creature lifted its head, and they froze. Charlie's legs suddenly felt like lead. He couldn't move. Behind him he heard Billy's sharp intake of breath.

'Talk to it, Billy,' Charlie whispered.

Silence.

'Billy?' said Gabriel.

'I c-can't,' Billy mumbled. 'I don't know what to say.'

'Anything,' said Charlie desperately. 'Say anything.'

All at once, the boa gave a loud hiss. It swayed ominously and its head swung down towards Charlie, who

stepped back, almost knocking Billy over.

To Charlie's surprise, Billy echoed the snake's hiss, and the creature reared up with a loud chuckling sound. Almost as though he couldn't stop himself, Billy crept past Charlie and began to climb up to the boa.

Charlie stepped down until he was standing in the passage with Gabriel. Breathlessly, they watched the small albino creep closer and closer to the glimmery blue coils. The boa's chuckling grew soft and intense, and Billy, who seemed to have found the creature's language, hummed and whistled in reply. When he reached the top step he sat cross-legged, gazing at the strange snake with its frill of feathers. And although Charlie couldn't understand its speech, it seemed to him that the creature had warmed to Billy and was trying to tell him a story.

In a quiet and hesitant voice, Billy translated the snake's words:

'It says . . . it was born a thousand years ago. Once . . . it lived with a king . . . who treated it well. But one day the king went away . . . and his son . . . tortured it, until it hated . . . hated . . . hated . . . and killed. The king's daughter found it . . . all curled up with fury . . . and . . . she . . .

almost cured it . . . with kindness. But it couldn't forget its
. . . yearning hug . . . its hungry embrace . . . so the princess
. . . gave it the power of . . . vanishment . . . not death.'

Billy looked down at Charlie and Gabriel. 'It's a good
snake, really,' he told them. 'Since the princess died it
hasn't spoken to anyone ever . . . until now . . . I think I've
made it happy.'

'Look out, Billy,' said Charlie.

The snake was gliding across to Billy, and the white-
haired boy turned back just as the boa slid on to his lap.
Billy gasped as the creature wrapped itself round his waist.
Gradually the lower half of Billy's body began to disappear.

'Hell's teeth!' cried Charlie. 'What have we done?'

'Ssssh!' hushed Gabriel. 'Listen.'

Billy had begun to murmur and hum again. He uttered
a series of short gurgling gasps as the boa encircled his
neck. It hung there, apparently listening to him, and
slowly, Billy's body became visible again.

'Wow! It can do it,' said Charlie. 'It really can.'

'Ask the boa if it can do the same thing to another boy,'
said Gabriel. 'A boy that it hugged into vanishment.'

Billy continued to hum and the boa replied with more

chuckling and hissing.

'It says . . . it will . . .' Billy told them, 'if we promise . . . not to put it in a jar . . . For hundreds of years it was kept in blue liquid . . . with the bones of a bird . . . until Mr Ezekiel revived it. That's why it's got feathers. I told it that we'd never put it in a jar. That we'd take it somewhere safe.' Billy glanced at Charlie. 'I hope that's true.'

'It is,' said Charlie. 'I promise no one will harm it.'

'OK,' said Billy. 'Now what?'

'We take it to the kitchens,' said Charlie.

Billy got to his feet and cautiously descended the rickety steps with the boa still happily wrapped round his neck.

'Hope we can get it off him,' Gabriel whispered to Charlie as they made their way along the passage. 'I wonder what it eats.'

'Who knows?' Charlie suddenly remembered another task. He took the jar of Best Strawberry Conserve from the pocket of his pyjamas and called softly, 'Ollie Sparks, are you there? I brought you some jam.'

But the building was still under the spell of wind and spirits. Charlie's words were drowned and there was no reply.

As they approached the main hall, the whistling and sighing of the wind intensified. Now and again a pale shape would glide beside them, and a shining spear or a feathered arrow would sail over their heads.

Billy, quite undaunted by all the supernatural activity, led the way, while the boa whispered into his ear.

They came to the landing and, looking down into the long flagstoned hall, beheld the source of the magical night. Two figures whirled and spun across the floor. They moved so fast their green capes looked like the sparkling wings of a dragonfly. It would have been impossible to tell them apart if it hadn't been for their heads – one black, the other a flashing, flickering yellow.

Billy was about to lead the way down the main staircase when he gave a shriek of horror. A giant spider had dropped from the ceiling and now crouched on the steps in front of him.

It was as big as Billy, with eyes like red coals and eight legs covered in coarse black hair.

'Keep calm,' said Gabriel. 'It's not what it seems.' He moved in front of the others and began to walk down to the spider. The giant creature suddenly leapt on to the

banister and swung into the hall on a silver thread as thick as a finger.

It landed in front of Tancred, whose whirling body faltered and then stopped moving altogether. His cape drooped and his shoulders sagged. He stared at the spider, his face white with horror, and the wild wind that had filled the building died away.

'Don't stop, Tancred,' called Gabriel. 'It's her – Yolanda. Don't be afraid. She can't hurt you.'

But Tancred couldn't move. Yolanda had chosen her shape with insight and cunning. Tancred was paralysed with terror, so Gabriel had to face the spider himself. Wrapping brave Mr Boldova's cape tightly round himself, he ran into the hall, shouting, 'Here, Yolanda! Here, old hag! What can you do to me, eh?'

The spider turned, her front legs reaching for Gabriel, her red eyes blazing. Gabriel leapt away, but one glance at that hypnotising stare had already made him dizzy. And then Billy walked past him, crying, 'You can't do it to me, Yolanda. I can't be hypnotised, not by anything.' And the boa, that was Billy's now, body and soul, lunged at the spider with a hiss that swept through the hall, making the

great creature shudder and shrivel.

Tancred smiled and raised his arms. With his green wings he stirred the air and the wind returned, sending the spider sliding across the floor.

The little troop, with Billy at its head, continued its journey to the kitchens. But just before they left the hall, a dreadful howl made them look back. The beast Charlie had seen in the ruin stood at the top of the staircase. It was surrounded by tall, ghostly figures in pale robes. Their arms were covered in gleaming bracelets and the tips of their long spears reached over their heads.

'The beast won't be moving far tonight,' Charlie said grimly.

The three boys hurried down the corridor of portraits, and Gabriel brought out his torch to light their way. Cook was waiting for them by the door of the blue canteen, with a wicker hamper at her feet. Uncle Paton had kept his word. The hamper even had wheels.

'My, oh my,' said Cook. 'You're a brave boy, Billy. Will your snake come into this basket, do you think?'

Billy whispered to the boa, but the creature still clung to him. He hummed and hissed in a soft, coaxing voice,

and gradually the snake loosened its grip. Billy lifted it from his neck and gently laid it in the basket. 'It will do what you want now,' he said.

'Thank you, Billy.' Cook closed the lid and fastened it with a leather strap.

'Everything is taken from me,' Billy murmured sadly. 'Everything.' And his eyes filled with tears.

'Not always,' said Cook. 'You'll soon be seeing a friend of yours. Rembrandt's the name, if I'm not mistaken.'

'Really?' Billy wiped his nose and beamed with delight.

'And what news of Ollie Sparks? To my shame, I haven't been able to get any food to the poor mite. That man Weedon has been watching my every move.'

'We seem to have temporarily lost him,' Charlie confessed, 'but we'll find him, Cook. We won't give up.'

'It had better be soon, Charlie.' Cook gave a sigh. 'Off you go now, you three. I'll take care of this.' She picked up the hamper and disappeared into the canteen.

Accompanied by the singing wind and a host of darting spirits, the three boys hurried back upstairs. They passed Tancred and Lysander, still working their magic in the great hall, but the spider and the beast had vanished.

Gabriel and Billy were ahead of Charlie, and he had just turned into the passage that led to his dormitory when a hand clutched his wrist. Charlie nearly jumped out of his skin.

'It's me,' said a voice. 'Ollie Sparks.'

'Ollie?' Charlie whispered. 'I've got something for you.'

'Jam,' said Ollie. 'I heard you.'

'Best Strawberry Conserve,' said Charlie. 'Here.' He held out the jam.

'Wow! My favourite. Thanks, Charlie.'

It was hard to see what was happening, but Charlie felt the jar being tugged out of his hand – and disappearing. 'Ollie, I've got some good news,' he said. 'We've found a way to make you appear. But somehow you'll have to get out of the building. Emma made this to cover your toe. Here . . . it's a spider.'

Ollie gave a low chuckle and the spider was taken out of Charlie's hand. 'This'll be very useful, but I'm not going out while I'm still invisible. Where would I go?'

Charlie gave him Miss Ingledew's address. 'It's close to the cathedral, and she'll look after you until . . . well, until you're cured.'

'How will I be cured?' asked Ollie suspiciously.

Charlie realised he would have to mention the boa. He described Billy's strange disappearing and reappearing act. 'It'll work, trust me,' said Charlie.

'The boa?' squeaked Ollie. 'No way. It'll finish me off.'

'But you are finished,' said Charlie, 'in a way. I mean, being invisible is a pretty miserable existence, isn't it? Don't you want to go home to your parents? Think about it. Don't you want your brother to see you as a real, whole boy?'

There was a long silence, then a sigh, and Ollie's voice came floating out of the dark again. 'Yes,' he said. 'Yes, I do.'

Charlie felt guilty about mentioning Mr Boldova – or Samuel Sparks. For a moment he thought of telling Ollie the truth, that they didn't really know where his brother was. But when he spoke Ollie's name there was no reply and he realised the invisible boy must have drifted away.

I hope he gets out, thought Charlie. Or it'll all be for nothing.

Cook carried the hamper back to her secret room behind the kitchen. When she got there, she stood on a chair and

opened the skylight in her low-beamed ceiling.

'Hmm. It'll just about fit,' she said to herself.

Three pairs of glowing eyes looked down from the darkness above her.

'Ah, there you are,' she said. 'Good cats. I've got a package for you. Here it comes,' and she lifted the hamper up through the skylight.

Any sleepless citizen glancing through their window that starry morning would have seen a strange sight indeed. Three large cats were running through the empty streets; one yellow, one orange and one a wild copper-red. Their fur was touched with fiery gold and their whiskers flashed like silver. Each cat held in its mouth the end of a leather strap and behind them they pulled a wheeled wicker basket. What could it contain? A stolen baby? Priceless jewels? Or a feast for a party? No one would have guessed the truth.

The bright creatures ran through the town until they reached a green door at the end of a narrow alley. The door opened and a very small man appeared.

'Well done, my beauties,' said Mr Onimous. 'Now let's have a look at your treasure!'

Ollie and the boa

To make his escape from Bloor's Academy, Ollie chose a door that not many children knew about.

Before the novelty of being invisible had worn off, Ollie had used the freedom it gave him to indulge his insatiable curiosity. One night he had discovered the back door. But it was locked, and even had it not been, he wouldn't have left the building. It was dark for one thing, and for another, where would he have gone?

This door was situated at the back of the green kitchen, where Mr Weedon's wife, Bertha, held sway. When Bertha wasn't

cooking, she would sit in a worn armchair, reading thrillers. She was especially fond of Agatha Christie's novels. But even when she appeared to be totally engrossed in her book, Bertha Weedon would have half an eye on the door. She liked to know exactly who was coming in and going out.

Outside the door there was a small yard for dustbins. The refuse collectors made a big fuss about these dustbins, and why shouldn't they? To reach the street, they had to wheel the huge bins up a steep ramp and then through two tall iron-studded gates.

All the deliveries came through these gates and down the ramp, or by a set of stone steps favoured by the postman, who had once slid from top to bottom down the ramp. (A mouldy banana had been blamed.)

On Tuesday morning, Ollie made his way down to the green kitchen. Emma's spider fitted his right toe perfectly and he enjoyed watching it leap ahead of him whenever he put his right foot forward.

The academy was unusually quiet and Ollie thought no one else was awake – until he reached the green kitchen. Mrs Weedon stood by the back door while the fishmonger

and his assistant staggered through with large trays of frozen fish.

'In there! In there!' shouted Mrs Weedon, pointing to the huge freezer. 'And be quick about it.'

Ollie waited until the two men were sliding their trays into the freezer, and then he took his chance. As he moved his right foot over the threshold Mrs Weedon spotted the spider and BANG she stepped on it.

'OUCH!' squealed Ollie, and almost without thinking, he brought up his left foot and kicked Mrs Weedon where it hurt most.

'CRIPES!' yelled Mrs Weedon.

'What's going on?' said the fishmonger, whose name was Crabb.

'Blasted spider – it's getting away!' shrieked Mrs Weedon. 'Get it – quick – my guts is winded!'

'You're joking,' said Mr Crabb genially.

'I am NOT!' cried the irate woman. 'I'm injured.'

'No, I mean you're joking about the spider,' said Mr Crabb.

'I am NOT!' yelled Mrs Weedon. 'GET IT!'

'What – a little spider?' said Mr Crabb incredulously.

'It's not LITTLE! It's got a kick like hell,' screamed Mrs Weedon.

'I see,' said Mr Crabb rather more seriously. 'Come on, Brian. Let's get going.'

The two fishmongers climbed the stone steps a little faster than usual, but not fast enough to see a large spider leap through the iron gates and bounce its way up the street.

Ollie hadn't been outside the academy for more than a year. He couldn't help making a few little skips and jumps as he hurried through the city. He was free. The sun was up and the dome of the huge cathedral shone in the early light.

'I'm out!' sang Ollie. 'Out forever. And soon I'll be me!'

When he reached the cathedral he gazed up at the ancient building, awed by its height and the crowds of stone creatures that stared out from the great arched doorway.

'I'm free!' Ollie shouted.

There was no one about, so he danced over the cobbled square, singing, 'Soon I'll be me, me, ME!'

Sunlight showed him a small window where large

leather-bound books were displayed against a red velvet curtain. 'Ingledew's,' said Ollie, reading the name above the door. He ran across and rang the bell.

A woman looked out from a second-floor window. She stared at the space where Ollie stood. Even at that distance she could see the large black spider her niece had made just a few days ago.

'Ollie?' she said.

'Hullo!' said Ollie. 'Yes. It's me.'

'Wait there. I'll be down in a second,' said Miss Ingledew.

A moment later the door opened with a pleasant tinkling sound, and Miss Ingledew appeared in a blue dressing-gown. She had a smiling, pretty face and Ollie immediately felt at ease.

'Come in, Ollie,' said Miss Ingledew, addressing the spider, for there was nothing else she could see.

Ollie stepped down into the shop and gazed round at the shelves of books. They looked very interesting with their rich, mellow covers and gold-tooled spines. 'What a great place!' he said.

'Thank you,' said Miss Ingledew. She glanced anxiously

round the room and found the spider crouching by the counter. 'I expect you'd like some breakfast.'

'Would I!' sighed Ollie. 'Have you got any jam?'

'Plenty. Emma asked me to get some in for you. But perhaps you'd like bacon and eggs as well.'

'Bacon and eggs!' Ollie cried gleefully. 'I haven't had anything hot for more than a year.'

'My goodness,' said Miss Ingledew. 'We must put that right at once.'

'And after breakfast can I be cured?' said Ollie. 'Can I see the blue boa, and will he make me appear again?'

'I think we'd better leave that for tonight,' said Miss Ingledew. 'The city is very crowded during the day, and I wouldn't like you to be crushed or – or lost.'

'Nor me,' said Ollie. 'OK. Tonight, then. Now could I please have some of that jam?'

While Ollie was eating his first hot meal for many a month, the children and staff at Bloor's Academy were just waking up.

As he made his way down to breakfast Charlie observed an air of embarrassment among the teachers who hurried

past him. It was even more apparent in the dining hall, when the staff climbed four steps and took their places round the high table, in full view of the rest of the school.

Dr Bloor kept clearing his throat, as if he were about to make an announcement. But not a word passed his lips. He looked in rather a bad way. His grey hair had a stiff, surprised look, and his face was very pale, for him.

The embarrassed, sheepish look appeared to have spread through the school. It had been an extraordinary night and yet no one wanted to discuss it. The truth was that most people were either ashamed of their cowardice, or, like Dr Bloor, humiliated by their failure to stop the invasion of such terrifying and unnatural activity.

The strange atmosphere lasted all day. Teachers couldn't look their pupils in the eye. Children glanced quickly at each other and then looked away. Everyone moved very swiftly, not in any way eager to get where they were going, but rather to escape whatever might be behind them.

Charlie reckoned it was like having a bomb in the building. No one knew where it was or when it would go off. Things finally came to a head in the King's Room after supper.

Tancred was the spark, if you can call it that. Although he was tired after such an energetic night, no one could help noticing that he looked rather pleased with himself.

Charlie had good reason to look pleased, but he knew it would be dangerous to show it.

The eleven endowed children were sitting in their usual places round the table when Tancred's expression became too much for Belle to bear.

'Take that smirk off your face, Tancred Torsson!' she said. 'You think your little breezes are so clever, but you're nothing, NOTHING!'

'Is that so?' said Tancred, his grin growing broader. 'Well, I honestly don't know why *you* bother to wear that pretty face any more. We all know what you're really like, you old hag!'

A shocked gasp of horror rippled round the table and Asa leapt up, snarling, 'Take that back, you brute!'

'Feeling brave now, are you, you mini-beast?' Tancred taunted.

Asa was about to spring across the table when Manfred grabbed him by the back of his collar. 'Shut up, everyone!' he shouted. 'Torsson, apologise!'

'Me? Why should I?'

'She started it,' said Lysander in a reasonable tone.

'You heard me,' growled Manfred. 'I mean it, Torsson. You're not too clever to be punished, you know. APOLOGISE!'

'Forget it!' Tancred tossed his shock of electrified hair. As far as wind was concerned, he had kept things remarkably calm, but now, not to be boring, he sent out some new weather. A few raindrops pattered on to the table, and everyone pulled their books on to their laps.

'Pitter patter,' sneered Zelda Dobinski. 'It's pathetic. Call that rain?'

Everyone wished she hadn't said that. The next minute the small black cloud that had been floating near the ceiling suddenly burst and a torrent of water poured on to their heads. It filled their eyes, drenched their clothes and soaked their books.

'Stupid boy!' said Belle in a deep and dreadful voice. 'Who do you think you are?'

Half-blinded by the deluge, Charlie saw something he hoped never to see again. Belle's pretty features turned brown and doglike. Two ears sprouted from her head and

two huge hairless wings began to spread out from her shoulders. Belle was turning into a giant bat.

The bat raised its naked wings and with a bloodcurdling screech, it launched itself at Tancred who cried, 'Yikes!' and dived beneath the table. So did everyone else – except Asa, who sat watching the bat with a look of rapt adoration.

The grotesque creature began to hover round the room, its wings catching at bookshelves and pictures. The clock crashed to the floor, a whole row of books was sent flying, and then, as Charlie peered out from under the table, he saw the picture of the Red King swinging violently against the wall. Charlie leapt up and ran to catch the painting as it fell.

'LEAVE IT!' thundered the awful bat voice.

But Charlie couldn't bear to let the King fall. As he caught the heavy gold frame the bat made a dive towards him.

It was Dr Bloor who, inadvertently, saved Charlie. The door suddenly swung open in front of him and the bat crashed into it. With a dreadful shriek, she dropped at the headmaster's feet.

'Good heavens . . . what . . . who?' stuttered Dr Bloor.

'Idiot!' screamed the bat.

'Oh. Is it . . . ? I do hope I haven't . . .'

'I'm not done for, don't you worry,' screeched the bat. 'You asked for my help, but you're not doing much to help yourselves, are you? You're letting them get away with it.'

To Dr Bloor's great discomfort, the bat crawled up his cape until she reached his shoulder, and then she launched herself through the door, screaming, 'Someone's in for a very nasty surprise.'

When the bat had gone, the headmaster shook his shoulders, straightened his cape and addressed the children who were now crawling from under the table. 'The noise from this room is intolerable. Manfred, can't you keep things under control?'

'Of course, sir,' said Manfred, turning a fierce red. 'Circumstances exceptional, sir.'

'Good Lord, you're all soaked!' Dr Bloor observed.

'Torsson,' said Manfred.

'Torsson, get a mop. The rest of you tidy this room. And BE QUIET!'

When the headmaster swept out it was already eight

o'clock, and the sixth formers had no intention of clearing up the mess. Billy was excused because he was beginning to fall asleep and Dorcas complained of a headache. The workforce dwindled to five.

'It's always us, isn't it?' said Emma, rolling up her sleeves.

'I wonder who's in for the nasty surprise,' muttered Charlie.

'I bet it won't be long before we find out,' said Lysander.

At half past eight, Miss Ingledew decided it was time to take Ollie to the Pets' Café. The streets would be empty and there would be no risk of him being walked into or knocked over. She had already made sure that all was ready at the café.

'Ready as they'll ever be, my dear,' said Mr Onimous's soft voice over the phone.

As Miss Ingledew locked the shop, she failed to notice a large bat hanging above the cathedral door.

'I think it would be best if you held my hand,' she told Ollie. 'Would you mind? I don't want to lose you.'

'No, I don't mind,' said Ollie. 'You remind me of my mum a bit. It's ages since I held *her* hand.'

Miss Ingledew was a little disconcerted to see her fingers disappear when Ollie's small hand clutched hers. But she told herself that she must expect this sort of thing now that she was part of Emma's strange world.

They hurried up to the main road, and then along to Frog Street, and although they didn't see the large bat fluttering in the shadows behind them, both Ollie and Miss Ingledew felt the slight tingle that people get at the back of the neck when they sense that something is not quite right behind them.

Several times, Miss Ingledew looked over her shoulder, but it was a crafty bat and managed to disguise itself as a dustbin bag, caught on a lamppost, a shop sign or a grimy windowsill. Mind you, a few people did see an extraordinarily large bat gliding past their windows. One man rang the zoo, and another the pets' rescue. But the size of bat they described was far too large to be believed. No such creature existed, they were told; it was probably a balloon, a kite or, dare it be suggested, a result of bad eyesight.

When Miss Ingledew and her invisible companion reached the Pets' Café, she rang the bell. The window was

dark and for one minute Ollie's heart plummeted. And then the door opened and he found himself looking at an extremely small man, and the man was looking him right in the eye. It was very comforting. Ollie had not been looked in the eye for such a long time. It set him on the road to feeling whole again.

'This is Ollie,' said Miss Ingledew, holding up her disappeared fingers.

'So it is,' said Mr Onimous. 'I'm very pleased to meet you, Ollie. Come in, both!'

Mr Onimous led the way through the darkened café to a cosy kitchen at the back, where Ollie was surprised to see three bright cats sitting on a freezer, a yellow dog snoozing in a basket, and a very tall woman making pastry, while a black rat watched from her shoulder.

'Aha!' said the very tall woman, who had a very long nose. 'The vanished one! Welcome, Ollie Sparks. I'm Onoria, dear. Mrs Onimous.' Her focus wandered a bit. She was obviously not as good as her husband at guessing where invisible people might be. But then she was a long way up.

Ollie couldn't help wondering how a man so small had

chosen a woman so tall to be his wife. In ordinary circumstances, Ollie would have asked. But these were no ordinary circumstances and instead he said, 'Is it here – the boa?'

'There it is, dear.' Mrs Onimous pointed to a large hamper quite close to her feet. 'I've been singing to it. The poor thing hasn't had an easy life.'

'I wonder,' Miss Ingledew said shyly, 'would it be possible to have a cup of tea before we . . . er . . . before it happens?'

'What am I thinking of?' cried Mr Onimous. 'Manners, Orvil, manners. Sit down, my dear.' He pulled out a chair and Miss Ingledew sat down gratefully.

Ollie said he would rather stand for the 'cure'. He thought the snake would find it easier that way. 'Can I see it now?' he asked.

Mrs Onimous lifted the lid of the hamper and Ollie beheld the dreadful boa that had once hugged him into invisibility. It was not quite as he remembered it. The brilliant sapphire skin had faded, and now it was a soft, silvery blue. It appeared to have shrunk as well, and something in its expression seemed to imply a gentler,

friendlier disposition.

The snake's silvery head reared up suddenly, and it chirruped like a bird. Ollie stepped back.

'It's a lovely creature, isn't it?' sighed Mrs Onimous. 'D'you take milk and sugar, dears?'

Miss Ingledew said, 'Just milk, please,' and Ollie said, 'Nothing, thanks. I expect I'll be thirsty later.'

While Miss Ingledew and the Onimouses sipped their tea, Ollie walked round the hamper. The snake followed him with its little black eyes. Obviously, it could see him. When Ollie stood still, the boa slid gracefully out of the hamper and began to wrap itself round his invisible ankles. Ollie held his breath.

'D'you think it knows what to do?' whispered Mrs Onimous.

'Let's hope so,' said her husband. 'Are you ready, Ollie?'

'Yes, I'm ready,' said Ollie. 'I'm thinking about seeing my brother. I'm thinking about going home to Sparkling Castle. It sparkles because my brother and my father can draw light from stones – did you know that?'

'And what do you do, dear?' asked Mrs Onimous. She thought of Ollie as a patient who must be distracted while

something painful was being done to them.

'I just play the flute,' said Ollie, who, at present, wasn't feeling any pain at all.

'I should love to hear you play,' said Mrs Onimous.

The boa was winding itself round and round in the air. As yet nothing could be seen within its shining coils.

'I'm going to close my eyes now,' said Ollie, 'in case it doesn't work. I don't want to be disappointed, you see.'

'Of course not,' said the adults.

Miss Ingledew put down her cup. She couldn't watch. It was all too much. The experiment wasn't working. Poor Ollie would be invisible forever, but she was already deciding what she would do. She would take him back to the bookshop and ring his parents. After all, an invisible boy was better than no boy at all. And then she saw the feet. First one, with a spider on its toe. Then the other. Bare, cold-looking feet, badly in need of socks and shoes.

'Here come the legs,' said Mr Onimous softly.

He might just as well have shouted because Runner Bean, disturbed by the impossible happenings, leapt up and began to bark.

'Hush, there's a good fellow,' said Mrs Onimous.

Runner Bean grunted and lay down, keeping a watchful eye on the proceedings, as more and more of Ollie was revealed. The cats gave the impression that they'd seen all this before. They remained quiet but alert.

'Oh, the poor boy, look at his trousers,' said Mrs Onimous, regarding the tattered bits of cloth that barely covered Ollie's knees.

The snake climbed higher, and now they could see a worn grey sweater, at least two sizes too small for its owner, the person whose bony wrists extended well beyond the threadbare sleeves.

'Bless me!' exclaimed Mr Onimous as the boa's neck curled round a head of tangled brown hair. A face appeared between the long brown strands; it had two large blue eyes ringed with shadows, a neat mouth and a pinched, inquisitive-looking nose.

'Oh!' sighed Miss Ingledew. 'Ollie!'

The snake encircled Ollie's head until it looked like a shining turban and Ollie's eyebrows shot up in surprise and excitement. 'Am I back?' he asked. 'I feel as if I am.'

'You surely are,' said Mr Onimous. 'You're well and truly visible, Ollie Sparks. Congratulations!'

It seemed appropriate to clap, and so everybody did, including Ollie, but very lightly, in case it frightened the boa.

The snake looked a little weary after its efforts, in fact it closed its eyes and snuggled into a comfortable position on Ollie's head.

Mrs Onimous lifted the creature off Ollie, and laid it in the basket. 'We ought to celebrate,' she said. 'Orvil, make another pot of tea, there's a love. And I'll find some cake.'

After a very jolly hour in which a great many decisions were made, Miss Ingledew left the Pets' Café and hurried back to her bookshop. She knew Ollie was in good hands. He was already having his first bath for more than a year. Mrs Onimous had everything under control. New clothes would be found for the poor boy. His hair would be cut, and he would be well fed and rested before his long journey home to Sparkling Castle.

Miss Ingledew was so pleased with the way things had turned out, she began to hum one of her favourite tunes. When she reached the crossroads, she almost carried on down to Filbert Street. She would have liked to share her news with Paton Yewbeam but this wasn't possible.

Grandma Bone's accusation still rankled.

'I am *not* a stalker,' Miss Ingledew muttered under her breath. 'And I will *not be* regarded as a stalker.'

She went on her way, a little slower now and slightly subdued, quite unaware that the large bat was still stalking *her*. Cloaked in darkness it flittered behind her, down Cathedral Close, and then it clung to a drainpipe and watched Miss Ingledew go into her shop and lock the door.

The bat flew on, down to Greybank Crescent and into Darkly Wynd. It hovered and flapped over the rooftops and popped into an open window at the top of the third number thirteen.

A few moments later Yolanda Yewbeam, a bat no longer, walked into her great-niece Venetia's basement workshop. 'Wonderful,' she murmured as she feasted her eyes on the garments spread across Venetia's long table. There were blue capes and green capes, silk dresses, velvet coats and breeches, coloured tights, necklaces, waistcoats, frilled shirts, woollen shawls and all manner of fancy belts and shoes.

Venetia was busily sewing sequins round the hem of a

long black skirt. Within her reach, at the edge of the table, there was a cluster of tins, jars and boxes. Now and again Venetia would dip her fingers into one of these containers and draw out a few grains of coloured powder, a sprinkling of herbs or a dab of liquid. These she would smear beneath the sequins before she sewed them on.

'Have you done the cape?' asked Yolanda.

'Not yet.' Venetia looked up and gave a little start.

'I suppose you'd prefer me to be that pretty little girl,' said Yolanda, whose age and nasty disposition showed all too clearly tonight.

'Not at all, Auntie. You surprised me, that's all.'

'I'm tired,' said Yolanda. 'I've been watching that interfering woman for hours. She had the boy, I'm sure of it. She's cooked our goose. Grizelda's right, she'll have to go. And so will her wretched little flying niece.'

'Have you fixed the belt?'

'Our little friend Dorcas is taking care of it.'

'Good. Now sit down, Auntie. Take the weight off your feet.' Venetia drew out a chair.

'I want to do the cape,' snapped Yolanda. She sat behind the sewing machine and pulled the green cape

towards her. 'That blasted kid, that little beast – thinks he's so-o-o-o clever. Well, he's got another thing coming.'

'Who, Auntie?'

'The Torsson boy. Called me a hag. A HAG!' screamed Yolanda.

A belt of black jewels

The girl called Belle Donner had vanished from Bloor's Academy. For most children this was a great relief.

But Charlie knew he hadn't seen the last of Yolanda Yewbeam. He'd discovered from Cook that Ollie's meeting with the blue boa had been entirely successful. This was great news, but Ollie had been asking for his brother. And no one knew what had happened to Samuel Sparks.

Charlie discussed his problem with Fidelio, who was feeling rather left out of things since the night of wind and spirits.

'We can't do much about it till the

weekend,' said Fidelio. 'And then Dad has booked me to play the violin at my cousin's wedding. But I'll give it up to help you, Charlie. The others seem a bit preoccupied.'

This was true. When Tancred and Lysander heard the good news about Ollie, they felt they had accomplished all that was required of them.

Gabriel had a lot of piano practice to catch up with, and Billy couldn't really be expected to help. He wandered around, dazed from his encounter with the boa and longing to be reunited with Rembrandt.

But it was Emma who had come off worst. Dorcas had bound her hands with unusually powerful cord, and ever since that night the fingers that had briefly turned to feathers ached continuously. The pain was so bad Emma could barely hold her pen. But she had promised to make a very special belt for Olivia, and nothing would persuade her to abandon the task.

Mrs Marlowe, the drama teacher, had been so impressed by Olivia's acting in rehearsals, she had decided to give her the role of leading princess. And Emma, excited by Olivia's good news, promised to make her friend the most beautiful costume ever.

The long dress was finished and hung on a rail at the back of the dress-making class. It was made of red silk with panels of shiny black. The sleeves were long and tight with cuffs of sparkling black net, and the hem was encrusted with tiny black sequins. Everyone admired the dress, and Olivia made frequent visits to Emma's class, just to stand and gaze at her beautiful costume. All it needed was a belt.

Emma was working on this now, but she was afraid that the belt would never be completed. Today she had stitched only two black beads in place, and already every joint in her fingers was aching.

'Shall I do a bit for you?' asked Dorcas, who was sitting opposite Emma at one of the large work tables.

'No thanks, I'll manage,' said Emma. She put another shining circle of jet in place. A small wire hook was fixed to every piece and the hook was sewn on to the belt, so that each bead moved independently, flashing and sparkling as it caught the light. The effect was stunning: a belt of black jewels.

Emma put up her hand. 'Please, can I get a glass of water?' she asked Miss Singerlee, the dressmaking teacher.

'Of course. Are you all right, Emma?' Miss Singerlee was concerned. Emma looked even paler than usual, and her work was progressing so slowly.

'I'm OK. Just thirsty,' said Emma. She left the classroom and began the long walk to the cloakrooms. When she'd had her drink she leant against the basins and massaged her aching fingers. Would she ever fly again? she wondered.

Emma wasn't sure how long she was away from the class, but when she got back, she found that someone had sewn a whole row of jet on to the belt.

'Thought you needed some help,' said Dorcas.

'Thanks.' Emma didn't know whether to be grateful or suspicious. Dorcas had been unusually friendly since Belle's departure.

The bell rang and Emma carefully folded the belt and put it in her bag. She would have to work on it over the weekend, so she rolled a handful of beads in her handkerchief and dropped them into her bag with the belt.

It was Friday and Emma was looking forward to a nice long sleep in her own comfortable room above the bookshop.

*   *   *

Charlie couldn't wait to see Ollie. In fact everyone who had been involved in his rescue wanted to meet him. Even Tancred and Lysander were willing to risk bats and spiders (should they appear) in order to get a glimpse of an invisible boy made visible.

'The old bat's probably flown off to Transylvania anyway,' said Gabriel as they ran out to the school buses.

'Don't bet on it,' muttered Charlie.

There was a surprise waiting for Charlie at home. Maisie was back. She was having tea with Uncle Paton when Charlie walked in.

After a lot of hugging and tears (on Maisie's part), Charlie's favourite grandmother made him sit down and eat a plate of fish and chips while she told him something very interesting.

'Listen to this, Charlie,' said his uncle solemnly. 'It might explain a few things.'

'OK. Fire away, Maisie,' said Charlie.

Maisie pulled her chair closer to his. 'Well, Charlie, as you know, I've been with my sister, Doris.'

'Is she better?' asked Charlie.

'Much better, thank you, Charlie. She's quite a bit older

than me, and knows more about the family. I'm not sure why she waited until she was at death's door to tell me this, but . . .'

At that point Charlie's mother walked in, and another long hugging session took place.

'Patience, Charlie,' said Uncle Paton. 'It's worth the wait.'

It wasn't until Amy Bone had her own plate of fish and chips that Maisie saw fit to continue with her story.

'Where was I?' she asked.

'Your sister was at death's door,' said Charlie.

'So she was. Well, all of a sudden she says, "Maisie," she says, "If I die, rescue my papers from the desk. Don't let them burn them." "Course I won't," I said, patting her poor white hand. And then she insists I get the papers and start sorting them right there and then. What a mess! She'd been hoarding useless stuff for years. I'd got most of it spread out on the floor by her bed, when I picked up an old paper bag and out came this roll of paper.' Maisie stopped and gazed at Charlie. 'It was a family tree, Charlie, and guess what it says?'

'Haven't a clue,' said Charlie.

'Well, at the top of the tree there's this person with a strange, unpronounceable name. When I asked my sister about it, she said, "Oh, him. He was a wizard, by all accounts. A Welsh wizard. That's why he's got an unusual name."'

'A wizard?' said Charlie, sitting up. 'Are you sure?'

'Positive,' said Maisie, beaming. 'So the Joneses aren't nonentities after all. We're as special as the Yewbeams. So there!'

Mrs Bone thoughtfully stirred her tea. 'But that means Charlie has got it on both sides,' she said. 'Power – or magic – or whatever it is.'

'Exactly,' said Uncle Paton, excitedly banging the table. 'You see, Charlie. The wand does belong to you. That's why it works for you and no one else. That wily old sorcerer must have stolen it from your ancestor. I've had a look at the dates – Skarpo was a lot younger – he could have been the wizard's apprentice. Maybe he stole it when the old man died.'

'Maybe that's why Skarpo didn't try to trick me this time. Because of the wand and my connection to the wizard.'

'He could have been a little anxious about what you

would do with that wand,' said Paton.

Charlie scratched his thatch of hair. 'Wow!' he murmured. 'Wow! I've got a double dose.' He wasn't quite sure how he felt about it, but he was certainly flabbergasted. 'D'you think Grandma Bone knows about this?'

'She might have guessed,' said Uncle Paton. 'Eustacia's clairvoyant, don't forget. Perhaps she had an inkling.'

Charlie stared at his fish and chips. 'D'you mind if we don't talk about this for a while?' he murmured. 'I want to think about it.'

'Course you do, love,' said Maisie. 'It's probably a bit of a shock, isn't it? But I'll give you the family tree to look at. After all, you are the last of our branch of Joneses.'

Charlie took the wrinkled roll of parchment up to bed with him. For a long time he stared at the strange names, the dates, the births and marriages, wondering if any of those other ancestors had the power. Had they used the wand and, if so, what for?

It had been a busy week to say the least. And now this. Charlie lay back and closed his eyes. Right now it was all too much to take in.

*   *   *

On Saturday morning, Julia Ingledew was about to open the bookshop when her eye fell on a beautiful jewelled belt. It was lying on her desk where Emma had left it the night before.

Julia Ingledew was not a vain woman, but she had an exceptionally small waist, and who could blame her for being proud of it? She picked up the belt and the black jewels glittered in the early light. It had been made for a child, but how would it look on her? Surely it would fit her to perfection.

Julia wrapped the belt around her waist. It was tight but . . . she drew in her breath . . . yes, it fitted. She closed the clasp and went to the mirror. The belt looked wonderful against the emerald green of her dress. Julia gave a little twirl and the dazzling jewels jingled mysteriously. 'Oo!' she sighed. She had never felt more beautiful.

She took another deep breath – for the belt was very tight – but she couldn't seem to get enough air into her lungs. She coughed rather violently. Her head felt as though it were being squeezed in a vice. The feeling travelled down her spine and Julia staggered from the

pain. She attempted to loosen the belt, but the clasp wouldn't open. Julia's heart began to beat wildly. 'Emma,' she moaned. 'Emma, help me!'

Charlie was having breakfast when the bell rang. On and on and on. Someone had their fist on the bell, or it was stuck.

'Hold on!' called Charlie, still chewing toast. 'I'm coming.'

'Help! Help!' cried a voice.

Charlie opened the front door and Emma almost fell into the hall. 'Oh, Charlie,' she cried. 'Something awful's happened to my auntie.'

'What sort of awful?' said Charlie, wiping his mouth.

The landing above him was all at once crowded with grandmothers, both shouting, 'Has something happened?' 'Who is it?' 'What's the fuss?'

'D'you want a glass of water?' Charlie asked Emma. The urgency of the situation hadn't quite sunk in.

'No,' moaned Emma. 'I want someone to come. Now. I want someone to help. I've rung the doctor's surgery, but I didn't know what to say, and I don't think they took me seriously.'

'What's going on?' said Uncle Paton's voice.

'Oh, Mr Yewbeam. It's my auntie,' cried Emma. 'I think she's dying.'

'What?' In four bounds, Uncle Paton had cleared the staircase. 'Let's go,' he said.

'Oh, thank you!' Emma shot out of the door. By the time she reached the pavement, Uncle Paton was already several strides ahead.

Charlie stood and shook his head. Things were moving too fast for him. But he was not too dazed to notice the nasty smile on Grandma Bone's face, just before she went back into her room.

'I'm going to the bookshop,' Charlie told Maisie.

'Good boy,' said Maisie.

Charlie leapt upstairs and got the wand from under his bed. He wasn't sure why it suddenly seemed so important, but since he'd learnt its history, he felt that perhaps it had a part to play in desperate situations.

By the time he was on the front step, Emma and his uncle had disappeared. Charlie raced up Filbert Street and along the main road until he collided with three dachshunds, whose master angrily told him to, 'Mind that stick!'

The bookshop door was still open, banging ominously in the breeze. Charlie latched it carefully behind him and made sure the 'Closed' sign was showing.

He found Uncle Paton in Miss Ingledew's back room, giving her the kiss of life. Embarrassed to see his uncle doing what he was doing, Charlie looked at the ceiling.

'Please, don't let her die!' cried Emma. 'Oh, please.'

Charlie moved closer. Miss Ingledew was lying on her sofa. Her face was a pale blue, her eyes open and staring, her mouth gaping like a fish.

Uncle Paton's kiss of life clearly hadn't worked and now he resorted to pressing his hands hard on to Miss Ingledew's chest. 'Loosen that belt, Emma!' he said.

'I can't,' wailed Emma. 'I've tried.'

'What!' Paton pulled at the clasp, and a blue spark shot across his fingers. 'Ouch! What the hell?' He pulled again, with the same result. He seized the belt with both hands and tried to tear it apart. 'It's impossible,' he muttered. 'What's this thing made of? We need a knife – a wire-cutter – something that can cut through steel.'

'It won't be any use,' said Emma in a small, scared voice. 'I think it's been bewitched. I left it, you see, to get some

water. It's all my fault.'

Paton stared at her aghast. 'This is how they punish people,' he said in a low voice. 'If Julia . . .' he choked on his next words, and then, falling on his knees, he took Miss Ingledew's pale hand and pressed it to his lips. 'Oh, my dear,' he sighed. 'I'm so sorry.'

Charlie looked on in horror. He was shocked to see his uncle in such a state. Was he going to give up, just like that? Was Miss Ingledew already dead? He couldn't believe it.

He felt something move in his right hand and his fingers tingled with warmth. Charlie looked at the wand. Why had he brought it here, if not to use it? 'I think I can help,' he said.

Paton looked at him. 'Can you, Charlie?'

'Yes,' said Charlie confidently. He walked up to Miss Ingledew's prostrate body and touched the jewelled belt with the tip of his wand. There was a bright flash and, for a second, the whole belt sparkled like a firework.

'It's burning!' cried Emma.

'No, it's not,' said Charlie firmly. '*Torra!*' he commanded.

The wand's silver tip glowed like fire, and the belt flew apart, sending showers of shining jet across the room.

'Good Lord, Charlie,' said Paton in an awed voice. 'How did you know what to say?'

Charlie couldn't tell him. Perhaps the strange word had been waiting in his head for years, never giving itself away until now.

The next minute, Miss Ingledew gave a huge sigh and sat up. 'Goodness,' she said. 'Did I faint, or something?'

'Oh, Auntie, I thought you were dead!' cried Emma, flinging her arms round Miss Ingledew's neck.

'Dead?' said Miss Ingledew, looking bemused.

'Oh my dear, dear Julia. I can't tell you . . .' Unable to say what he wanted to say, Paton blew his nose very loudly.

'Paton, did you save my life?' asked Miss Ingledew.

'I'm afraid not. Charlie did that.'

Miss Ingledew looked at the wand resting in her lap. 'Really? Was it that bad then? Thank you, Charlie.'

'That's OK,' said Charlie, withdrawing the wand. 'It wasn't just me, it was – us. Me and the wand.'

'I see. Well, thank you both,' Miss Ingledew gave Charlie one of her wonderful smiles.

'Are you feeling quite better, Julia?' said Paton, getting to his feet.

'Quite,' said Julia brightly. 'I'm sorry to have been such a silly.'

'Never, Julia,' said Paton fiercely. 'Never silly. But if you're feeling quite better, there's something I've got to do.' He strode to the door, saying, 'Look after your aunt, Emma. I'll be back later.'

Charlie bounded after his uncle who was already halfway down Cathedral Close. 'Where are you going, Uncle?' he called.

'You know very well,' shouted Paton.

Charlie did know. It was broad daylight but Paton had thrown caution to the wind. Careless of shop windows and rear lights, his long legs carried him through the town like a dark whirlwind. There was a small accident at the traffic lights, but luckily only the amber light shattered and before anyone could think what had caused it, Paton was on his way again.

Charlie caught sight of him turning into Greybank Crescent, but he was gone in a flash. Charlie didn't see him again until he ran down Darkly Wynd, and there was

his uncle outside the door of the third number thirteen. He didn't knock or ring the bell. Instead he brought up his foot and kicked. The old wood splintered and cracked. Paton kicked again and the whole door fell in.

Charlie tore up the steps and through the open doorway. His uncle was just descending the back stairs. Charlie followed, down the stairs, across a narrow passage and into Aunt Venetia's workroom.

Yolanda was sitting behind a sewing-machine, on the other side of a large table strewn with coloured clothes and material. There was a length of green cloth under the needle.

'Paton, we meet again, at last,' said the old woman. 'I hoped you'd come a-calling.'

Paton stared at her, almost in disbelief. 'You hoped?' he said.

'Of course. After your girlfriend's sad demise. She is dead, I trust? You don't have much luck with the ladies, do you, Paton? First your mummy and now your lady friend. You'd be much better off working with us, you know.'

'WHAT?' thundered Paton.

'You heard me, and so did that little wretch standing in

your shadow.'

Charlie clutched his wand tightly. He wondered when he'd have to use it, but there was no need after all. He saw where Paton's furious gaze was directed, and knew in a split second, before Yolanda, what was going to happen.

There was a look of horrified surprise on the ancient woman's face as she lifted her hands from the machine – too late.

The light on the sewing-machine exploded and the whole thing glowed white hot. With a dreadful shriek, the electrified woman behind it shot into the air. She spun like a top and a stream of wraith-like creatures came spilling out of her. They floated across the ceiling – bats, birds, spiders, dogs, cats, fish, monsters – and there was pretty Belle, waving long, stringy arms – and disappearing.

'What's happening?' cried a voice, and Venetia tore into the room. She took in the burning machine, the singed cloth, the scorched table. 'What have you done?' she screamed at Paton. 'Where's my auntie?'

'Where d'you think?' he replied.

'How could you?' she cried, backing away from him. 'How dare you? You fiend, you despicable tyrant. You . . .

you stupid man!'

'I should have done it a long time ago,' said Paton, wiping his hands clean of some imaginary dirt.

By now an army of little flames was licking at the garments on the table. Sparks caught on the velvet curtains and the room was filled with the dreadful acrid smell of burning.

'Come on, Charlie. Let's get out of here,' said Uncle Paton.

They rushed up the stairs and out into the fresh air, coughing and choking on smoke. It wasn't long before Venetia followed them.

The fire engine had a hard time getting down narrow Darkly Wynd, but it managed eventually. By then number thirteen was blazing on two floors. A crowd had gathered to observe the gruesome spectacle. People muttered about faulty wiring and old wood. No one was very surprised to see the old house burning.

The four sisters stood apart, watching in grim silence. They wouldn't even look at their brother.

The firemen had almost got the blaze under control when someone spotted a figure standing at a top-floor

window. A small platform was raised and, amid cheers of 'Well done!' 'He's all right!' 'He's alive!' the window was broken and the survivor stepped out on to the platform. It was Mr Boldova.

The Yewbeam sisters said the young man had been giving them some advice on costume design. 'He's an artist, you know,' said Eustacia.

Mr Boldova was saved just in time. A few moments after his rescue, the roof of Venetia's house went up in flames, and the walls of the top floor fell away. For a brief second, the gasping onlookers saw the dark outline of an upright piano, perched on the highest point of the burning building. And then the instrument came tumbling down, its scorched keys playing an eerie tune as it crashed on to the basement steps.

'I remember now,' said Mr Boldova. 'Someone was playing a piano.'

But there was no one left in the ruined building. The firemen made quite sure of that. So whoever had been playing the hidden piano had got out of the house before it was too late.

'Strange,' said Mr Boldova. 'I never saw the pianist, I

only heard the notes. That's all. Just wonderful music.'

Charlie thought of his father. Was it possible that he'd been kept up there, in Venetia's loft, with only a piano for company? And if so, where was he now?

Uncle Paton tapped Charlie on the shoulder. 'You've got something to tell this gentleman, haven't you, Charlie?'

'Have I?' said Charlie dreamily. 'Oh, yes. Of course.' And he told Mr Boldova all about Ollie.

'This is the best news I've ever had in my life!' said the art teacher. 'Can you take me to him? Now? And please, do you think you could call me Samuel? I'd rather leave the Boldova part of my life behind.'

'Course, Mr Sparks,' said Charlie. 'Ollie's not far away. And my uncle . . .' He looked around, but Paton had slipped away. Charlie reckoned he'd gone back to Ingledew's bookshop.

On Sunday, seven friends with assorted pets met at the Pets' Café. They all wanted to see the invisible boy. With new clothes, a bath and a haircut, Ollie looked completely normal. It was quite disappointing. But the

disappointment didn't last long.

'I want you all to come to Sparkling Castle,' said Ollie. 'Samuel says it's half-term soon, so you could come for a week. I haven't had a friend there for ages, and if it wasn't for you lot, I wouldn't be here.'

Who cared about learning lines, practising scales or painting scenery, when a whole week could be spent in a castle?

'It's not a real castle,' said Ollie, 'but there's lots of room. And there are mountains and streams and forests and fields.'

It sounded perfect.

Charlie got his wish. Uncle Paton hired a people carrier. He wasn't going to buy one, he said, because they weren't exactly his style. But for carrying eight children, an art teacher, a lady bookseller and a dog, it was obviously necessary.

They all met outside the bookshop on the following Saturday. Just after dark, Uncle Paton rolled up in a long silver people carrier. Rucksacks and sleeping bags were stowed in the boot, sandwiches and drink pushed under the seats, and everybody piled in.

Miss Ingledew sat beside Uncle Paton in the front. Charlie and Fidelio sat with the Sparks brothers in the next row, with Runner Bean spread across their knees. And the other five squeezed themselves into the back.

As they left the city lights behind them and plunged into the dark lanes, Ollie said, 'Where's that other boy? The one who made the boa change?'

Charlie felt bad about Billy. 'They won't let him leave the academy,' he said. 'But one day, we'll get him out. You know, Billy's probably braver than any of us.'

There was a murmur of agreement from the others, but before their mood became too sombre, Gabriel said, 'Right now, Billy's OK, actually. I managed to get Rembrandt into the kitchens. I bet they're having a great time together. Oh, and by the way, Blessed's got his tail back. Cook took him to see the boa!'

Samuel Sparks said he was glad to know that Rembrandt had someone to talk to. He had never been sure if the rat was happy. 'I don't think he liked these,' said Samuel, and he took two stones out of his pocket and let them sparkle across his palm.

'Animals don't like magic,' said Gabriel, whereupon

Runner Bean stood up on Charlie's knees and gave a long howl. 'You see?' said Gabriel, and everyone laughed.

It was a long journey and several times Charlie fell asleep. He would wake briefly when Runner Bean licked his face, or changed position. But the last time Charlie woke up, the car had jerked violently to a halt. They had reached a fork in the road and, looking through the window, Charlie saw a signpost. There were two names at the top. The left sign said Sparklestones, and the right said Yorwynde.

'Yorwynde?' said Charlie sleepily. 'What does that mean?'

'It means that the road leads to Yewbeam Castle,' said Uncle Paton solemnly.

Charlie felt a cold tingle of fear run down his spine. What had Yorath said to his uncle? 'If you harm my dear one, you'll pay for it with your life.' And Paton *had* harmed Yolanda. So what would Yorath do? Better not think about it yet, Charlie decided.

Miss Ingledew put a hand on Paton's rigid fingers, and he turned to her with a smile. 'That's one road we won't be taking,' he said.

The car lurched forward and followed the sign to Sparklestones. The road became steep and twisting, but they hadn't gone far when Ollie cried, 'Look! We're home!'

And there it was, standing on a sharp rise just ahead of them. Sparkling Castle. And it *was* sparkling. In every window of the strange, rambling, turreted house, there was a row of flashing, sparkling lights.

A lost boy was coming home and a father had recovered his sparkle.